Mafia Possession

BWWM Dark Arranged Marriage Mafia Romance

Boston Irish Mafia Romance
Book 4

Jamila Jasper

Edited by
Haley O.

ISBN: 979-8-3303-6255-4

Ingram Spark.

Thank you to my Patreon subscribers for your support with this book.

❀ Created with Vellum

Boston Irish Mafia Romance Series

Mafia Playmate

Mafia Property

Mafia Surrogate

Mafia Possession

Mafia Stalker

Click here for the complete collection:

www.jamilajasperromance.com/catalog

From Jamila

Dear Reader...

Sometimes the characters you need jump off the page at you. This has been the case for all the books in this series to one extent or another, but this is even more true for Callum and Zariyah's story.

I think we're drawn to the strongest, toughest heroes when we need the most strength and protection.

I know I write heroines who speak their mind when I feel the most silenced, when there's a lot on my mind that I just can't speak.

Zariyah and Callum have a special love story to me with some parallels to Darragh and Kamari's Story (Mafia Property).

This is another second chance romance and another "forbidden" brother's best friend romance story. Unlike some of my other books, I don't fixate on the age gap here as much as I fixate on the darkness and pain associated with loving someone who has hurt you in the past.

From Jamila

Because we're talking about interracial romance, I don't shy away from writing about different types of pain and emotional hurt that touch the deepest part of our psychological fears and desires regarding loving someone of another race. What if our darkest fears are true? What conditions can love begin and survive under?

These are **romance novels** so I tend towards an optimistic perspective. Whether the optimism is "realistic" is besides the point. I'd rather create realistic characters in a world where everything works out. I think we deserve that much out of our fantasies – at least we get our happy endings there.

Callum's *personality* in this story is a gruff, demanding, strong silent type alpha, but he's very different from Rian in his openness with his emotions.

Zariyah, our first biracial female lead in a mainline series novel, is the one who hesitates and I think when you read the story, you will side with Zariyah.

Readers often ask me if any of my books are based on real life. If we're talking about plot… hell to the no! As much as I love reading and writing about kidnappers and killers, my peace has to come over the thug life.

But every character has bits and pieces of a person or people I knew. With my female characters, this tends to be less direct, because I want the female leads to reach **your** heart and I fixate less on specific personality details and more about **common emotional motivations** that I can transform and personify in a single character.

Oh but the men. My inspiration for my alphas is as twisted and complicated as they are. I carve bits and pieces out of enemies, friends, and lovers, shaping and reshaping the words until they form someone distinct – a character that embodies a flawed yet realistic person that allows me to explore a certain dynamic, emotional landscape, or connection.

The characters are deeper than a fantasy and in dark romance, I can play with the villains in the shadows from the safety of my desk. I can explore fantasies of healing. Tease out the darker side of attraction. Make myself and my readers question **why** we find ourselves drawn to certain taboos.

I certainly hope the world is never exactly like my romance books. They are realistic, but they are not real life. Consider this story a psychological and romantic exploration of a complicated first love – loving a man who holds horrific beliefs.

Does time change him? Are there some parts of him that can never heal? Do we believe that people can be like book characters, and hold such contradictory beliefs within themselves – loving and hating all from the same heart?

Welcome to the darker side of interracial romance. This book has some scenes that I'm especially proud of and I am so grateful that you're here, reading this author's note.

Please use this email address if you would like to write me: author@ jamilajasperromance.com

Enjoy the book.
XO
Jamila

P.S. I send a text when I have a new release and if you visit this link, I can send you one:
bit.ly/textjamila

Part One

Chapter One
Zariyah

Then

The night of my combo birthday and graduation party is my last night in Boston and I have the perfect last hurrah planned out to perfection. Tonight, I'm confessing my feelings to Callum Murray – my older brother's best friend. I've been waiting to turn eighteen so I can sacrifice my virginity at the altar of the sexiest man alive, and I have my two closest friends as my support team to give me the courage to make my dream come true. I don't want to leave this city a virgin.

Callum is *everything* and tonight, I'm going to give him all a guy ever really wants – sex. He's tall as hell, about 6'8", lifts weights, has a thick head of hair, an ass like two watermelons, an enormous body stacked with muscle, and he has this sexy deep voice that instantly gets you wet. It's not like interracial relationships are taboo like they were when my parents got together – I can get a white guy if I want to. There's nothing wrong with wanting to lose my virginity to a fine ass white guy, even if he's my brother's best friend.

I mean... that makes it even better because it's like an adventure, secret, and conquest wrapped in one. My brother Lamonte doesn't control me and even if he finds out, Callum could totally kick his ass. I just have to get Callum to act on the desire I know he has.

It's his best kept secret, but I *know* that Callum Murray is into me, even if he hardly says three words in my presence. I've been dumb, I've been naive, and I'm only eighteen, so I get it. But I know Callum's different.

There's something that bonds us together even if I've always been too young for him and totally off-limits because he played football in high school *and* college with my brother. Those limits won't matter tonight because I'm finally eighteen years old and I go after what I want. Always have. Always will.

I fluff out my curls in the mirror and spin around to take a look at my ass. It's flatter than a pancake. I thought a long teal gown would make my booty pop, but it didn't work at all.

I'm one of those unlucky black women who didn't get much of an ass. I quickly turn around to avoid the hot shame rushing to my cheeks. My boobs look good though, so instead of fixating on my lack of assets, I scope out my chest in the mirror to make sure I'm ready for my night of seduction. Thankfully my boobs are less disappointing. I hope they get bigger…

My best friends Kalani and Sophia are in my bedroom with me getting ready for the party and vying for space in front of the mirror. I move aside so they can check out their outfits.

Because of my brother's new NFL contract, he's going all out on this combo party for me and I'm so freaking excited. I've never had a celebration like this for my birthday and Lamonte got a professional party planner to plan everything down to the very last detail. He bought my parents this new house last year, and it's weird to live on the rich side of town over in Brookline after growing up in a tiny apartment with my brother and parents.

Everyone we know will be here soon, my brother's friends from his college football team before he got drafted, and family from out of town. The house has over fifteen bedrooms in it, so it'll be easy to drag Callum off somewhere to do the deed without getting caught by my brother, parents or anyone else.

Everyone in New York City starts having sex when they're like… twelve. I don't want to be the only person at NYU who hasn't done it yet.

"How do I look?" Sophia asks, checking out her ample ass in the red dress she picked for the party from my closet. As she whips her braids around, Kalani and I examine her outfit closely. She looks way better in that dress than I do and red goes great with her skin tone.

Sophia has tawny skin and she's biracial too, although she's mixed with black and Chinese. I give her a thumbs up to show my approval for the dress. She looks hot as hell.

Sophia is the shortest of our friend group, only five feet tall and plus-sized, but she has an ass that could make anyone envious of her figure. Kalani gives her some verbal encouragement before moving in front of the mirror to scrutinize her own outfit.

"You look damn good, girl," Kalani answers loudly before I can. "Red is your color. I should have tried this dress on before today. The teal makes me look weird."

Kalani squeezes her boobs together and shakes them in the mirror before releasing them, apparently satisfied at how well the dress holds her boobs together, even if she's not a fan of the color. Kalani has a video vixen body with perfect proportions and she's been that way since we were all in middle school.

"Shut up," Sophia says with a smile. "Yellow does *not* make you look weird. You would look good wearing a trash bag."

"Not with all these damn rolls," Kalani mutters, grabbing her stomach and jiggling some of her belly fat in front of the mirror. Belly fat or not, Kalani has a body that a lot of women would pay for. I meticulously pull apart a few of my curls to make the pattern more defined, but I'm ready to leave my new bedroom and head downstairs to the action. *Callum will be here soon.*

I want to go downstairs to the food table so badly and soothe my anxiety with jumbo shrimp, but I wait for my friends to finish messing with their dresses and their hair. When they're finally ready, Kalani links arms with both of us.

"We're doing it," Kalani says. "We're graduating and starting a bookstore together while going to college. Life is gonna be awesome."

"And," Sophia adds. "Zariyah is gonna get some dick tonight."

"Sophia, please… Don't hype it up," I tell her, suddenly embarrassed now that I'm wearing a revealing dress and moments away from seeing Callum again in real life – not just talking about it.

"You haven't stopped talking about him all week," Kalani calls me out. "Don't act like you ain't excited to see Callum's fine ass."

I can feel my cheeks getting red with embarrassment even if it's true. Kalani loves watching me squirm and get all embarrassed when I have to talk about my feelings for Callum. It's one thing to stare at the way he fills out a t-shirt, but emotions are another story entirely. Sex is cool, emotions aren't. That's the rule in our generation.

"Whatever," I say noncommittally. "We *all* need to get some dick tonight. Let's go get some snacks so we can get our energy up."

I'm not an expert on sex but I know it burns calories. I bet having sex with Callum could burn thousands of calories, he's so damn big. I'll need to eat at least a dozen jumbo shrimp.

"We don't need snacks," Kalani says. "We need *drinks*. If we get drunk, sex will be easier. We can easily sneak liquor without your parents noticing."

I nod along with Kalani's plan. She's my local sexpert since she's had a boyfriend.

"I already planned for that," Sophia chimes in as we walk towards my bedroom door together. None of us can walk in heels, but we're determined to make this our night. We're young, we're happy, and as far as the three of us are concerned, there's nothing that could possibly change that.

"Where's the liquor then, hoe?" Kalani asks her, opening my bedroom door with a raised eyebrow. Sophia grins and reaches between her boobs for a small flask that none of us knew she had in there. Sophia loves hiding stuff in her bra – debit cards, stolen pens, her cellphone, and apparently we can add liquor to the list now.

Chapter One

We pour back as much as possible in the hallway before Sophia returns the empty flask to her bra and we walk downstairs together. My brother hoots and hollers so that the entire room full of guests stops talking once I appear at the top of the stairs. The DJ lowers the volume on the music and all eyes in the room turn to me. I wish I was desensitized to seeing my brother next to his famous teammates, but I have a physical reaction seeing him next to football superstars like Duke Callahan. It's surreal that normal people like us could be anywhere near celebrities. My brother *is* a celebrity. But to me, he's still just Lamonte. I remember what he looked like before he played football – just a skinny ass light skinned boy who was all elbows. He's nothing like that now. To millions of Americans, he's a damn legend. *Weird.*

"Everyone, welcome the birthday girl to the party," Lamonte says with a commanding voice. "Zariyah, congratulations on turning eighteen and graduating high school. You were probably the first person I ever tackled, so I have you to thank for everything, really."

He pauses so everyone can laugh. Lamonte was always much better than I was with people. I think maybe he *was* built for fame. He's lucky he has his path all carved out for him. I feel so lost compared to my brother. But he's my rock, and watching him work a room makes me feel so much better.

Lamonte continues his speech with a broad, white smile, "Happy Birthday, little sis. I hope this is the best night of your life. Everyone, let's sing Happy Birthday to my little sister."

I walk down the stairs with my best friends in tow as everyone sings to me like a princess and right when I get to the foot of the stairs, Callum Murray appears next to my brother with his arms wide open for a hug. He looks better than ever – taller, more muscular, and he's clean instead of wearing his usual ratty gym clothes and a Red Sox hat.

He dressed up for my party – at least by Callum's standards. Blue jeans. A red henley shirt that hugs his muscles and has a button undone to accommodate Callum's thick neck. *He looks perfect.*

"Happy Birthday, kid," Callum says in the gruff deep voice that I'm totally in love with. Then, my crush scoops me into his arms and spins me around.

Tonight is gonna be perfect.

Chapter Two
Callum

Now

Fuck it, I don't want to move. I'm tired from my deadlift session last night. It doesn't matter how many eggs you eat for breakfast, it's not easy pulling 800lbs. A man just needs sleep. Deep, restful, peaceful, sleep.

I throw the covers over my head and pretend that I can't hear Aiden's aggressive and shrill car horn blaring outside. Queenie starts howling along with the car horn. *Damn it.* He's slamming down on it like he's getting paid to piss off my fucking neighbors. I don't give a fuck. I'm enjoying my bed too much. My muscles sink into the latest investment in my body – my California King mattress. The only thing I'm missing in this bed is a woman to put my dick in.

Still, it's pretty fucking great in here. Soft. Warm. Comforting.

I'm not getting out of this bed – I don't care why my brother thinks he needs me. I need sleep. Lots of sleep. I work out hard and it kills my body. I need rest to grow these muscles and plenty of it. Aiden can fuck off. I've done everything he asked without question the past few weeks and I need a vacation.

After hitting that heavy ass deadlift last night getting cheered on by the entire gym, my legs are tired as fuck. And my back. The only thing that could get me out of this bed right now is a hot chick. A really hot chick with a skinny little waist and a nice big ass. Not fucking Aiden Murray. I don't want to see my brother right now. Maybe he'll miss the truck parked outside and assume I'm not home.

I close my eyes and sleep for two more minutes, completely forgetting that my asshole big brother has a key to my place.

His loud footsteps wake me up as he stomps down the hall, right before he throws his wallet straight at my head. I should change the locks. Queenie, of course, was no help. Aiden easily subdued her with a treat and I can hear her flaps and folds as she slobbers on whatever bone Aiden brought her outside my bedroom. That hound is only loyal to her damn stomach…

"Fuck off, I'm sleeping," I growl at my brother, pulling my navy blue comforter over my head and pretending I can escape Aiden. His leather wallet smells like ass. I groan. There's no way he's leaving my bedroom until he gets me up. I hate my brother.

"Wake up, asshole. It's an emergency," Aiden commands unsympathetically.

He has absolutely no respect for the dedication it takes for me to look this big. My muscles *need* this sleep.

I grunt back stubbornly, "No…"

He paces for a few steps around my room. My oldest brother doesn't have a shred of respect for me. I think it's because he watched me grow up and he can't ever respect a man he saw in diapers. I'm totally fucked. There's no way he's leaving, but I'm still in denial about it. Aiden somehow makes his surprise appearance even worse.

"You need to get married," Aiden says. "Urgently. Now wake the fuck up."

What the fuck is Aiden talking about? I groan and roll over, sitting up in bed to see my pissed off brother preparing to throw a book at my head. All my brothers have a few screws loose, but Aiden is the worst because his insanity just expresses itself in an extremely hot temper. Nobody wants to be around when Aiden explodes. I think it helps that he has other good leadership skills. People fear him and respect him.

"I just woke up, bro. Give me time to think," I groan, pulling my blanket around my torso. The blanket is too tiny to conceal me from Aiden. I need to get rid of him. The last thing I want to talk about right now is marriage.

"You don't have time to think," Aiden says sharply. "I sent you fifteen texts about this shit last night. What the fuck were you doing?"

Trying to forget her – it's what I've been doing since high school.

"Nothing. Work. Gym. Thinking about buying a new truck."

Aiden gives me a look of intense disappointment. Hey, I might be a piece of shit, but I'm more responsible than Odhran. Aiden forgets that. I don't need to think complex thoughts all day. It's more peaceful to think about work, the gym, and buying a new truck. I also like the Patriots, but that's about it.

Aiden's voice tightens and he doesn't let go of his stupid proposition.

"Okay Callum. Great," he says with a voice that drips sarcasm. "You're running out of time and I need you to take this seriously. We have tax issues and the lawyer says we need to act now."

"You haven't explained shit," I answer, yawning loudly. Aiden looks like he wants to squeeze my neck until my head pops off. He's so fucking Irish. Pissed off first thing in the fucking morning. "Can I at least get some Dunkin' first before we start getting serious?"

"I brought Dunkin'," Aiden says through gritted teeth. "Now get your ass out of bed and tell me you're seeing some chick you can marry tonight."

Tonight? Does it really have to be so soon? Aiden has finally fucking lost it but at least he made himself useful and brought coffee.

I FOLLOW the scent of the Dunkin' to my kitchen where Aiden has clearly made himself at home. Three donuts are missing from the open box. Queenie follows us into the kitchen sitting attentively in front of the box of donuts with her tongue hanging out. *Hm.* No way in hell does that dog need anymore donuts. She'll eat whatever you put in front of her. Large black coffee sits on the kitchen counter beckoning me over. Aiden glares at me as I yawn and stumble over to my breakfast.

Aiden folds his arms and glares at me impatiently as I take a few welcoming sips of coffee. It's like a shot straight to my brain and it feels *so* fucking good. I wouldn't trade this buzz for anything. I. Love. Dunkin'.

"Name a wife," Aiden says. "This is *urgent*, Callum. I need you to take it seriously."

Aiden repeats himself whenever he talks to me because he thinks I'm an idiot. It takes me a while to understand stuff sometimes, but I'm not an idiot. Just because I'm big, strong and don't like to think too much doesn't mean I'm stupid. I've got wisdom beyond what Aiden's ready to recognize.

"It's marriage," I grunt, ignoring Aiden's bad mood. He's always in a bad mood, so if I paid attention to all his bad moods, I'd be quite fucking busy. I wouldn't have time to lift, which is extremely important. "Who gives a fuck?"

See? That's wisdom. Aiden married a bombshell of a black woman, so I bet he's gonna disagree with me. Instead of falling for my bait and fighting with me, he stays on task.

"Your cavalier attitude will help you adjust to your circumstances. Now, give me your girlfriend's name. I'll get her to agree."

Like most smart guys in the mob, I typically keep my personal affairs a secret. I'm the guy who knows everybody's secrets – nobody knows mine.

"I don't have a girlfriend," I respond, running my tongue along the inside of my mouth. Aiden might mistake my nervous response for deception, but that isn't the case this time.

"Bullshit. Where the fuck are you every night when you're not working? You're somewhere from seven to eleven p.m. every night," Aiden accuses.

Does he think I look like this by accident? My brother has to acknowledge how fucking hard it is to put on this much muscle at my height. I have to eat and train like a beast so I can look like one.

"I'm at the gym," I grunt back at him, failing to hide my annoyance that he could even suggest I would be anywhere else.

Pumping iron is the only way I can live with the shit that I've done. I've seen so much shit in the world that would terrify a regular person. I'm not a regular person and I want to look like it. I want to look like the monster that I am. Aiden has nothing to worry about.

"Then I'll assign you a wife," Aiden says. "And I expect you to be fine with whoever I assign. I don't have time to waste and you're getting married. It's an order."

"What does it matter? Why are you here at the crack of dawn to bug me about this shit?"

I don't want to think about marriage. I thought about it before. *Just once.* There's only been one woman in my life that I've given a crap about. She doesn't live in Boston anymore. She always had big dreams, far bigger than me. She didn't want anything to do with a dumbass football player like me.

There's another problem too. She's black. Well, not completely. Biracial. She has a black mother and a white father, not like that matters. She's still not right for an Irish mobster. I took a vow just like my brothers... and Zariyah would never agree to marry me. Not for anything.

"We have an urgent financial problem. You need a wife, or you'll owe the IRS $435,654 this year. I can't bail you out. The feds are up our ass over the last three strip club fires and we have to lay low for a while."

"I don't have that kind of money. They can't take what I don't have."

"It's the IRS, you fucking idiot," Aiden snarls impatiently. "If they don't get their money, they'll send your ass to prison."

"For how long? I'd have a lot of time to work out there."

Aiden gives me a look like I'm the dumbest guy he's ever met. You get sick of that look after a while. I know I'm not the smartest guy, but

I'm not a complete idiot. If I can get off doing nine months behind bars for something, I don't see the problem. Why sentence myself or some poor chick to a lifetime of misery?

I'm the furthest thing from husband material.

Aiden grinds his jaw back and forth as he struggles with his desire to knock the wind out of me. When we were younger, he would always hit me twice in the stomach when he thought I was saying something stupid as fuck. That changed when I grew taller than him. As I grew addicted to gaining more and more muscle on my previously lean physique, everyone treated me differently. I became a weapon.

I might not love it the same way Rian does, but there's a part of me that's still a Murray and I still love the fucking power of walking into a room and owning it.

"You aren't going to prison, you stupid fuck," Aiden says. "If you won't give me a name, I'll find one."

"I don't care. Find me a wife, then. As long as she's Irish."

Aiden doesn't say anything, but there's a flicker of rage behind his eyes as I say that. My three older brothers broke their vows, but I have no reason to break mine now. If I'm not marrying for love and I'm just marrying for duty, I should go all the way and stick to the plan.

Zariyah would hate me for this. She always thought that I was so much better than what she called "racism". It's easy for her to judge me as a racist. She's one of those liberal hippie types with a white father who thinks the world is all sunshine and roses and that we can all get in bed together and sort out generations of crap by fucking or falling in love.

She's wrong.

"The IRS won't give a fuck what race your wife is and neither will the accountant," Aiden says. "Wouldn't this be much easier if you gave me the name of one woman you've had a romantic entanglement with?"

"That would be a good way for her to end up killed," I respond. "Sorry, Aiden. You're on your own."

"Or I could call Darragh and ask him."

"Darragh doesn't know shit," I blurt out. There's not enough coffee in the world to make meddling Aiden tolerable, but I've probably just given him more than enough information.

"Fine," Aiden says. "Have it your way. When I see you again, I'll have a wife for you and I will need you to do exactly as I say once I make that happen."

"Got it."

"How are you this lazy about your love life?" Aiden asks, unable to resist one final jab.

I grunt in response. It's not laziness. I've just given up. There's only one woman I could ever love and she hates me. It's not just that she hates me, she ran away and she'll never come back to Boston if she knows I'm here.

IF I CAN'T HAVE her, it doesn't matter who the fuck Aiden forces me to marry. If I can't have Zariyah, I should accept my fate without complaining.

Chapter Three
Zariyah

Now

Kalani came to help me move the last of my things from Brooklyn. I should have joined her years ago when she opened the new store in Boston, but I didn't want to admit that what we built together in New York had completely fallen apart. I sit in the passenger seat of Kalani's Toyota Camry with the urn on my lap. I didn't want to risk sending it with the moving company, but it still creeps me out to have it.

My best friend slides into the front seat and sighs.

"How's Sophia?"

I glance down at the urn. *The same.*

"She's the same."

Kalani shakes her head. "I can't believe you kept that thing."

"I couldn't toss out our friend," I say to Kalani, holding the urn tightly. "Her parents wanted us to have some of her ashes. Have a heart."

"I *do* have a heart," Kalani says. "It's not my fault Sophia's haunting us."

"She is *not* haunting us," I tell Kalani, giving her a pointed glare. "Life is just fucked up. There's nothing superstitious about it."

"Don't worry, girl. That'll change once we get to Boston. New York is dead anyway."

"Yeah. Sure."

Kalani turns up the radio and I wonder when she started listening to country music. She bailed on New York three years ago when the mob activity from Long Island spilled into our neighborhood and we found bullet holes in our shop window. But I stayed for our dream. For Sophia. But I couldn't keep the dream alive. When mobsters killed my neighbor's boyfriend and the Italian mob started stalking my neighborhood, I knew I had to get out.

Chris Stapleton croons on the radio and Kalani cheerfully turns the music up as she navigates New York City traffic like a true Bostonian. I don't think I'll catch my breath until she gets out of the city. I try to act like her newfound love of country music (which she always hated before) doesn't bother me, but it does.

I can't listen to country music anymore because of Callum Murray. I used to love country music because it was his favorite, even the new stuff. He didn't just listen to the mainstream stuff though, he listened to Jelly Roll and Ryan Upchurch. I could kinda get into his stuff but... now it just makes me sick to hear those twangy accents and annoying ass guitars.

Callum ruined it. He ruined Boston for me and he ruined my life. The only reason I'm sitting in this car is because I'm running away again, running back to the place I left originally. The bookstore burned down after all the mob activity reached a violent peak. I have nothing left here. I press my head against Kalani's car window and try not to think about Callum.

Then Tennessee Whiskey by Chris Stapleton comes on. That was his favorite song. He looked so hot when he sang and with his voice, he was always good at it. I stop myself from smiling. I can't let thoughts of Callum make me smile. I have to let the good memories perish along with the bad ones. *He's been out of my life for years and it doesn't matter how hot he looked when he sang.*

If he hadn't been so handsome, I would have never been stupid enough to get mixed up with him.

It's been years since I've seen him. My brother, Callum's best friend throughout high school, moved to Tennessee to play professional football down there, so I haven't seen Callum since my eighteenth birthday.

Kalani pokes me in the side, distracting me from thoughts of Callum. It's been ten years... He's probably not even in Boston anymore.

"Hey, cheer up and stop thinking about making Sophia's ghost happy," Kalani says. "We'll be much better off in Boston. I've been doing great the past six months and with you here to help, the bookstore will take off and we'll be rich."

I hope Kalani's right. She promised me she would do everything to get our second location on its feet and I hope we have a shot like she thinks we do. The insurance payout from the bookstore burning in Brooklyn will help us out, but I just want it to be enough. I want this to work *so* badly and it's not just for Sophia.

I haven't even told my parents that I'm moving back to Boston yet. They still think they have a shot at getting me to move to Tennessee with them to be closer to Lamonte. I'd rather sit curled up in a corner with a book than watch football – no offense to my brother. I don't want to just follow him around because he's a famous football player now. I want to have my own life. I spent enough time being Lamonte's little sister.

"We can't be sure the bookstore will take off," I tell her. "But we can still hope. You're right."

The urn jostles on my lap and I hold the lid down tightly to make sure we don't have any tragic accidents.

"Exactly," Kalani says. "We can still hope. Plus, Boston has way hotter guys than New York. Maybe we'll meet a rich guy to take away our problems."

I scoff at the suggestion. It's a nice fantasy, but it's never going to happen. Everyone dreams about meeting a rich guy who solves all their problems, but how many people does that really happen to?

"We're not going to find a rich guy in Boston that's our type who wants to take away our problems. All the guys in Boston are white."

Meaning, they aren't interested in black women like that. I learned that the hard way. Kalani doesn't get how deeply cynical I am about interracial love because I've never told her exactly what went down the night of my birthday party after all the texts and after my fight with Callum. She knows that I want nothing to do with him, but I spared her the details of our falling out. That he refused to take accountability. I tried to reason with him, but he didn't care about me enough to change.

"So?" Kalani says. "Ain't your daddy white? Why should you care about race like that?"

Kalani has always been the darkest one out of our friend group. She isn't biracial, just a standard issue black woman with two black parents. She's never made me feel out of place for having a white parent though. I've been super lucky that I've never felt like I had to choose a side. I've always been black, always been drawn to black folks and always had best friends who were mixed like Kalani or black like my mama.

There's never been a question about where I fall if it comes down to picking sides. I thought race didn't matter when I was younger. What I learned growing up was that I didn't *want* race to matter, but race mattered. Race *matters*.

"I'm not the one who cares about race."

Kalani snorts. "Okay. Whatever you say, Z."

"I'm not."

"You told me that you automatically block any white guy who follows you on Instagram."

"I don't want to be some guy's fetish. Is that so wrong?"

Kalani shakes her head. She's always been the better one at avoiding a fight so she changes the subject and tells me about my new apartment in Boston. Kalani likes living alone, so even if we're running the business together, we won't be living together. She got me a sweet deal on a studio in the building across from hers, so at least we'll be close enough that I can run over for a cup of milk or a stick of butter in an emergency.

The drive back into Boston is longer than I remember, even with Kalani's flagrant disregard for the speed limit. At least her driving keeps me awake the entire time. When we get to my apartment, she helps carry my things upstairs and then she has to leave to head to an appointment with her personal trainer. She's trying to lose a few pounds for her older sister's wedding.

We promise to meet up for dinner the next night once I'm settled in. After thanking my best friend for driving me and helping me move, I give her a hug and try to give her money for gas which she refuses profusely. I slip it into her purse after tricking her into a second hug and watch her saunter off with her typical charismatic strut.

I admire Kalani. I don't know how she can stay so happy when there's so much shit falling apart around us all the time. We thought life would be perfect if we just left Boston, but nothing has been as carefree and beautiful as it was in high school. Not friendship. Not love. I hate thinking that those were the best years of my life.

I get about halfway done with unpacking before I'm too tired to continue. It's close to midnight and Kalani has sent me several updates via text message about how hot her personal trainer looks today and how she wants to "sit on his blond beard and put a baby in him". I don't know how she expects *that* to work.

After putting my phone on silent, I walk over to my bed – the first thing I set up in my apartment. Yes, I'm one of those women who has a special affinity for her bed. My bed is soft. It's warm. It's mine. I don't want to leave it. I don't even go through my bedtime routine even though I know my hair will look a damn mess in the morning.

I definitely don't remember falling asleep. But I remember waking up because I'm startled awake by the sound of loud footsteps in my room. It's a studio apartment, not a gigantic house, so I know I'm not alone the second my eyes snap open. Panic is immediate.

The footsteps are too heavy for them to be Kalani's. My body refuses to co-operate and I remain frozen in my bed. I take in a sharp inhalation, my body instinctively preparing itself to scream when a large hand clamps over my mouth so forcefully that the hand pushes the air out of my nose.

I can't scream. But I can fight. With the air knocked out of me, I attempt to move my legs, but I'm trapped by the covers. I thrash around violently, the trapped feeling sending me into a dull panic, and I make contact with what feels like a very firm chest. I hear a heavy South Boston accent scream, "Fuck!"

The covers shift away from my skin, exposing me to the cool air. I scream and try to use the opportunity to fight. My hand thrashes out in a closed fist, but nothing happens. That's all I remember before a tiny pinch in my side. I can feel the needle sinking into my skin and I flail around trying to scream again. But that's it. One pinch and I'm unconscious.

I yelp as my body jerks away and my eyes snap open. I can tell I'm in the trunk of a car because of the way my head slams against the fabric interior and the jostles of the tires going over bumps. The sharp scent of bleach invades my nostrils and my body violently shakes again, but I have no control of my limbs.

I'm tied up. Holy shit, I'm tied up. And I have no memory of what happened except for the pinch in my side. I try to cry out but my voice is hoarse and I'm breathing too fast for me to make any audible sounds. I'm trapped. The car goes over another bump and I hit my head again, letting out a loud shriek. No. This can't be happening.

After everything I've done to avoid my life turning out like this, I can't let this be the end of Zariyah Armstrong's story. I have to fight my fear. I stop struggling for a second and focus on my breath and establish some type of rhythm of movement in the trunk of the car. Modern cars have these escape tabs in the back of trunks exactly for situations like this. Sure, my hands are tied, but once I identify the tab back here, I can use my teeth.

I can do something other than wait here for these maniacs to rape me and dump my body on the side of I-495 somewhere. Okay, thinking about them raping and murdering me does nothing to calm me down. I push those thoughts out of my head and tell myself that I can do this. After a few minutes, I steady my breathing and gain some semblance of control.

I move my body with the bumps just enough that I don't whack my head on the bottom of the trunk. I ignore the smell of bleach and pretend it doesn't confirm my suspicions that whoever took me wants to kill me. My eyes take longer to adjust to the darkness, but I see the faintest glow of a green escape tab once I calm my breathing and look around. I'd have to risk turning over on my face and hitting my head pretty hard if we go over a large bump to get to the tab, but then I can get the trunk open and get someone's attention.

If that doesn't work, I can try kicking the tail light out, but that would probably require a bit more effort. The bleach scent feels like it's suffocating me back here. With each passing bump, I could be even closer to the point of no return with my kidnappers. I lean forward and try several times to drag the tag open with my teeth, but it doesn't work. I have to kick the tail light out.

I grunt and wriggle until my bound feet are roughly where I expect the tail light to be. I kick as hard as possible and nothing happens. Fuck no. I'm not giving up this easily. I keep kicking until I'm dripping with sweat. I can feel the plastic zip ties around my wrists sliding over them. I wriggle my hands in hopes I can free myself as I continue slamming my feet into the trunk.

I hear a loud crack and then a pop. A gust of air whooshes into the back of the trunk and I let out a loud scream, "HELLLLLLLLLP!!!!" I move until my feet stick out of the little hole. I wasn't wearing any shoes because I was asleep, so I just have white socks sticking out flailing around. It's working. The car behind me honks loudly. I whoop excitedly but... it's too soon.

Something's changing. The car I'm in slows down and turns. We're exiting the highway. Oh fuck. I scream for help and wriggle my shoes again but I can't see out the hole so I can't tell if the person who honked saw me, if they'll call the police or if the person who honked will do anything to help me aside from slamming on their horn.

I scream again and then move my hands in just the right way that one of my wrists pops free from the ziptie, lubricated by my sweat.

Yes! I scramble forward but the car takes a sharp right turn and I'm thrown against the back wall of the trunk. I yelp again and the car takes a sharp left, tossing me again so I hit my head.

It's almost like they're doing it on purpose. My stomach churns with nausea as the car takes four more sharp turns — left, right, right, left and then comes to a sharp stop. I don't hesitate. Nausea be damned, I lunge for the escape tab in the trunk and yank on it so the trunk pops open.

Before I can jump out, I hear a loud, threatening click and sit up to stare down the double-barrel of a large pistol. I freeze, but not just because of the pistol, but the man standing behind him. A ghost from my past that I'd rather leave dead.

"Hello, Zariyah," he says, cocking the pistol. "Do you remember me?"

Chapter Four
Callum

Then

Zariyah looks beautiful tonight. She's always been a pretty teenager, but she's grown into a sexy as fuck woman. I know it's wrong for me to think that, but I'm a guy and we're pretty much thinking about sex 24/7, even when we're not thinking about it.

Her looks aren't the only thing getting me going tonight. She smells fucking amazing as I hug her, trying to make the hug look more innocent than I feel. I smile, giving her that "proud older brother look" and I let her go from that hug even if it's the last thing I want to do. If there's one woman in the world off-limits to me, it's Zariyah Armstrong – my best friend's little sister.

It's her eighteenth birthday today so she's technically old enough for me to show interest in, but I don't know. I can think she's damn sexy but acting on my impulses is another story entirely. She needs time to grow up and I don't want to interfere with that.

Chapter Four

Age isn't the only thing keeping us apart. There's my family to worry about too.

I know how my dad feels about black women – who he calls the worst of all the colored women – but when you're the fourth son out of five, you learn tricks to get away with what you want.

Reality doesn't kill my fantasies about her though. I'm like my older brother Rian. I've always liked black women. I like their features. Lips. Noses. Hair. Butts. Legs. Did I mention butts?

Zariyah thinks she doesn't have a great ass (she posts about it on her social media page), but I think it's cute. Cute, but too young for me.

I try not to look like I'm checking her out, even if it's impossible not to stare at her. *She looks fucking incredible and all grown up – like the woman I've been waiting for.*

"Have a great birthday, kid. If any high schoolers get handsy, come get me and I'll kick their ass."

"I'll let you know," she says, giving me a broad smile before her friends drag her away giggling. High school girls giggling never fails to make me nervous as fuck, but whatever. At least they distract Zariyah long enough that I can watch her walk away. She's got great legs that show through the slit in her long dress to match her perfect ass. I never realized how much of a leg guy I was until I met her.

Lamonte puts his hand on my shoulder, shaking the fantasy clear out of my head. Her brother would probably put me through a wall if he knew what kind of thoughts I had about his sister. He's the third and most important reason I need to stay away from Zariyah.

"Yo, man," Lamonte says. "I got the good tequila in the third kitchen. Join me and the guys for a few shots," he says. I shrug and follow him through the hallways of the giant mansion he just bought for his parents. I feel his sense of pride as he struts through the halls. Lamonte always grew up with less than I did but I knew he would be famous one day. He went to all the practices I skipped. He made football his life. He didn't have a mob boss father to fall back on.

When we get to the bar in the third kitchen, I see why Lamonte pulled me aside. He has three hot chicks dressed in skimpy clothing serving drinks to his NFL buddies who lean over the kitchen bar like they've never seen a woman before. I can smell the high end tequila the second we enter the room. I'll feel like shit when I hit the gym tomorrow for my squat day, but I'll worry about that tomorrow. Tonight, I need to get my best friend's little sister out of my damn head. *She looked too fucking good in that dress.*

Tequila. She's a fickle mistress. I drank so much tequila in college with Lamonte that I can't even taste it anymore. I remember tequila *had* a taste but now I can drink it straight out of the bottle. The Mexicans are right – it's better that way.

He introduces me to other players on his team but I recognize every last one of them before the introductions. I've always been able to be a social butterfly when I needed to – the consequence of a big family – but it's getting hard to hide how badly I need a drink. Lamonte pulls through and presents me with my very own bottle of Clase Azul Reposado. Best damn tequila you'll ever drink.

"Surprise," he says. "I kept this unopened bottle just for you. It's Zariyah's last night in Boston, so it'll probably be my last night here for a while. I'm gonna miss you, bro. I want us to go out in a blaze of glory."

"If I drink this much tequila, it's gonna kill me."

Lamonte grins. "Better get started brother. I'm way ahead of you."

He holds up a matching bottle of tequila that he's already drained a quarter of. Christ. Lamonte could never outdrink me before college but clearly, he's been training more than his routes in the NFL.

If I can't have her, I might as well have booze. That's how dad handled everything and he's just fine. I toast Lamonte and clink our bottles of tequila together before I empty as much of the liquor as possible down my throat in one gulp.

TEQUILA BLURS time within the hour. I finish the bottle Lamonte gives me and start on a bottle of gin. Oh, the gin is fucking good, but I'm so drunk it tastes like water. I don't know how Lamonte can still stand this. The next time I gain any awareness of what time it is, it's midnight and I don't like how out of control I feel. I'm 6'8" so it takes a hell of a lot of liquor to get me drunk, but I've somehow managed it.

I hear Lamonte say, "Hey man, you okay?"

"I'm fine. I just need some air. I'm going outside."

"Do you know the way out?" Lamonte asks. I grunt and wave him off. He should be having a good time tonight and taking care of his sister, not looking after my drunk ass.

"I'll be fine," I grunt, feeling my way along the walls as I struggle to remember my way out. My phone buzzes relentlessly, making it more important that I find the door. It takes longer than I'd like, but I get there, stepping out into the fresh air and answering my phone.

"It's not a good time, Aiden."

"Where are you?" Aiden barks, completely ignoring me. *Fuck.*

"A party."

"Are you drunk?"

He'll get pissed if I answer the question honestly. Aiden knows how I get when I drink too much and I should technically be steering clear of all liquor. I fucked up by taking too long to answer.

"Fuck's sake, you are drunk," he says. "Are you with Lamonte?"

I don't want to answer that, either. Aiden is just as bad as my father – an outright racist who wants nothing to do with black people unless he can make money from them the way he does with Darragh's friend, the boxer. But again, I take too long to answer, so he figures it out quickly.

"I won't tell dad if you help me out with something," he says. "I have a problem. A blackmail problem."

"Tomorrow," I promise him. "I'll call you tomorrow when I sober up."

"Thanks."

Aiden hangs up with an abrupt click. I was so focused on my phone conversation that I didn't hear anything else happening outside, but now that I'm off the phone I hear quiet sobbing coming from around the corner of the house. The large stone patio wraps around the mansion with two potential sliding door entrances. I came out of one entrance, but someone must have left the party from the other entrance.

I put my phone in my pocket and walk around the corner towards the crying sounds. At first, it's too dark for me to make out more than a slim figure with wild curly hair hunched over and sobbing into her hands. I drunkenly lurch forward towards her, attracting her attention.

She gasps and says my name. Her body relaxes once she recognizes me. I move closer towards her, the dim outdoor night light illuminates her face as I approach. Man, I'm drunk.

"Callum. It's just you," she says softly in a voice that can get me instantly hard. I can't help it, especially not with this much liquor in me.

Zariyah.

MY CHEST IS STRANGELY tight as I walk closer to her. Why is she crying out here alone in the dark? This should be the happiest night of her life, so if anyone fucked that up for her, I'll kick their ass.

"Yes. It's me," I answer, closing the space between us and grunting as I sit next to her. In some ways, she's like a little sister to me. I gave her a pep talk before her AP US History exam, even if I was fucking terrible at school. Football gave me a head for pep talks and I think I made her feel better even if I was a goofy dumb ass college kid.

"What are you doing out here?" she sniffles, quickly wiping her tears away with her hands and stiffening up her facial expression as if that could stop me from noticing her tears.

I don't fucking know what I'm doing out here, but it feels like I was looking for her. Like I was meant to find her. I glance over my shoulder to look at her. She looks fucking tiny next to me, even if she's a completely average height for a woman. Her heels are off, making her look even smaller and her feet extend from beneath the length of her pretty dress ending in cute toes, painted a pretty royal blue.

"I'm drunk. Needed some air."

I struggle to get the words out, Zariyah's beauty suddenly reducing me to the conversational skills of a fucking teenager. The liquor and the instant hardness from seeing her and hearing her voice certainly don't fucking help.

"I'm drunk too," she says, sniffling again and failing to hide a tear streaming down her cheek. Instinctively, I do something very, very foolish.

I REACH over with my thumb and wipe Zariyah's tear off her cheek slowly, appreciating the softness of her skin beneath my hand as I touch her, setting events in motion I could never take back.

Chapter Five
Zariyah

Now

It's been years since I've seen Rian Murray, even longer than since I've seen his brother Callum. I'm not entirely surprised he has a gun pointed at my face, but I am surprised to see him. I freeze because he has a weapon and I'm not an idiot, but I don't think Rian will kill me.

"Of course I remember you," I answer as calmly as possible. "You're another racist Irish asshole. How could I forget?"

Rian makes a sound halfway between a snort and a grunt, like he somehow thinks there's something funny in what I said. I don't see the humor in it.

"Cut the sass, princess. Tonight's gonna be the best night of your life."

"Where are we and why the hell did you kidnap me? Where's Callum?"

Rian doesn't bother hiding his amusement this time. "You'll see him very soon, princess."

Chapter Five

"Call me princess again and I will kick your *ass.*"

Rian's hand hovers over the lid of the trunk like he's threatening to slam me in. I don't know how he keeps such good control of the pistol with one hand as he does it, but everything about him suddenly makes me nervous. He might not kill me, but if Rian's anything like Callum, he's not above hurting people to get what he wants.

"Okay, Zariyah. I got it. Now get out of the trunk. We're here."

"*Where?!*" I yell at him as Rian impatiently grabs my forearm and yanks me out of the trunk. I wrestle my arm away from him immediately and prepare to slap him but the second I raise my hand, he turns the pistol back on me, so I lower it and serve him up my meanest stare instead. Just because I'm mixed doesn't mean I can't throw hands. I grew up with a football player for a brother and he never went easy on me. *Ever.*

Despite my desperation to stay in control of the situation, my feet wobble as I stand on my own. Too much time tied up and in the back of the car has made all my limbs stiff, giving Rian an additional advantage aside from the firearm. I hear the driver's side car door close and more footsteps coming my way but I don't dare take my eyes off Rian's gun, even as my heart races with terror.

"What's the hold up back here?"

Rian lowers his firearm, apparently satisfied by the back up that just materialized. I glance over my shoulder now that he doesn't have a gun pointed at my fucking head and see another Murray brother. I don't know this one's name, but I recognize him. He's blond and roughly Rian's height with blond hair.

"We're catching up. I've met Zariyah before, remember?" Rian answers, unconcerned with the terrifying blond man's increasingly reddening face.

"Fuck, Rian," the blond man growls. "Darragh has the priest at *gunpoint* in the backseat. We need to get a fucking move on."

"We won't get struck down for exchanging pleasantries. Zariyah, this is Aiden."

I give the terrifying blond man another quick glance. He doesn't look pleased and he also doesn't look sympathetic to me or to Rian.

Zariyah

"I don't care," I say to Rian, pleading with him. "Just tell me why you kidnapped me and what I have to do so you let me go. I haven't seen Callum in *years*. If this has something to do with him–

"Quiet," Aiden interrupts. "Yes, this has something to do with my brother and we will answer all your questions but for now, we need you to shut up and get ready. Rian?"

"Ready for what?!"

"Your wedding," Rian answers, a smirk returning to his annoying face. I want to sink into the earth. I start blubbering, but Rian grabs my forearm and drags me around the front of the car, giving me my first chance to properly scope out where we're parked. It looks like an abandoned church and our surroundings are noticeably desolate.

It sounds weird to say, but it still *smells* like Massachusetts, and I doubt we're far off from Boston, knowing what I do about how deeply Callum and his family are intertwined with the city's life. Rian pushes me in front of him and presses his pistol into my back.

"Walk," he commands, pointing towards the church door. So this isn't a joke. I hear the car door opening behind me and more footsteps.

A loud, thick Boston accent declares, "What would your father think of his son marrying one of those people, eh? I don't want to do this, Darragh..."

"Rian..." I start to protest but Rian just shoves the gun hard into my back. Message received: shut the fuck up. I walk forward towards the door of the church with no chance at escape. I'm a little better off than the priest since Darragh has his weapon pressed against the priest's temple and it's a sawed-off shotgun.

Marriage. A wedding. No. This has to be a prank. I enter the noticeably cooler stone church and can't deny what's happening anymore, even if Callum isn't in the church at all. It's empty and dusty enough that it must *really* be abandoned. Rian pushes me down a hallway into an empty room that looks like it's for the priest or nuns to get ready in.

There are two pews, a closet, a rickety metal chair, and hanging in the stained glass window, a wedding dress.

Chapter Five

I try not to gasp dramatically, but that's how I feel internally, like something just smacked the air straight out of me. It's not just a wedding dress, it's the one I always dreamed of, since I was a little girl. I drew it over and over again in sketchbooks. I talked about it. It's…

Beautiful.

I DON'T EVEN CARE what Rian does to me at this point. This is too weird and crazy for me not to fight back. I can't stand here and put on a wedding dress, and I definitely can't marry Callum.

I turn around once I take in every detail of the dress. I can tell just from looking at it that it will fit me perfectly. Whoever planned this actually planned it and if this is Callum's idea of a joke or revenge, I don't find it funny. I bolt for the door, making my best efforts to tear past Rian and take my chances at escape.

Apparently, I don't stand a chance because I thud straight into Rian's arms and he tosses me away from him with a forceful thrust.

"You're not getting out of this, Zariyah. Put the dress on. Callum's waiting."

"Is this Callum's idea?"

"Put the dress on," Rian says firmly, giving me a warning look. "Callum hasn't seen you in years and I'd rather not screw up your pretty face for him."

The dress isn't alone. There's a pearl thong with the dress. My stomach lurches. Does he expect me to put that on too?

"I don't want to see Callum!"

"This is for your own good, Zariyah," Rian says. "Trust me."

"I'm not wearing that."

"Yes you are. And you're wearing the panties too. Callum will appreciate that later."

OH HELL NO.

. . .

Zariyah

"WHAT THE FUCK is wrong with you people?! If you hate black people, why don't you just stay the hell away from us!"

My panic heightens. I'm not the naive eighteen-year-old I was when I left Boston. I understand how the real world works now. It's not all sunshine and roses. Hot white guys can seem like the sweetest guys in the world until you look beneath the surface and find... darkness.

Darkness like what I saw in Callum all those years ago. I don't want to marry him and I don't want to marry anyone. Your first love is supposed to be innocent and sweet, but Callum took that away from me. He fucked me and then he fucked me up. Rian doesn't react to my outburst, which only makes me heave and act more anxious. Great...

"I have a black wife," he says. "And you're very much mistaken about me, which doesn't matter in the slightest because I need you to put the wedding dress on. We can do this the easy way or the hard way, Zariyah..."

I choose the hard way and after twenty minutes of screaming like a banshee while Rian forces me at gunpoint into sexy panties and my dream wedding dress, I'm finally clothed. He pushes me against the wall the second he has the final clasp hooked and pulls out his pistol again, pointing it straight at my head. He's red in the face from the effort of getting me into the dress and I'm probably red-faced too.

I fought like hell, but Rian's twice my size so I just made his job difficult. There's no one coming to get me. If I can scream for twenty minutes and nothing about my situation changes... I'm at their mercy. I put my hands up. The dress is comfortable and after all this effort, it would be a shame for me to go out like this.

"Okay," I say, gasping for breath and ignoring the bead of sweat running down my cheek. "I'm done fighting. I'll go do it. Crazy motherfuckers."

My insult doesn't appear to have even the slightest impact on Rian. I got him real good with a couple of scratches, so the blood streaming down his face may be distracting him from my slick comments.

Rian keeps the pistol leveled at my head and his expression doesn't change. He gestures towards the door with his head.

Chapter Five

"I wish Callum the best of luck dealing with such an insufferable and impossible beast."

"Who the hell are you calling a beast?" I snap at him, trying to hide my sniffling again. I'm shaking as the reality sets in that they're really going to make me do this. I have to marry Callum — a man I swore I would never look twice at again. I haven't even seen his face in years. I haven't looked him up on social media... I never ask Lamonte about him and he doesn't exactly call up his little sister and keep her updated on his relationship with his best friend.

My brother is too busy with professional football to call me up often anyway. It's not like he neglects me — he helps all of us out financially — but we just don't talk like that. He would kick Callum's ass for this and Callum knows it.

So what the hell is going on?

"Come with me," Rian says and then he adds in a much kinder voice. "For what it's worth, you look beautiful. If he's smart, he won't screw this up."

There isn't going to be a "this", but I don't tell Rian that. I just nod and obey his commands, walking towards the door and towards my fate. An arranged marriage.

I can feel Rian behind me and my instincts heighten my awareness of everything, including the gun he has pointed at me as he guides me out of the dressing room and into the main part of the church. It smells dusty and I try not to let out a sneeze. My dress is beautiful and despite the circumstances, I don't want to mess it up or do anything unladylike.

The wedding march plays in the background from an organ. I glance over and there's a very pale boy (or maybe a young man) with black hair hunched over it playing the song. I'm getting married... I feel woozy and it gets worse when I turn down the aisle and see him for the first time in years.

My situation only grows more surreal as I realize how many people are here against their will. Darragh holds the priest at gunpoint, Rian has me at the end of his pistol and Callum doesn't even look at me first. He's busy glaring at Aiden, his blond racist brother with the cruel stare.

When he turns to look at me, I really mean to look away, but I don't and our eyes lock from across the church. Callum's face softens instantly and I don't know what happens to my face because I'm not thinking of myself at all. After all those years, my mind logically knows I should hate Callum and find the very sight of him repulsive, but seeing him again flips the logical switch off and my emotional response to seeing Callum Murray again is deep.

He looks... bigger. He's gained about forty pounds of pure muscle since I last saw him and it's not like he was a stick when he was a football player. As I walk down the aisle and to my fate, I can't help but notice how different he looks. I've never seen Callum dressed up like this. He's a blue jeans and flannel type of guy, not the type to wear a suit unless he's going to a wedding.

His wedding. Our wedding. I freeze as I approach the altar. I could faint. They can't make me marry him if I faint, right? I might not have a choice but if I do, I decide that I won't let myself faint in front of them because that would only make them marry me to Callum faster.

"Go on," Rian goads me in a low murmur and I have to force myself to take another step forward. I move my eyes away from Callum again. I shouldn't be noticing his new neck tattoo – a pair of dice. Or the new roses tattooed on his hands. The priest's outraged expression grabs my attention away from Callum again.

"I have to protest one last time," the priest says. "I do not want to perform a mixed race marriage. I have done many things for your family and kept many secrets. I will keep this one, but it goes against everything I believe to marry this woman to a Murray."

Aiden doesn't even flinch. None of them do except Darragh whose finger nearly moves over the trigger of his gun. He moves it back and swallows slowly instead, holding himself back. My only thoughts are to stay standing and not lose hold of myself because even if they force me to do this, they can't force me to stay with him.

"I understand your concerns, Father," Aiden says unmoved. "If you wish to continue performing work for my family and receiving large sums of money donated to the church as a result of that work, you will perform the marriage and then forget that you performed the marriage."

"Your father would hang himself before he let this happen."

"Trust me, Father," Aiden says calmly. "I would prefer not to use your services. However, my preferred priest is in Ireland, so you will perform this task."

"What would Padraig Murray think?" the man repeats, as if stuck on a loop. I can feel the energy in the room shift as the brothers grow more annoyed. I suppose they wouldn't kill a priest, but I can't be certain.

"My father is dead," Aiden continues. "I'm the boss now and I need my brother Callum married to this woman."

"I will do as you ask, Aiden."

"Thank you, Father," Aiden responds. He looks at me and nods with approval that does absolutely nothing to make me feel any better. What the fuck is wrong with this priest? If I didn't have a gun pointed at my back, I would have blurted that out. But I don't.

The priest looks at me and then at Callum before gesturing for the two of us to come closer together so he can perform the marriage ceremony. As I draw closer to Callum, my chest tightens. For the first time in years, I can smell him. He smells like Dr. Bronner's lavender soap and Old Spice deodorant which mix so perfectly and distinctly with his scent that it's nearly enough to make me faint on its own.

He towers over me as he always did and he's so close that I can feel the warmth emanating from his body.

"Stay calm, Zariyah," Callum murmurs, ignoring the fierce look from his older brother. "Everything will be okay."

I whisper under my breath to the man I'm about to marry, "Fuck you, Callum."

AND I DAMN well mean it.

Chapter Six
Callum

Then

"**W**hy did you do that?" she asks me when I pull away, giving me a strange look. I don't know if it's just because she's been crying or if it's something else.

"Because... I don't like seeing you sad."

"You don't care about that," she says. "I haven't seen you all night."

I chuckle. "It's a high school party. Your brother dragged me off to drink with the big boys."

"That is *so* annoying and immature."

Funny. That's what Lamonte used to call her when we were in high school and she was just a kid. They've grown closer over the years. Zariyah was always her brother's biggest fan. She followed him everywhere and she always wanted to do whatever the boys were doing. I always liked that she marched to the beat of her own drum and that she had those wild curls.

I could never think about her as more than pretty though. I don't know what the fuck is wrong with me tonight because it feels like I started thinking of her different long before the liquor, around the first time I saw her in that dress tonight. She looks great in that shade of teal and her pale caramel-colored skin only highlights her pretty dark features – thick dark brows, a mass of black curls and dark brown eyes that are insanely difficult to break away from once I get to looking at her.

But I'm the older guy. The *drunk* older guy who knows better than to touch his best friend's sister or indulge in any of his drunk or sober thoughts about what it would be like to get her out of that dress and into his bed.

"I have to stay away from you, kid," I say with as much assurance as I can muster. "Nothing annoying or immature about that."

There. I did it. I turned her down and put this behind me so I don't do something stupid tonight…

"I'm not a kid," Zariyah protests. "I'm a grown ass woman and I'm leaving my hometown. I want to live my life. I want to have adventures, fall in love… kiss someone for the first time."

I don't mean to give her the look that I do, but we're both looking at each other and the word "kiss" hangs in the air between us like a promise. Or like a threat. My chest heaves as my gaze drops to her lips. I've never let myself look at them before and I finally understand why. Zariyah's lips are a thick, full dusky pink that I instantly picture wrapped around my cock.

The dirty, depraved thought flashes into my mind and I shudder, exhaling loudly enough to thicken the tension between us. She won't stop staring at me and then she runs her tongue slowly over her lower lip like she's thinking about it too.

I lean over and let myself do something so fucking stupid and out of control. I know it's a mistake, but I tell myself that I'm too drunk to stop myself even if it's not entirely true, and that I want her too badly. I tell myself that I need this without giving a second thought to her brother, the future, or anything else. She's pretty, I like her, and I want to kiss her. That's all I'm thinking about.

Our lips meet and the connection feeds me an instant high. Her breath hitches as our lips first touch and I stop fighting the urge to hold her.

I pull Zariyah close as I kiss her and let myself feel everything at once. Her lips. Her hands on my chest. She smells amazing. I part her lips and slowly push my tongue into her mouth. She's awkward and uncertain about it at first, but I calm her down by kissing her slowly. I push my tongue into her mouth and tease hers slowly.

She's a naturally good kisser and she pushes her tongue back against mine. I could stay here kissing her forever but a twig snapping in the treeline forces me to pull away from her. This is fucking nuts. Her brother's inside. I don't have to say anything for her to know why I pulled away.

"Lamonte's not gonna come out here."

"We should go somewhere."

What the fuck is wrong with me? I'm not thinking clearly. I shouldn't be taking her anywhere but inside with her family.

"No," I say quickly. "Never mind. I should leave. You go back to your brother and have a good night…"

She reaches for my forearm quickly and grabs me. She's never touched me like this before. I know, because I would remember. Her nails dig forcefully into my forearms. I love the way her hands feel, I don't even care about the pain. It isn't that bad and it's fucking worth it to have her touching me.

"No," she says. "I don't want you to leave."

"Zariyah…" I plead with her, but I don't pull my arm away, even if I'm perfectly capable of it. I can't stop looking at her face. Round. Pretty. Everything I want. It's too bad I can't have her and I have to fight this, even if she won't let go of me. Even if I don't want her to.

"You *stole* my first kiss," she says, giving me a fierce look that only momentarily induces guilt. Smart ass kid. There was nothing stolen about that kiss. Her lips were perfect though and I haven't kissed her enough.

"You wanted me to kiss you," I say to her, shifting closer to Zariyah against my better judgment. I'm close enough to kiss her again. If I leave tonight, maybe that's what I'll leave with. One more kiss. I'll master my restraint and leave this beautiful, unsullied woman alone before my fucked up life ruins her.

I just can't seem to pull my arm away from her.

"I never asked you to kiss me," Zariyah cracks back, but she still doesn't let go of my forearm.

"But you wanted it. You still want it. But I have to do the right thing and let you go."

"What? Who says that's the right thing?" she protests, continuing to claw at my arms as she shakes her curls away from her face.

"I do."

"Why?"

"Lamonte."

She digs her nails into me harder and her face gets all pouty and angry. I know it pisses women off when we say it, but she looks fucking hot when she's mad.

"That's not a good reason," Zariyah says. "I'm eighteen. I can do what I want. I don't need Lamonte's approval."

"It's a mistake to get involved with me."

"Then why did you kiss me?"

"Because. You wanted it."

"Bullshit," Zariyah says. "I have a brother, Callum. I'm not stupid. You kissed me because you wanted me and I bet if I kissed you again, you wouldn't even stop me."

I tell myself she's wrong but then she kisses me again and completely fucks with my head. I don't stop her. She pushes her tongue in my mouth and then grabs my cheeks. I fucking lose it once she does that. I grab her hips and drag my best friend's little sister onto my lap, kissing her like this isn't the most dangerous shit in the world.

I might be in the mob but Lamonte's in there with famous football players who could gang up and beat the shit out of me if they wanted to.

That doesn't stop me from grabbing her hips and moving my

hands to Zariyah's perfect bubble butt. My cock gets instantly hard as I grab onto her butt. I know I need to stop myself but my hands are clutching a perfect handful of ass and I'm a red-blooded Irish man holding onto a beautiful woman who wants me.

She presses her hands to my chest and grinds her hips forward. The slight movement of Zariyah's hips drives me fucking wild. She pulls away from me to catch her breath and I force myself to take my eyes off her for a second.

"We have to get out of here," I grunt. "I'm not taking any chances."

Her hands move to my cheek and she runs her fingers through my short beard. Women have touched my beard before and I've felt nothing. Maybe a little annoyance. Zariyah's fingers running through my beard feels like heaven. I want her to keep stroking my beard all night.

"Where can we go?"

"My place."

"You have a place?" she asks, wrinkling her nose. I nod. She's only ever been to my parents' house, and only when my dad wasn't around, but I moved out a couple years ago. I've got my own place and we won't have to worry about Lamonte there.

"Yes. And I want to take you there... even if it's a fucking terrible idea."

Her thighs clench around me as she straddles me, making it impossible to control myself. Her body is so soft and it's been a long time since I've been with a woman. Not so long that I've forgotten what to do but... you get to a point where casual sex doesn't make you feel anything. I want to *yearn* for a woman and Zariyah fits perfectly in the palm of my giant hands.

This is the first night I've allowed myself to feel anything for Zariyah and it's rushing into me all at once.

"Take me," she whispers, her fingers running through my strawberry blond beard again. Fuck, I love the way she touches my beard. I want to belong to her just as much as I want her to belong to me tonight. If she's never been kissed before, she's definitely a virgin. And this is the last time I can stop myself from ruining her life.

Chapter Six

I pull away from her and take in just how fucking pretty she is. This is my last chance to turn back. I run my thumb over her lower lip. It's wet, soft and swollen from how much I just kissed her. She's perfect tonight. Perfect for me.

"Are you sure, kid?"

"Stop calling me a kid," she says. "I'm not a kid."

"I don't know what else to call you, Zariyah... I've known you-"

"Shut up," Zariyah interrupts, pressing her finger to my lips. "Just take me to your place."

SHE WANTS ME. And it's enough for me. I lift her up and carelessly carry her across the backyard all the way to my truck. After I got my last assault charges dropped, dad bought me a brand new forest green Ford F-150. I carry her all the way to the passenger side door and don't think twice about driving off.

Zariyah furiously texts friends and I assume she gives her brother some excuse if he messaged her. I drive us towards my new place quietly, just appreciating her presence and the scent of her perfume. I can't get over how magical she looks tonight. I'm just sober enough to drive, but I still take it easy through the twisted Massachusetts roads. I don't live too far from the new Armstrong place, so it takes less than ten minutes.

When I park I look over at her and damn. She's so fucking pretty that I could do her right here in the front seat of the truck. Maybe some other time. She's a virgin and Zariyah deserves better than in a truck for her first time. Zariyah looks back at me and flashes me a nervous smile. *I've never noticed how nervous she gets around me until now.*

"What?" I whisper, looking back because I'll take any opportunity to drink her in.

"Nothing," she says. "I just... you're really hot."

Fuck, she's so innocent.

"Come on," I whisper. "Let me get you upstairs, baby girl."

"Baby girl?"

"You don't want to be a kid anymore, right?"

Callum

"I just want you," she says, still smiling.

I could fall in love with her. I think I've been forcing myself not to…

Chapter Seven
Zariyah

Then

We're clearly here for one reason, but Callum still treats me like a gentleman. He carries me out of the truck like I'm a new bride and I wrap my arms around his broad shoulders. It's better than my fantasies because it's real and I can smell him, actually touch his body and soon... even more than that.

I want to keep holding on forever, but he sets me down gently in the entryway of his home. Callum helps me take my fancy shoes off and he gets me a glass of water before a brief tour of his house. My desire for him burns... I don't know how "going back to a guy's place" works, but I'm starting to worry that we won't even have sex.

Then he opens the bedroom door. He saved showing me the biggest room in his house for last. It's the most Callum place I've ever seen – and I've never seen it before. The last place I ever thought I would end up is my brother's best friend's bedroom. I can't wait to tell my friends, but first...

Callum puts his hand on the small of my back and I feel a strange throbbing between my thighs as he touches me.

"Like what you see?"

He has a normal, extremely masculine bedroom. The walls are a marine grey color, his bedsheets are white and there is sports paraphernalia *everywhere*. His bedroom isn't messy, but it smells strongly like a guy. Like Callum.

"It's... manly."

He makes a low chuckle in his throat and his body is so close and protective over me that the strange thigh throbbing intensifies.

"Did you tell your brother you left?" he asks. I don't want to think about Lamonte right now. I texted him and my friends, but Lamonte is the only one who hasn't texted me back, not like I told Lamonte the truth or anything. Sophia and Kalani want me to text them live updates about what's happening, but I don't want to spend the night glued to my phone when I'm here about to do what I've wanted to do for so long.

Callum wants me. He might call me "kid" but if he thought I was just a little girl, he wouldn't have brought me here to his sacred space. His sex dungeon... or whatever. I only got that phrase from the romance novel Kalani assigned me to read last minute to help me act sexier. Clearly, it's working.

I step inside Callum's room and shiver unwillingly. He puts his hand on my shoulder protectively and warmth spreads through me instantly.

"I didn't tell him where I was going. He's too drunk to notice what's going on with me, anyway."

"Good," Callum says. "I hope you know what you're getting yourself into, baby girl."

I turn around to face him as he ducks to enter the doorway to his bedroom. Callum has always been too tall to fit through door frames since I was a very little girl. He grins as I look up at him. Callum always looks at me like I'm an angel and right now it means everything.

"I know what I'm getting myself into. I thought you were avoiding me all night."

His face turns to stone. I've never seen him this serious before and it's almost scary, a feeling I don't really associate with Callum.

"I *was* avoiding you, Zariyah."

"Why?"

He puts his hands on my hips. They're so big that they wrap all the way around my hips and I'm not even that small. My throat tightens as I gaze up into Callum's golden brown eyes. They are the prettiest color, almost more gold than brown.

"Because the second I put my arms around you, I thought about bringing you back here and making love to you all night long."

I want to believe it, but it just seems so unrealistic. Callum is gigantic, sexy and he could have any woman he wants. I'm happy to be in his bedroom but...

"Are you serious?"

"You look stunning, Zariyah. Absolutely stunning."

He kisses me again, and I can tell that he means it from just how good it feels. I've only been kissed once before now, but I'm already obsessed with kissing. I can't tell if it's Callum or the act itself. His grasp on my hips tightens as we kiss slowly.

Callum's scent is everywhere and it's the perfect mix of Old Spice and Dr. Bronner's... and him. I don't even care about the taste of liquor on his lips because he smells so good otherwise. His natural scent is deeply masculine and arousing to me. As Callum eagerly parts his lips to push his tongue into my mouth, I reach up and touch his beard. I love that he's grown it out this much. I run my fingers through the thick hair on Callum's sharp jawline and appreciate the warmth of his lips on mine.

He pulls away from me, but I don't stop touching his beard, nor do I want to.

"Hm," he whispers, pulling away from me and letting his face get all serious again. My heart flutters with mild nervousness. His hands tighten on my hips, making me feel more secure in how he feels for me. He doesn't even have to say anything for me to feel the energy shifting between us. He wants me. I'm done questioning it.

"I like how your hands feel, baby girl. But I need to see you out of that dress."

I freeze a little bit and touch my hand to my shoulder. Callum meets my hand on my shoulder and gives me a smile that makes his intensely masculine face look very cute. The throbbing between my thighs intensifies. I want him so badly and it's not just the liquor or my childhood crush. Callum is 6'8" of pure man and I would be *crazy* not to feel attraction to him.

Plus... he's Lamonte's best friend and I won't lie, I love the rush of doing something that I shouldn't. I'm eighteen and I've always been the good girl. Never had sex. Never ever been kissed. Tonight, I want to get with Callum – the guy my brother warned me about since I became a teenager. He never trusted Callum alone with me, and he made sure to tell me the worst rumors about Callum like that could scare me away.

All the rumors about the bad boy only made me want him more...

"Let me help you," he grunts, pushing the strap of my dress over my pale tawny-colored shoulder. I shudder as he exposes my bare shoulder to his cool bedroom, but Callum doesn't let me stay cool for long. He presses his lips to my shoulder and the kiss makes me shudder and lose hold of myself as he removes the other strap and slides the dress over my strapless bra. As usual, my tan strapless bra slipped down a bit over the night, so now it barely covers my nipples. Callum's face turns bright red and he hasn't even seen me with my bra off yet. Just the sight of my breasts pushed together in my bra has an immediate effect on him.

"Fuck, I'm going to hell," he growls.

After that, he doesn't care about leaving my dress in tact. Callum grabs my hips and practically rips the dress off before unhooking my bra. My breasts swing into view and Callum presses my body against him. I feel a hard bulge against my lower abdomen as Callum holds me. That's his dick.

I've never seen a guy naked before and I've never been this close to an aroused, adult male. I kiss Callum slowly and reach my fingers nervously for his bulge, desperate to feel it through his pants. He makes an uncomfortable grunt as I touch his dick through his pants and I pull my hands away. Did I hurt him?

"No," he grunts. "Touch me…"

He kisses me and I touch him through his trousers again, allowing my fingers to feel the contours of his cock through his unnaturally formal clothes. My dress is on the ground and my panties are soaked and sticking to my thighs and my pussy. I've never been in this state before and I feel a little bit gross and a little excited.

"You're a virgin," he groans as I curve my hand over his dick and I pull my hand away again. Was I somehow doing it wrong?

Callum puts his finger under my chin and tilts my face so I'm looking at him.

"Why did you stop?" he asks.

"You said I was a virgin."

"You are," He says. "I was making a mental note, not telling you to stop. Keep touching my dick."

My hand returns to his dick. It's very warm and big. Are they supposed to be that big? I run my hand over it in slow movements around Callum's dick and his body tightens so all his muscles flex as I touch him. I gently squeeze his cock, hoping to figure out how big it is and Callum makes a low grunt in the back of his throat.

"Okay virgin," Callum says, his voice all deep and growly. "Give me another kiss."

I tiptoe as far as I can, but Callum still has to hunch over to reach my lips. He's so ridiculously tall that it's almost terrifying. He looks like a giant but he feels like home. I've known him for so long and feel so safe around Callum, that everything about the night feels perfect.

I press my hand against his chest and kiss him like he demands. I would give him anything he wanted. *I've wanted him for so long…*

After another perfect kiss, Callum slowly slips his hands into my underwear. I gasp as he fingers my lower lips like he's getting to know me down there. I squirm and feel warmth rushing to my cheeks as a strange tightness spreads through me. I gasp and squeeze my thighs together, trapping Callum's fingers between my pussy lips.

He smirks delightedly and pushes my thighs open before he rubs his fingers around my outer pussy lips and then he pushes his thumb in slow circles over my clit, touching me somewhere no other man has. I gasp loudly and Callum chuckles.

"Okay, virgin. You're the sensitive type."

"I'm not..." I start protesting, but then gasp again as Callum does something else with his fingers. It feels *so fucking good.* It's almost too much and I jerk away from him. He chuckles and takes his wet fingers out of my underwear, pushing his fingers into his mouth. My eyes widen as I watch him do that.

Callum grins and bites on his lower lip cheekily. "Don't look so scared, virgin. You taste good."

He's going to call me "virgin" all night, isn't he? I roll my eyes and Callum finishes licking me off his fingers very thoroughly before he kisses me again and his fingers slip back down into my underwear. I squeeze my thighs together again but Callum roughly spreads them apart, rubbing my pussy more thoroughly. He uses his other hand and pulls my body against his as he touches my pussy until my pleasure heightens to a point I can't handle.

"Callum... Please..."

I gasp and squirm in his hands but Callum just tightens his grasp on me and then starts rubbing my clit more intensely. I lose control of myself in a brand new way. Pleasure starts in my core and then I erupt with more intense euphoria than anything I've ever experienced. My first ever orgasm crashes into me and I let out a really loud moan that's almost embarrassing.

Callum presses his lips to my neck and sucks on my neck as he plays with my pussy while I cum. It's intense and I want so much more of him than this. As he wraps his arms around me, I impulsively leap into his arms. Callum lets out a surprised grunt, but he catches me easily.

He smiles once he's holding onto me and his hands go straight to my butt. Callum's fingers dig into the flesh of my ass cheeks and I feel the bulge between his legs stiffen more as he holds me against him and then drags me over to his bed. My heart quickens as I face the reality of tumbling into bed with Callum Murray.

It's finally happening. I grab his cheeks again and run my fingers through that sexy ass beard as I fall with Callum into his bed. He knocks the air out of my chest as he falls on top of me. Callum's weight feels fucking great and I don't even care that I can hardly breathe.

He adjusts his weight and moves his body so our faces are close to each other. He doesn't bother turning the lights off and I'm not the most experienced or confident person, so the lights on definitely makes me nervous. Callum grabs my cheeks and takes my mind off my flutter of insecurity as he kisses me slowly.

"You're fucking hot, baby girl," he says. "So fucking hot it hurts. I'm gonna eat your pussy until you scream…"

I want to hate the pet name but hearing it gets me so wet coming out of Callum's mouth. He slides my underwear off all the way and I shudder as his tongue presses against my lower lips. Is he going to make me cum *twice* before we have sex? I don't know what to expect and I can't ask because I lose myself moaning as he teases my pussy open and flattens his tongue against my clit.

"Callum…" I gasp and he rubs his tongue faster against my clit. *Oh my God, I'm gonna cum again.*

Chapter Eight
Callum

Now

Father Muldoon proceeds through the rest of the ceremony slowly. My brothers are absolutely crazy for dragging him here. There are much more forward-thinking priests, but apparently, most of them have left Boston for some sort of convention, so I have a racist priest performing my ceremony.

I was never much for dreaming about my wedding day, but I didn't imagine this. Zariyah won't look at me as he asks us to repeat our vows. He repeats his complaints about conducting an interracial marriage, but then we say our vows and he tells me that I may now kiss the bride. Only then do Zariyah's eyes snap to mine.

She looks at me like she wants to kill me, but she's still the most beautiful woman I've ever seen and even if all of this is fucked up – even for Aiden – I want to kiss her. I *really* want to fucking kiss her. I grab her cheeks and give her a wedding kiss that reminds me of the first time I kissed her.

Her lips are just as soft. She yields to me after a few seconds, even if I know it won't change how she feels about me. But I don't stop kissing her, and I don't want to. My brother has a gun to her back. This is probably the craziest night of her life and she deserves at least one thing that makes her feel fucking good.

When I pull away from her, the look on her face is pure hatred. But I didn't have a choice. This was Aiden's choice. I didn't even know she was the one they found and I definitely didn't know they would force her. But Aiden's my boss. I have to do whatever he asks… *I must.*

"Thank you, Father," Aiden says calmly. "My brothers will see you back to Boston and he'll give you our usual fee for marriages."

Father Muldoon's face steels and he turns to Aiden, boldly asking, "Mr. Murray, I think for a matter like this, I would request an additional bonus."

Aiden nods. "Darragh and Rian, get him out. Callum, take your truck back to Boston. I'll hire a car to get back to the city tomorrow. I have business to conduct here. I'll keep you informed."

"Got it, boss," Rian says. The church is uncomfortably quiet until Aiden dismisses us. Rian lowers his weapon and the transfer is complete. Zariyah's my responsibility and somehow, I'll have to get her ass back to Boston. My brothers must realize that if it took multiple firearms to get Zariyah here, it'll take some effort to convince her to leave with me back to Boston.

It doesn't matter what she wants, does it? *She's my wife.* In the mob a wife can be whatever a man wants – his partner or his possession. I never thought I would be in this predicament of turning a woman into my possession, but if my brother orders it, I must comply with his orders. My role is not to question Aiden, but to trust him.

I take a step towards Zariyah and she hisses, "Don't you dare touch me."

"Zariyah… I won't hurt you–

"Stay away from me!" she yells, her face wild and angry, her hair in a gorgeous halo around her head. Fuck, all those years and I swear she hasn't aged a damn day. She looks just as hot as she did when she was eighteen – hotter, because she's grown into all her physical features.

Rian intervenes. "Listen, Zariyah. Callum is more likely than any of us to treat you well. We're hours away from Boston and you have no money, and no ID. He's your husband. *Go with him.*"

Zariyah turns over her shoulder to glare at Rian, who doesn't move. He's always been the best at being stoic and it never bothered him how little our father paid attention to us. He wasn't like me. I always thought I had to be the biggest, the strongest and the toughest kid out there to get dad's attention. It worked but... it wasn't worth it.

Now that he's dead, I have so many fucking regrets about my past. One of my regrets is standing right in front of me in a white wedding dress like I dreamed all those years ago. Right now, marrying her doesn't feel as sweet as I thought it would. Zariyah takes a step towards me this time and I glance at Aiden for permission to leave.

"Don't lose track of her," Aiden commands. I put my hand on the small of Zariyah's back and pretend I don't notice her flinch when I touch her. She doesn't trust me. All those years later, she hasn't come any closer to forgiving me. She's like her brother that way – stubborn.

She's still mine. It doesn't matter how much she hates me, she's mine.

I guide Zariyah out of the church and point to my latest truck. She makes a disgusted snort.

"Another trashy lifted truck. Why am I not surprised? You racists sure love your dumb ass trucks."

She won't give me a break, will she? I keep my hand on Zariyah's lower back and ignore her comment as I walk her around to the passenger side of the truck. She doesn't fight me or try to run away when I open the door, but she glances at the seat with skepticism that she can make it up with her dress on.

I grab her hips and easily lift her into the truck. She whips around with fury written on her face. "How dare you touch me."

"I was just helping you get in the truck, kid."

It's instinctive, but the second I say it, I regret it. My face turns all red and I can see the outrage on Zariyah's face heightening as she pinches her lips together and knits her brows in absolute fury. She hates me and it hurts like hell. As I get into the driver's seat of the truck, my phone buzzes with a text message from Aiden.

. . .

Chapter Eight

AIDEN: Consummate that marriage, Callum. I don't care how you do it.

FUCK, he's busting my balls over this. He doesn't bother giving me an explanation that makes any fucking sense. Just marry the woman who broke my heart. The woman I've loved for years. The woman I never fucking got over. I swear, my fucking family is filled with sociopathic Irish fucks who deserve a hit in the fucking face.

They're the reason I spend so much time at the goddamned gym. I start the truck and turn to look at Zariyah again. She stares straight ahead with a stubborn, outraged expression on her face. She holds that stubborn ass position the entire drive back to Boston, refusing all my efforts at conversation with her. If Zariyah doesn't give a single fuck about me, how the fuck does my brother expect me to consummate a marriage with a woman who hates my guts?

He wants me to do something dark, or at least he doesn't care if that's how he gets what he wants.

I have a new place since the last time I saw Zariyah. I moved to be closer to my gym – which I bought after dad died. My house is only a couple blocks away from the gym now. I pull up and park the truck in my street spot outside the row house. It's bigger than my last place.

I lost the only woman I ever wanted to do that with. Well. I thought I had. There's only one bed in my apartment, which my brothers knew when they commanded this. I thought they would have at least found someone willing. *She doesn't want a fucking thing to do with me.*

Once I park the truck, I expect some acknowledgment of my existence from Zariyah, but she says nothing. She just folds her arms and waits. I get out of the truck and walk around to her side to open the door. She acts like she's gonna hop out of the truck in her fancy dress, but I can't let that happen. I take her hand and before she can snatch it away from me, I let go of her hand and reach for her hips to grab a better hold of her. She doesn't exactly protest as I set her down, but she looks upset.

I don't want to let go, even if Zariyah looks like she wants to slap the shit out of me.

"You look fucking beautiful, baby girl," I whisper. She's still so fucking small and fragile in my hands. I regret ever letting go of her.

"Fuck you, Callum."

My heart twists in a knot.

"I'm sorry," I tell her in a soft voice. "But I promise, whatever the fuck is going on with my family, I won't hurt you."

"Let go of me, Callum."

"No," I say to her, reaching for her wrist. She gives me an indignant look as I hold onto it. I'd much rather hold her hand but clearly, she's not ready for that. Despite her frustrated grunts, she doesn't make much effort to get away from me. Any efforts to escape me would be futile anyway, she's still short as fuck compared to me, more than a foot shorter than me. All the spunk in the world can't save her if I decide to throw her ass over my shoulder and drag her upstairs.

Hopefully it doesn't come to that. As we approach the front door, I can already hear Queenie howling from the other side. Poor girl gets lonely. I adopted her a couple months after Zariyah left Boston and I rarely leave her side, except when I'm working or lifting heavy.

I open the door to the rowhouse and take my shoes off. Zariyah glances at me nervously and then follows suit. I turn the light on and whistle for Queenie. I close the door behind us and my chest flutters nervously. Aiden's text message throbs in the back of my head. Zariyah walks ahead of me barefoot, even if she doesn't know exactly where she's going.

The hallway leads into the kitchen on the right and the living room on the left. The staircase right in front of us leads to the bedrooms. She's probably using her instincts to avoid going there, but she can't avoid it forever. Technically my row house has two bedrooms, and an office, but I didn't see the sense in furnishing the place with two beds.

One of the two bedroom's is Queenie's, she has a doggie door and a giant doggie bed – a fact I take great lengths to conceal since it doesn't exactly fit with expectations for a mobster. Or whatever it is I am right now. Aiden hasn't asked me to work in ages, so it's just been business at the gym, business at the casino and now… sudden marriage.

Zariyah wanders into my kitchen and then quickly whirls around to face me, pressing her back against the white marble counter, her hair and dress rustling the large pothos plant I've been growing for the past three years. Queenie lets out a little bark and rushes towards Zariyah, curious about the new person in our private space.

She's the first person outside of my family I've ever let into my house. It's weird to have another person here, especially a woman who I never thought I would see again. She made it clear that she wanted nothing to do with me. Her words cut me like a knife and numbed me to love for years. *And now she's mine.*

"I assume you asked your brothers to do this?" she snaps at me. "What the hell, Callum? There's no one here with a gun. I can call Lamonte *right now* and he'll kick your ass."

I have her cell phone in my pocket. Aiden slipped it to me after the ceremony and told me it was up to me if I wanted to give it back to her. There's no way for her to call Lamonte without sticking her hands into my pants pockets. I duck to enter the doorway and hang onto the frame, allowing my body to take up as much space as possible.

"I don't see what that will accomplish. We're already married," I point out to her.

I'm so large that I nearly have her pinned against the counter and I've barely entered the room. Queenie sniffs at her feet a little more and gives up once she realizes Zariyah won't be giving her any treats. She scurries off and I hear her waddling up the stairs to her dog bed all before Zariyah responds.

"Why the hell did you do this?"

"I'm following orders."

"What orders? Whose orders?"

"My brother's orders," I respond honestly. I can't explain any more than that and it's not because I don't want to.

Zariyah shakes her head in disbelief. "What the hell do I have to do with whatever bullshit your racist family is up to?"

Her accusation still cuts deep, even all those years later. You grow up thinking you're a good person and that your family is filled with good fucking people who mean well and love each other. Then you hear someone else, an outsider, say that all those good people are really bad *racists*. The word feels like a stain, an insult, and a diagnosis of poor moral character.

Nobody wants to be racist. But maybe she was right about me. Maybe back then, that's exactly who I was. And I'm still ashamed of it. I'm still ashamed of how I've hurt her. I'm ashamed of the beliefs I've held and the things I've done to please my family. If it weren't for Aiden, I would have done more and more until I became the monster she thought I was.

"I don't know what you have to do with it. All I know is that my brother commanded me to marry you and I do whatever my brother asks."

Zariyah rolls her eyes and folds her arms. That wedding dress is so fucking sexy that when she crosses her arms, the fabric pushes her breasts together, making them look fucking delicious. I'll never forget how it felt to see her naked for the first time and run my finger over those large, dark nipples.

Just looking at Zariyah gets me hard, even if she wants to kill me.

"I don't understand why I'm involved with this."

"Because after all this time, my brothers know you're the only woman I ever loved. They think they're doing me a favor."

I scowl as I admit it out loud to myself. Aiden doesn't want me fighting this, so he's put me in an impossible position. Surely he knows that I haven't seen Zariyah in years. I don't even know how the fuck he tracked her down.

"I have an apartment, Kalani's expecting me at work tomorrow and I have an entire life, Callum. I'm not staying here."

"Tonight, you are," I tell her, allowing myself to block her only exit. "My brother wants you here and he wants us to make love."

Zariyah glares at me fiercely. "Absolutely fucking not. I am *never* going to have sex with you again, Callum Murray. *Ever.*"

Chapter Nine
Zariyah

Then

Callum's tongue slides over my clit so he touches all my sweetest spots, and I lose control of myself as the tightness between my thighs grows before I explode all over his tongue. I can feel juices gushing out of me and at first, an embarrassing flush spreads through me, but Callum instantly makes that self-consciousness go away by licking all over my thighs, sucking the juices away and then teasing the flesh on my inner thighs until dark hickeys form on my pale tawny skin.

His kisses make my thighs shudder uncontrollably. It feels like I have no control over myself and that's something new about sex that I weirdly enjoy. I don't even know if I have permission to do it, but I put my fingers through Callum's hair. Apparently, it's the right thing to do because he continues his ministrations between my thighs and eats me out until I cum two more times.

When my body trembles with the intensity of those climaxes, Callum hovers his body over mine. He's still wearing all his clothes, but I can feel his cock straining through the fabric and pressing against me.

"I need you to take my clothes off," he growls. "I want to feel your sexy fucking hands all over me before I make you mine, virgin."

I wish he wouldn't call me kid, or virgin, or any of those pet names, but even if I hate them, I have to admit to myself that they get me soaking wet. I don't hesitate to follow Callum's orders to undress him. I've wanted to see Callum naked forever. I've seen him shirtless before while playing football with my brother, but that's very different from getting up close to him and touching him.

My fingers rush to the buttons on Callum's shirt and I quickly peel the buttons apart until Callum's broad muscular chest eagerly pops out of his formal shirt. I can't believe how fucking sexy he looks in a formal shirt. It feels like it should somehow be illegal how damn good he looks. As his chest pops into view, I notice Callum how big and sexy his chest looks.

He has tattoos everywhere, including large four-leaf clovers that yield into a Celtic knot cross surrounded by barbed wire all over his chest. The piece must have taken ages and woven into it are other symbols and words that I recognize as Gaelic. I pull the shirt over his shoulders and struggle to get it over the bulging muscles.

Callum grunts and helps me get his shirt all the way off. He has tattoos on his shoulders too – *I shall fear no evil* on his left shoulder and Gaelic script that I don't understand on his right shoulder. I touch his yummy, muscular shoulders and then run my hands over his back until Callum grunts and thrusts his hips forward. His cock strains through his pants and the bulge I felt earlier somehow feels even bigger than before. My stomach lurches, but Callum doesn't give me time to freak out.

He kisses me with his shirt off, letting me touch him all over. My hands wander all over his body, touching his shoulders, his incredible deltoid muscles and then his chest. I eventually end up touching his beard again and sinking my fingers in the rough strawberry blond strands as I pull Callum's face to mine for another dreamy kiss.

Nothing could ruin tonight. As I wrap my thighs around him, he grunts and pushes his hips forward. He kisses me until my lips feel sore but when he pulls away, I don't even want him to stop.

"Get my cock out, virgin," Callum commands, easing his hips forward and giving me space to reach for his trousers. He's wearing pants belted with a black leather belt decorated with a Celtic knot belt buckle. I work the belt buckle loose and Callum's bulge thrusts forward as I struggle to get the trousers over his muscular ass and hamstrings.

He has the best defined legs out of anyone I've seen and it's a struggle to get his pants over his muscles. More wetness pools between my thighs. I bite down on my lower lip as I grab the waist of his underwear and pull them over Callum's thighs.

His dick hits my thigh with a loud smacking sound. My throat tightens and I can't get air in. It feels like something the size of a can of Arizona Iced Tea just hit my leg. *This can't be right.* I'm almost too scared to glance down, but I don't even have to look. My body responds instinctively to the monster cock that Callum unleashed from his tight black boxer briefs.

This has to be the biggest dick in existence and it feels so fucking wrong. Like... it's not even human. I glance down despite my body's trembling and the nervous goosebumps all over my skin. Callum's dick is just as thick as a can of Arizona Iced Tea and slightly longer. His thick meaty girth tapers into a smaller cock head that allows cruelly little preparation for the rest of his monstrous dick.

Pre-cum oozes from the head of his cock in a large, almost threatening drop of clear fluid. He dribbles it onto my thigh as he runs his cock over my thigh. It's nearly the length of my femur. I'm a virgin. There's no way in hell I can handle this. As I whimper and try to scramble away, Callum grabs my wrists and pins them over my head.

I push against him instantly, but he easily overpowers me and keeps me in place.

"Not so fast, baby girl. No backing out now. I made you cum... it's your turn to give up that tight ass pussy."

I push hard against Callum's wrists, but there's no give. I grunt and push against him again, but a wicked smirk crosses over Callum's face and his grasp tightens significantly.

"You knew what you wanted when you came up here," he says. "Now you're in my bed, you got my cock nice and hard, so it's time for you to give up that control, baby girl."

Callum's body makes me feel crazy things that I've never felt before but now that I see his dick up close and feel his hardness pressing against my thigh, my thoughts race faster than I can handle. His dick is too big. Callum is an impressively sized man, but his dick is beyond impressive. It's terrifying.

"Giving up control is not my thing," I answer Callum, my chest heaving as he holds me nearly naked beneath him.

"Too bad," Callum says. "When you're in bed with me, you're mine to do what I please with. Those are the rules."

I pout and wriggle again, but that doesn't influence Callum at all. He leans down and runs his tongue along my neck until I moan. Once I release that first unwilling moan, Callum presses the head of his dick against my entrance. My chest tightens nervously as I feel droplets of warm liquid and then something soft probing at my entrance.

The soft head of Callum's dick won't do anything to prepare me for Callum's rigid and incredibly thick staff. He keeps my hands pinned to the bed so I can't brace myself against his body or push him off if he thrusts his dick into me fast.

"Callum, please..." I whimper as he pushes forward slightly. My tightness barely gives way to Callum's dick.

"Trust me, baby girl. You come into my bed, I need you to trust me."

"I'm a virgin," I shoot back. "I don't even know what you're doing..."

He gets close to me and nibbles on my neck until I calm down. Then Callum presses his lips to my ear and whispers, "I'm making you feel good. I'm claiming your pussy. I'm making you mine... and you don't need to fuss about it, baby girl."

I can't protest because Callum thrusts at least the first two inches inside me and I cry out loudly as he stretches me. It hurts. It hurts so much more than I thought it would. Heat rushes to my face and panic makes my heart race. I know Callum has barely put his dick in me and there's more of his length to go.

"Easy," he whispers. "You're just really fucking tight. It feels good baby…"

I bite down on my lower lip since it's the only thing that I can do from this position aside from using my feet to push Callum away, which wouldn't really work on him.

Callum braces himself on the bed and moves his hips forward to drive another couple inches of his dick inside me. Now I feel real pain as his thick shaft stretches me really wide. Callum has my thighs pinned lewdly apart so he can enter me leaving no defenses against his invading cock. I didn't know sex would be so painful… I want it to feel good but it doesn't.

Not at first.

"Almost there," Callum growls, running his tongue along my neck again. I can't help but moan in pleasure as he stimulates my neck, even if there's only pain between my legs. I have to trust him. He still has me pinned to the bed so I can't escape.

I close my eyes and allow him to take me. I stop fighting Callum and spread my legs wider. He grunts and buries the rest of his shaft inside me. The sharp pain subsides once he has his thickness buried inside me. I know once he starts to move, the pain will return but for now, Callum's fullness begins to bring pleasure to me deep inside me, touching parts of me I didn't completely know existed.

I at least didn't know these parts of me were so sensitive. He releases my hands once he buries himself inside me. I don't even notice completely until he cups my breast with his hand and then runs his tongue over my nipple, still holding his dick still inside me. I moan and buck my hips up instinctively to meet him.

"Good girl," Callum whispers. "I love your tight virgin pussy. You feel so fucking good… Best I've ever had…"

Callum's first movements between my legs bring back the pain of his first entry. I cry out loudly and my hands thrust instinctively against his chest. I meet a wall of muscle and my fingers curl against it. Wow. He has such a good body. Callum's hips withdraw from me slowly. I forget the pain as my fingers sink into his chest.

"Fuck…" he grunts as he slowly pushes back into me and my pain yields to pleasure. "You feel so fucking good."

"Callum…"

"Let me fuck you, baby girl. I want to make your tight ass pussy cum all over my dick…

Callum's dirty talk sends a deep throb surging through my body. I can feel my pussy clenching around his dick, sending pleasure to every inch of my body as he thrusts into me.

I feel more pleasure than pain from his cock and I can appreciate now how his dick takes me completely, forcing me to surrender to his desires. My body yields to him as heat rushes through me. I moan his name and Callum's thrusting increases its pace. Throbbing intensifies between my legs and my body approaches climax as Callum pounds into me harder.

"God, baby girl, you feel so fucking good," he growls. "I can't wait to feel your tight ass pussy cumming around my big dick."

Callum's dirty talk and how it feels to have his big dick plunging into me forcefully are more than enough to push me to the edge. My hands move from appreciating his chest as he pounds into me to stroking Callum's mess of auburn hair. As his large body hovers over mine and he slows down his pace to push me over the edge, my emotions are at an absolute high.

"I'm close…" I gasp, opening myself up to Callum and climaxing hard around him. I lose control of my body as I cum all over his dick and Callum holds me close to him as my thighs squeeze his gigantic body. He's so big compared to me that it makes me feel like he's protecting me, even as he fucks me hard in his bed.

"Good girl," Callum murmurs as I cum, taking my lower lip between his and nibbling on my lips as he kisses me. His gentle nibbling kisses turn into a full-blown make out session. His lips are full, delicious and he pushes his tongue into my mouth like he doesn't even care about what I've been eating or drinking.

Chapter Nine

It feels hot and dirty, especially because he still has his dick inside me and especially because he deflowered me in his bed. I'm his…

"Now it's your turn," I whisper to him. Callum grins.

"Trust me, baby girl. I plan on cumming inside you tonight," he says. My pussy throbs again and Callum moves his hips like before.

This time he feels even better. My first climax around Callum's dick makes me even more sensitive to his ministrations between my legs. He kisses my neck and then teases my breasts as he thrusts inside me and when Callum finally climaxes between my legs… I cum with him and it's amazing. Euphoric. I've never felt anything like it.

Callum withdraws from me and kisses me until I come down from my orgasmic high. He plays with my curls and I feel like I'm the most beautiful girl in the world beneath him. The way Callum looks at me is different from the way anyone else has. I didn't even know he saw me this way. I wonder what we're going to do about my brother. Or the future. But I know bringing that up to a guy after sex is like the worst idea ever, so I don't say anything.

I just let him touch my hair and then touch him back, stroking his hair and then his beard until we're both too sleepy to move more. Callum moves his body off mine and then pulls me tightly in his arms, holding me close.

"Mine," he murmurs. "You're always gonna be mine, baby girl…"

Chapter Ten
Callum

Now

One look on Zariyah's face and I know she wants to kill me, but she doesn't have a way out of this.

"Aiden has a good reason for wanting this. So we might as well get it over with."

"Easy for you to say," Zariyah hisses, spit blasting out of her mouth from the passion of her words.

I want to go easy on her, but I don't give a fuck what Zariyah wants. I have my orders and I've been ordered to make love to her tonight. It's going to happen.

"You can fight me if you want to, but I'm getting under that dress tonight."

If I'm going to do that, I'll need to get properly drunk. If I'm going to make love to Zariyah at all, I'll need liquor. This woman doesn't know what she does to me. What she did to me. I accept that she had every right to want me out of her life. I'm not the good guy. I might not be as mean as Aiden, as blatantly fucked up as Darragh, or as cruel as Rian. But I do terrible things and I don't mind doing them. I believe in the strength of the Irish people and what we've survived.

Zariyah has every right to want nothing to do with me. But she's still the woman who broke my heart into a thousand fucking pieces. And I still love her. After all this time, I still love her more than she can ever know.

"You aren't going to rape me," she says accusatorily. Her nostrils flare with frustration. God, it's so Zariyah. I've missed how she looks when she's angry. I normally saw her flaring those nostrils at her brother, Lamonte, but I don't even mind her turning her rage on me because at least she's giving me something. It's the most I've had from Zariyah Armstrong in years.

No. Zariyah Murray. She's mine.

My cock lurches at the thought of her belonging to me. Everything happening in this room right now is fucking impossible for me to handle.

"Christ, Zariyah… You know what my family is capable of doing. If I don't obey my brother's commands, I don't know what the fuck he'll do."

"I'd rather die than have sex with you again," she says angrily. "So if your dumb ass brother wants to kill me, I'll wait until tomorrow and he can do just that."

My baby girl. I remember her sass being a lot easier to handle when she was a teenager. Now that she's in her twenties, Zariyah has become even more of a pain in my ass. Doesn't matter. I'm still not gonna let her die or get in trouble with Aiden. Marriage hasn't changed my brother as much as he likes to think. He still has a dark side.

"I won't let that happen," I answer her calmly, trying not to let Zariyah get under my skin. I'm a pretty calm person, but if there's someone who stands a chance of riling me up, it's her.

Zariyah can't possibly think I'm doing this purely because I want to. If I wanted to kidnap her ass of my own will, I would have done it years ago.

"I'm trying to follow orders," I continue. "Not hurt you. It's sex, Zariyah. We've done it before."

That makes her cheeks get bright red. But I think it's from anger, not because she wants me. Her voice rises with anger again.

"You might be an asshole, but you wouldn't dare put your hands on me," Zariyah says, so fucking sure of herself. "You're not that type of person."

She doesn't know what type of person I've become since I left her. I steel myself for what I have to do and close the distance with one quick step. Zariyah sizes me up and wrinkles her brows.

"I'm not fucking afraid of you."

"Good," I growl. "Because I don't want you to be afraid."

Taking her by surprise, I wrap my arms around Zariyah's waist and easily throw her over my shoulder. She loses her fucking shit, which I knew would happen, but I steel myself to prepare for the onslaught of violence from Zariyah. Her fists slam into my back as hard as she can hit me, and it's pretty fucking hard.

"PUT ME DOWN!" Zariyah screams. I have to tune her out and get her to my bedroom. There's only one bed anyway and I have no intentions for either of us to sleep on my couch. She's coming with me and she's getting out of that wedding dress. "CALLUM!"

I ignore her screaming and kicking until I get her to my bedroom. I duck through the doorway and toss Zariyah's stubborn ass on the bed as hard as I can.

She shrieks as her body bounces off the bed and then she lands in a splash of white fabric that she can't get out of easily. That leaves me a few seconds to take control of the situation, which isn't very long. I shut my bedroom door and lock it. Zariyah shrieks my name and still seems stuck in the skirts from her dress. I toss a throw pillow from my bedroom chair at her head to keep her busy.

Zariyah yelps as the pillow narrowly misses her head, but that gives me enough time to increase my defenses. I shove a desk chair under the door handle and then put my hands on my hips, staring at Zariyah who pokes her head out of the mess of white fabric even angrier than before.

"LET ME OUT OF HERE!" she yells at me, scrambling to the edge of the bed with the pillow I threw at her head grasped tightly between her fingers. I keep watching her with my hands on my hips, letting her yell and act all crazy while I figure out how the fuck I'm gonna subdue her and get her ass naked beneath me.

"Not a chance," I huff as Zariyah swings at me hard with the pillow. It's like there's a tiny pretty butterfly in a white dress swinging at me. I glance down at her as she wallops me aggressively with the pillow.

"I hate you!" she screeches.

"I didn't ask for this, baby girl."

The pet name slips out of my mouth too easily, intensifying Zariyah's rage. She leaps up and slams the pillow into my head as hard as she can.

"How dare you call me that," she screams at me. "You have no right to call me any cute nicknames."

"What about Mrs. Murray?"

"UGHHH!"

"Can you calm your ass down?"

"NO!"

I narrow my gaze. There's nothing that will calm this hellcat down except... the one thing she claims she doesn't want. But I'm her husband, my brother gave me my orders, and maybe she won't like it at first, but I know I can have her begging for me.

"Fine," I growl. "Then I'll calm your ass down for you."

When Zariyah realizes I'm gonna lunge for her again, she makes another effort at escape, tossing her pillow like a decoy and attempting to run for the door. I hardly have to move before I catch her. I seize her forearm and ignore Zariyah screaming as I maneuver her so I can pick her up by the hips and toss her on the bed again.

She screams and tries running away again as I push her back on the bed and attempt to hold her hips steady as she fights against me like she's fighting for her life. The only thing that stops her furiously kicking my head is a loud rip that obviously comes from the fabric of Zariyah's wedding dress falling victim to our physical struggle.

"You ripped the dress!" she screams. I glance at her stomach where I ripped the seam between the top part of the dress and the skirt. Her exposed, pale caramel stomach gets me instantly hard. An uncomfortable moment of silence descends as Zariyah examines the tear and I can't take my eyes off her stomach undulating with each nervous breath.

I reach my hands inside the tear and rip the rest of it. Zariyah yelps loudly as I expose what she's wearing under the dress. *Holy fuck.* She's wearing a lace black thong with a pearl string. I can see the pearls wrapping around her hips and my cock lurches as I imagine the pretty pearls nestled between Zariyah's perfectly round ass cheeks.

The black lace thong barely covers her mound. Her hands rush to pull the ripped white fabric over the thong so I can't keep looking at her. Zariyah gives me a concerned look. *I'm scaring the crap out of her, but at least she hasn't lost her shit completely yet, so I'm all good.*

"You ruined the dress…"

"What do you care?" I answer callously. "You don't want this marriage. You don't want me. But I can't care either, baby girl. You're caught in a mobster's web and things will be much easier for you if you just do what I say…"

"Fuck off."

"No," I answer, taking the fabric from Zariyah's hands and exposing her stomach, thighs and of course her sexy ass pussy covered by that tiny shred of black lace fabric. "I'm not gonna fuck you yet, baby girl. I know you don't want this, so I'll go easy on you. It's been a while for me but… I still know how to make a woman cum with my tongue."

Zariyah shrieks loudly and shoots her foot out so the bottom of her bare feet press against my forehead. It'll take more than that to get me away from her. I grab her foot and gently pull her leg aside while holding her other leg down, causing Zariyah to yelp loudly and call me a long string of rude names.

Ignoring her protests, I drag my finger beneath some of the lace and tug it away from her body.

"Don't you dare," she says, struggling for breath as she increases her efforts to fight me off. Zariyah may be older and stronger than when we last saw each other, but I'm still more than double her size. She doesn't stand a chance. I yank the fabric harder and it rips away from Zariyah's mound. She screams after the loud sound of fabric tearing away from her body and makes another effort to scramble away from me on her elbows.

Zariyah's efforts to escape only drag her deeper into my bed. She's mine tonight and my heart races as it hits me hard. Aiden did everything he could to ensure this marriage wouldn't be a punishment, but maybe it's more than that. Maybe he intends for this to be my reward — the one who got away.

I grip Zariyah's hips and pin her to the bed as she pushes her hands through my hair, sticking to silent grunts of protest instead of screams now that she's tuckered herself out. I kiss the top of her exposed belly button, losing myself in the skirts of her pretty white wedding dress.

"I'm not gonna hurt you, baby girl. So you can calm down and let me say hello…"

She grunts again and attempts to smack my head. She can't reach and it doesn't matter, because I bend my head to her sweet pussy lips and suck on the outer ones, French kissing Zariyah's sweet ass pussy after years of painful agony away from her.

I remember everything about how she tasted the first night I brought her into my bed. She tastes the same and I fucking love the flavor. I run my tongue over her outer lips slowly, sticking my pink muscle into the crease of her thighs before diving between her lower lips again. Tasting every inch of her gets me rock hard and even more ready than before to make her cum and consummate our marriage.

"You taste sweet as fuck," I grunt, stifling any protest by finally pressing my tongue against Zariyah's clit and tasting her little nub with slow, purposeful movements. I remember exactly how to make her cum, exactly what her sweet ass pussy likes, and within a few seconds of my tongue teasing her clit, Zariyah's pussy dribbles those sweet fucking juices all over my lips and tongue.

She gets real quiet, those grunts turning into soft moans until I wrap my lips around her clit and suck on it hard. The soft moans yield into a loud, exhilarated moan. Zariyah might hate my guts but her body can't help but respond to me. I told her the first night we slept together — she's mine.

Nothing, not even time can take this woman away from me.

I don't just want to get her moaning. I want to turn her into a writhing mess with my tongue and eat her pussy so good that she gushes juices all over my face. I want to eliminate every fucking doubt in Zariyah's mind about me. I won't deny that I was a dick all those years ago, but I wanted to change. I have changed.

And I did it all for her.

Picking up the pace between Zariyah's thighs, I feel her edging closer and closer to a big one. She raises her thighs around my head and instead of fighting me off, she squeezes them slightly to hold my face in place as I eat her pussy. She doesn't bother hiding her moans and she gets louder when I lick the drops of pussy juice off her lower lips and then spread her wide with my tongue as I tease her clit.

"Cum for me, baby girl," I murmur, rolling my tongue faster around her clit and then pressing an index finger along Zariyah's entrance. My cock is about to burst from remembering how tight she was back then. I exhale slowly, warming her pussy with my breath before resuming my ministrations to her clit. I slide my index finger inside her as I lick her soft ass pussy and the force of my finger entering her tightness pushes Zariyah over the edge.

She grabs my hair as she climaxes, yanking on the long strands harder than she probably means to as she loses herself in a hard, passionate climax. Her long black curls are a tangled mess around her pale caramel skin and I thrust my finger deeper into her as I watch her cum beneath me.

I kiss her pussy as she calms down from the intense orgasm. I know it'll only be a matter of time before she's yelling at me all mad again. I have to get inside her before she does that. I take my pants off quickly and then pushing Zariyah back, I spread her thighs and climb on top of her so my dick lines up perfectly with her tightness.

She braces herself against my chest, grabbing onto my firm,

muscular torso with a measure of resistance. Zariyah looks at me and it feels like the first fucking time she's seen me since we got married.

"I don't want to hurt you, baby girl," I growl. "But I'm taking your sweet pussy tonight. It's been way too fucking long for me. And after all this time away from you… I'm still completely in love with your wild ass…"

Chapter Eleven
Zariyah

Then

I wake up in the middle of the night with a stomach ache. I don't really handle my liquor well. Callum always has bottles of Gatorade because of the gym, so I know he must have a stash somewhere in this place, even if I've never been here. I don't want to rudely go through his kitchen cabinets though, so I try to wake him up.

"Callum," I whisper a few times. Then I push on his gigantic tattooed shoulder, taking a second to observe his tattoos. They're sexy and they say a lot about him. I've never asked what they mean or anything, but I desperately want to know more about them. More than what he told me before.

"Callum," I say in a normal speaking voice as I push on his shoulder trying to wake him up again. It doesn't work. I tell myself that he's tired from sex, which seems reasonable considering I feel sore and tired myself. *He was so good.*

He doesn't wake up, so I get out of his bed and search for clothes. I find my bra on the ground and my underwear too, but my underwear doesn't even have cheeks to cover my butt so I'm freezing. My dress is too tight and uncomfortable for me to bother forcing myself into it. Callum has to have something I could wear. We just had sex – he wouldn't let me freeze to death after the night we shared together. Callum's not an asshole.

I tiptoe over to his closet, glancing over my shoulder in case he wakes up. He makes a little snoring sound that sounds stupid and cute coming from a guy that big. I can't help but smile. He's so good looking. I can't *believe* a guy who looks like that was my first.

Without thinking anything of it, I open Callum's closet door, expecting to find the clothing I normally see him wearing. He's said it himself that his wardrobe consists primarily of gym clothes – joggers that highlight his ass, tank tops that make his arms look like semi-automatic weapons, big t-shirts and hoodies. But this is the furthest thing from normal. Right on the hanger in front of me is a big white t-shirt with the stars and bars printed right on it.

The confederate flag.

You don't see those too often around Boston. I mean, you couldn't get any deeper into "Union territory" if you tried. Southerners might have excuses if their family members fought in the war, or if they simply have misguided notions about what the flag means. But up here, in Boston fucking Massachsetts, it's pretty fucking clear what this flag means.

I DON'T LIKE black people.

I *hate* black people.

And I support the institution and government that wanted to enslave black folks at any cost.

DOES he think I won't care because I'm mixed race? I glance over my shoulder at the gentle giant sleeping in the bed behind me. My stomach tightens in a knot. I let him take my virginity but obviously, he doesn't have any respect for me. I bite down on my lower lip and try to let a sane thought take hold.

I don't know what to do. I still need a shirt and goosebumps are breaking out all over my legs. Obviously, I don't want to wear Callum's confederate flag shirt, so I move it aside, finding a normal lime green shirt that says *Irish Pride* in white, celtic-looking font, but only after I've seen three more t-shirts with confederate flag variations. How many shirts with confederate flags on them does he fucking need?

Under normal circumstances, I wouldn't have minded the *Irish Pride* shirt or even thought twice about it, but considering the other articles of clothing in Callum's closet... I'm questioning everything. It's the first shirt I've come across that isn't explicitly racist, so I throw it on.

He's huge, so it fits me like a dress and I'm instantly warm. His shirt smells like him, which makes me feel that painful knot in my stomach again. *You have to get out of here, Zariyah.* I search the pocket of my formal dress (I chose well) for my cell phone and then tiptoe out of Callum's room clutching it and pretending that my hands aren't shaking with anxiety and fear.

Callum is racist. Lamonte tried to warn me and I didn't listen.

If I weren't at Callum's house, I would call Lamonte to come pick me up. He wouldn't hesitate to bail me out of any other situation. But he'll lose his shit if he finds out what happens and that will only make this bad situation worse. I easily find my way to Callum's kitchen. This time, I don't want to wake him up. Not until I know what the hell I'm going to say to him.

I send out an emergency text message to the group chat with my friends.

ZARIYAH: SOS. Found confederate flag shirt in Callum's house. HELP!

· · ·

Chapter Eleven

I'M surprised my friends are awake, but they ping back instantly.

KALANI: Not his?
  Sophia: He's racist. Run.

THE SHIRT IS DEFINITELY HIS, but I appreciate Kalani giving him the benefit of the doubt. He doesn't deserve it though. The longer I'm awake, the more it sinks in, the more the discovery hurts. I text back after a painful minute of consideration.

ZARIYAH: The shirt is his. I lost my virginity to a racist.

TYPING it out just twists the knife. Pain explodes through me, but I do everything in my power not to cry. I grew up with an older brother who would always make fun of me for crying, and I always tried not to be that person growing up – the *baby*. My discovery about Callum hurts, but I'll have to handle this my way. No crying.

Kalani texts back next, which makes me think they're in the same room and considering their answers together.

KALANI: Search his house for more shit. Find the truth.
  Sophia: Be careful.
  Zariyah: I should leave.
  Kalani: Learn. The. Truth.
  Sophia: Do it.

I'M in a daze because of my emotions. I'm hurt, totally confused, and I don't know what the rules are for confronting a white guy you've been in love with all your teen years over the darkest secret you could learn about someone.

He just has them… maybe there's a good reason.

My friends' text messages get in my head, interrupting any excuse or justification that I could possibly make for Callum. I feel crazy as I start swinging open kitchen cabinets and drawers, as if he would keep klan robes with the Dunkin' Donuts coffee beans. His kitchen turns up empty after I turn the whole thing over. I don't find anything racist, but I find other alarming signs of Callum's darkness.

First, there are two pistols under the kitchen sink and then he has mysterious black plastic bags shrink wrapped on top of his fridge. *He's a criminal. A racist criminal.* I can fill in the blanks with my imagination. He's a drug dealer who sells to black people and then kills them, I tell myself. It's dark and it fuels my searching frenzy.

SOPHIA: Find anything?

I UPDATE my friends with my findings and they goad me to search his house more. He doesn't have that many rooms – two bedrooms, a living room, a couple bathrooms and the kitchen. I could get through the rest before he wakes up, I tell myself, ignoring that what I'm doing feels totally crazy, even if there's a part of me that feels justified too.

Whatever. It's time to search his living room. It doesn't take long for me to find what I didn't even know I was looking for. I'm no stranger to finding hiding spots in a house filled with nosy ass people (yes, I'm talking about Lamonte again) so I make a beeline for the couch cushions and lift them up.

More fucking flags?

He has another confederate flag that looks hand-sewn and old enough to have been in the Civil War. It's folded beneath the couch cushions like it's special. Like it *means* something to him. I want to throw up. There's another yellow flag with a coiled up snake on it. Several older American flags.

Chapter Eleven

Messing with the flags causes something to thump around beneath the couch. I get down on my hands and knees and find the source of the thump – more guns. These ain't any damn pistols. They're huge semi-automatic weapons like someone in the army might have.

I move away from the guns and sit back on my heels, frazzled and confused about the man I thought I knew. I spent the past few years romanticizing Lamonte's hot best friend, but clearly, I didn't even know him. All that kindness he showed me, the way he acted like he wanted me last night... It was all fake.

"What the hell are you doing?"

I jump and gasp out loud embarrassingly. Fuck. I glance around the room nervously and it doesn't take long to find where Callum's standing. He's still impressively large, but instead of feeling protected and warm in his presence, a cold terror shoots straight down my spine.

I'm not the type to let fear fuck me up. I don't even think before I act. I just leap to my feet and yell at him.

"I'm learning that the guy I lost my virginity to is big fat fucking racist," I yell at Callum. Anger has never gripped me so completely before. I feel betrayed in a way I've never been – in a way I didn't think was even possible in the present day. In my mixed race family, I guess I had a naive view of how the world worked. How some people still considered me and my types of people to be lesser just because of our skin color.

"Zariyah," he starts... But I can't let him finish because this isn't something I can forgive. I can't look past what I've found or what it means. If Callum thinks the fact that I'm mixed race makes me a "watered down" version of a black woman who would be okay with this type of thing, he's wrong.

"I don't want to hear it, Callum. I just want to go home."

He frowns deeply. "I don't want you to go."

I can tell that he means it, which makes what I'm doing even harder. Callum sounds hurt, but it can't possibly compare to what I feel. I thought I loved him.

"I have to go," I tell him. "And I don't want to ever see you again. *Ever*."

I sound so convincing. His eyes flicker to mine. Callum, the tough guy, doesn't bother hiding his emotions. I can see how he feels about me written all over his face.

"Zariyah…"

"I'm serious. Just take me home and… *leave me alone.*"

"I don't want that."

"I don't care," I say to him. There's no screaming, no big drama, just that – a sad, soft ending to what I thought could have been something special.

I thought I loved him, but clearly, I don't even know what love is.

Chapter Twelve
Callum

Now

"I don't know what you feel for me, Callum Murray," Zariyah hisses. "But it isn't love. You are a deeply racist and troubled man. One orgasm at your hands changes absolutely nothing between us."

She can't push me off her even if she tried. I'm even more muscular than the last time I got into bed with her. I remember the way she grabbed onto my body and bucked her hips spectacularly as I thrust into her. She loves my muscles and they get her all hot and wet, even if she wants to deny it.

I'm even bigger than the last time I slid my dick between her pretty pale brown thighs and with all the tension between us, fucking her will be the release that we both desperately need. My cock strains against my trousers as I rip the rest of her wedding dress apart so I can access Zariyah's body.

She squirms beneath me, but when she opens her mouth to protest me drawing closer to her, I run my tongue over her neck in a slow stroke until she moans. That makes her slap me across the face. Hard.

"Bastard," she says. "You can't just ignore what I say. You've already done that enough."

I make her cum and somehow, I'm the bad guy. My face stings a little from where she hit me, but I don't mind. I like any time she touches me. I like that she's back in my bed, even if she hasn't yet accepted that this is where she belongs.

"I apologized, Zariyah. I got rid of the stuff you had a problem with. I haven't screwed up, not once, since you left. I've been a better person."

"You proved that completely by having me kidnapped, dragging me to your bedroom and forcing me into your bed. Consider me completely convinced of your improved moral character."

She sassily pushes her foot against my thigh like she's still trying to push me off her. I know we're past that. For all her tough talk, I still know the little girl she used to be. She might be a strong, grown ass woman now, but that innocent little girl is still in there somewhere. I just know it.

"I'm talking about the race stuff," I say to her, pushing her curls away from her face so I can get a better look at her pretty high cheekbones and those dark eyes that just draw you in like a whirlpool.

She gives me an uncomfortable look and unconsciously bites on her lower lip which she normally does when she's trying to stop some impulsive ass comment from flying out of her mouth.

"Isn't this proof that I've moved past that?" I murmur, kissing her neck and thrusting my hips forward to push my hardness against Zariyah's thighs. Nothing about her, or her heritage repulses me. I grew up the fourth of five brothers, so I grew up knowing that if I kept my mouth shut and said what I had to say, I could do whatever the fuck I want.

Hanging out with Lamonte as teenagers meant all the hottest black, Hispanic, and even Asian women flocked to both of us. Football helped get women, which was my main goal in life until I graduated high school. I wasn't too picky back then. I did find most Irish girls boring, but I hooked up with a couple South Boston girls from my part of town.

After high school, I got too busy with lifting and dad's business to chase women. I pretty much spent time with one girl – Lamonte's younger sister who tagged along with us everywhere 'cause his mom thought Zariyah needed constant supervision. I might have been a dumb ass kid who didn't realize the weight of certain things, the importance of certain parts of history.

I never was too good at school or listening or understanding stuff outside of my world. Losing her changed that and I want her to fucking believe it. But I guess I say the wrong thing because Zariyah only pushes against my chest more forcefully.

"Your dick getting hard isn't proof you're a good person."

"I'm here. I want you. If you conduct a complete search of this apartment, you will find no racist paraphernalia except… *one* confederate flag."

She slaps me again with a frustrated grunt and tries to push me off her with both her feet this time. I force her legs apart again and hold her open so she can stop her damn kicking.

"What is wrong with you?" she huffs as she continues her futile efforts to push me off.

"It's the personal battle flag of some confederate general and it's worth a lot of money. It's a family heirloom. But it's in a safe. Not like that would stop you."

"What kind of sicko would pay a lot of money for that?" she grumbles. *Man, she's sexy when she frowns. I'm getting impatient about getting between her legs.*

"I don't know, Zariyah," I reply with frustration. "But it's not like I have the damn thing flying out of the back of my truck. I learned my damn lesson with you. I'll prove it to you every day of our marriage if I have to. But you aren't getting out of this."

She stops struggling for a second and considers me with a very serious look, like she's trying to guess how much I care about her. After tonight, there's no fucking way I'll leave Zariyah guessing. I never thought I'd get a second chance with her. She's always been stubborn as hell and the only person who can change Zariyah's mind is Zariyah.

I promised myself if I got a second chance with this impossible fucking woman, I wouldn't waste it. Now I have her in my bed with a torn wedding dress and exposed pussy... I can't take this shit for granted. It's too fucking lucky.

I kiss her neck again. She squirms for a bit, but yields to my kiss eventually with a soft moan. That's much better.

"You can't keep me as your wife-prisoner for the rest of your life."

I can damn well try.

"I don't see why not. I was single until my brothers brought you to me. I need a pretty little baby girl like you to get my dick wet."

"Kalani will call the police if I don't show up to her house tomorrow like I promised. We have important business to discuss."

"Then you'll show up to her place tomorrow. With me. Is that enough for you?"

"No."

"Too damn bad..." I murmur.

I stop the protest about to leap out of Zariyah's mouth with a kiss and move my fingers between her lower lips. She gasps into my mouth as I kiss her and tease her soaked clit. She spreads her lower legs wider and I rush my dick out of my pants. My dick lands on Zariyah's thigh with a loud smacking sound that makes her flinch.

"I forgot how big that thing is," she says, her feet scrambling against the sides of my thighs as she attempts to push me off.

"I'll go easy on you, baby girl," I murmur, kissing her neck again. I kiss her on the lips as I press the head of my cock against her entrance. My dick remembers just how tight that sweet ass pussy was. Not much has changed about Zariyah's body. She's a bit thicker than I remember, but all the weight on her hips and tits gets me even harder. She's grown up now... *and mine.*

"There's no going easy on me with a dick that big..."

"Then lie there and let me please you, Zariyah. It's been a long ass time since I've been with someone and... you're very damn tempting even with that smart ass mouth."

Chapter Twelve

"Don't be foolish, Callum. I know what you were like in high school. You couldn't go five minutes without a girl on your arm."

"That all ended after you, Zariyah."

She grabs my cheeks and kisses me, but I can tell it's not from sheer desire, but because she wants me to shut the hell up. I don't mind because her full lips feel fucking amazing against mine. I push her lips open and stick my tongue in Zariyah's mouth. She teases my tongue for a while and then makes an effort to push my tongue out of her mouth.

I don't mind. I suck Zariyah's lips until she moans and then press the head of my cock against her entrance to find her nice and wet. Damn, she gets really fucking wet. I can't wait to get my dick inside her pussy. I push against her entrance and Zariyah cries out as I push just the head past her entrance.

Holy fuck. I thought I remembered how tight she was, but I was so goddamn wrong. She's even tighter than I remember. Her pussy is fucking perfection and it's like she's squeezing the life out of my dick.

"Wait," she gasps, pushing against my chest with more resistance again. "What about protection?"

I growl and push my hips forward, burying my cock several more inches inside her.

"You're my wife. We don't need protecting from each other."

"Callum…"

It's too late. I push my dick all the way inside Zariyah and kill every last bit of her resistance. Her pussy wraps tightly around my dick and instead of pushing me away, Zariyah finally stops resisting and her thighs squeeze me inside her.

Chapter Thirteen
Zariyah

Now

It's too late. All my fighting led to nothing. My attraction to Callum overpowers my morals and I moan loudly as he buries the full length of his enormous dick between my legs. I haven't let another man this close to me in a long time. I saw a couple guys, but none of them meant anything to me and none of them could get deep inside me like this.

Callum moves his hips to withdraw his cock with a slow rhythm to allow me time to adjust to his dick. The first few thrusts feel so damn good that I almost forget the big, sexy giant making love to me is a man that I loathe completely.

Before I can make my protest known again, Callum slides two fingers around my clit while he thrusts his dick inside me to the hilt again and I respond with an embarrassingly loud moan of pleasure. My moans and the euphoria of having Callum's big dick rubbing all my sweet spots forces my pussy to tighten around his dick.

He groans as my pussy clamps down on his dick and Callum's pale, freckled skin turns bright red, so red that it makes his auburn hair look darker as he pumps into me. He speeds up his pace, thrusting

Chapter Thirteen

into me with reckless abandon while he rubs my clit. I can feel how badly he wants me with each thrust. Each time he bottoms out inside me, I can feel myself getting close to cumming.

Instead of fighting him now, I'm moaning with each thrust, tilting my head back and allowing myself to feel the ultimate pleasure of having Callum's dick touching the most sensitive parts of my pussy when it's been a *very* long time since I've been with a man. I can feel an orgasm getting closer, so I let it happen. I grab onto Callum's meaty, muscular shoulders and move my hips to encourage him to take me deeper.

It's so wrong and I know I should fight him harder, force him to take accountability for the things he's done, for his beliefs, for who he...

"Oh my God..." I gasp as an orgasm crashes into me. It's so strong that I cry out again and drag my fingers through Callum's hair, pulling his face to mine so he can kiss me. I haven't cum this hard in forever and I forget that I fucking hate the man who just did this to me. He's an asshole, but damn, that orgasm was good.

I grab his lips between my teeth and bite as Callum keeps driving his dick into me.

"You like that?" he growls, picking up the pace and making me moan louder as I start to feel another orgasm about to hit me. "All that time and you still get so wet for my big white dick."

I moan in protest, but Callum doesn't stop thrusting into me and he doesn't stop that filthy ass dirty talk either.

"That's right, baby girl. Your pussy gets so wet for my big white dick. I love how tight you feel."

I cum really hard. I don't even pretend like I'm fighting him anymore. I drag his body close to me and let Callum nibble me all over with kisses while he slows down his pace and makes love to me. That's how I know he's getting close. He loses himself in passion and when he's ready to cum, he takes it nice and slow, appreciating the fuck out of me.

I remembered every damn detail of the night I lost my virginity to him. He's still always been the best sex of my life. When your first time is with a dick like that, nothing else can compare to it. I dig my nails into his back and watch the thick skin beneath my nails redden.

He smells so good. His weight on me feels incredible and his dick is just about to make me cum again with his slow, intentional strokes. I grab onto Callum's thick, muscular butt and draw him into me.

"You're mine, Zariyah..." he growls. "Mine..."

With one final thrust forward, I feel Callum's dick throbbing inside me and a gush of hot cum. It's more than I expect and his dick pushes an enormous amount of his semen out of me so it splatters all over my thighs. Callum drives his dick into me one last time, pinning me to the bed with his huge torso and gigantic, thick cock.

He kisses me for several minutes after he finishes. We're still intertwined, still closer than I've been with another person in a *long* time. How can things still be this good in bed between us? I swore my first time with him was a fluke. I had to tell myself there was no way a racist guy had been that good in bed when I swore him off completely.

"This ain't the only way I'm different," he says before pulling out of me. "Last time I had you in my bed, I was a fucking idiot and I let you go. I promise you, that will never fucking happen again."

"You can't keep me locked up like a prisoner forever, Callum."

And I don't just mean because I'll obviously try to escape the first chance I get. Callum might be a lot of things, but I don't think he could hold another person captive the way he's suggesting. He might have been angry with me, but the way he just held me and made love to me tells me everything about where his head is at.

It scared the fuck out of me to see those emotions on his face all those years ago, and it still scares the fuck out of me now.

"I'll do whatever the fuck I have to, Zariyah. I'll even call your brother up and tell him about us myself if that's what you want."

"I do *not* want that," I spit out, the flash of panic at the thought of Lamonte finding out about this reminding me why I shouldn't be beneath Callum at all, much less lost in an orgasmic sex haze with him.

"We can't avoid telling him forever."

"Do you want to die, Callum?"

Chapter Thirteen

"Sometimes."

"Ugh! No, Callum. You do *not* want to die. My brother will kill you if he finds out about us, and considering you snatched me off the streets and forced me to marry you, I have enough problems."

"Okay."

I exhale with relief that he doesn't press this particular issue. We can tell Lamonte after we've been married for a decade. By then, he'll have too many sports injuries to murder Callum. It sounds cold but it's probably the only hope this impulsive giant has of surviving Lamonte. He's always been protective of me and he's warned me away from Callum since he noticed my extremely obvious teenage crush.

My brother never found out how or why I got over Callum so quickly. If Callum wasn't stupid enough to spill the beans to my brother then, I hope he hasn't gotten dumber somehow.

"I'll take you to see Kalani tomorrow," he says. "No guarantees about your job. My brother must have brought you of all people into this for a reason. I'll have to do whatever he asks."

"So you let your big brother boss you around? Aren't you almost thirty?"

"It's not that simple, Zariyah," Callum whispers before kissing me again and removing his body from mine. I hate that I feel cold so quickly and that my instincts make me want to snuggle up next to him. Callum is my enemy and my husband, not my snuggle buddy or my friend.

"Nothing is ever simple with your annoying ass."

"Hm," he murmurs. "I guess I am pretty stupid for letting you go. Don't worry. That has definitely changed."

He throws a gigantic arm over me and drags me against him for what I guess is mandatory wifely snuggling. I'm too cold and naked to protest. Callum has a great body. It's impossible not to feel completely dominated and protected by his huge muscles and the size difference between us. He's the biggest man I've ever known.

And the most dangerous…

But I guess I'm past that now. I'm his wife and if there's any danger here, I'm already in the thick of it. I yield to Callum's cuddling and sleep for a few hours in his arms after he turns the lights off. I wake up in the middle of the night the way you do when you're in an unfamiliar bed and your body just screams "wrong!" as you sleep. My eyes flutter open and as my senses adjust to my waking state, Callum's delicious scent overwhelms me.

No. I can't let his hotness become a distraction this time. I have to pull it together. Men don't have fewer secrets as they get older, they have more. Callum might have scrubbed his house of confederate memorabilia, but there has to be something here to prove that he hasn't changed at all. Not like it would matter. I'm still not going to be his wife.

His past is enough for me to stay away from Callum. I can't let good sex cloud my judgment. I just need him to think I'm okay with him until I get to Kalani. She'll help me out. I try waking Callum up, but he's still a hard sleeper. That doesn't make me overly confident about escaping, because he could still be pretending. I don't know what lengths he'll go to considering he already had his family members kidnap me – or at the very least, he didn't stop them. I climb out of bed and look around, finding a pair of sweatpants and a t-shirt before trying to find a way out of the bedroom.

After quietly removing the chair from under the door handle, I gently turn the lock and open the door before sneaking out. Getting out of the bedroom was easy enough, but the rest of the house seems to be on lockdown. I tiptoe out of Callum's bedroom and head to the living room. That was where I found all the worst stuff last time. I check the doors and windows, but like I suspected, they're all reinforced. *Crap.* Sure enough, there's no Wi-Fi internet or landline phones, and deadbolts on all the doors with no keys left out.

I'm trapped with Callum, but I'm also trapped with all his secrets and he's fast asleep. This isn't the same house he had when I was eighteen. He upgraded big time. This house is big enough to house an entire family. I always knew Callum and his family had money, but considering the state of Boston real estate, this house must be over $1.2 million dollars. It's gorgeous.

I sneak back up the stairs into his room to continue my search. I don't find anything when I search Callum's bedroom. He doesn't even wake up as I open drawers and closet doors searching through his things again. I don't regret what I did last time. I have bigger regrets from that time in my life. Sophia died shortly after I left Boston and… I still don't know what happened to her. I have more regrets about her than about Callum.

Being in this situation again just reminds me of that crazy graduation party, one of the last fun nights we had together. Both my friends would have endorsed this. If Callum keeps his promise to take me to Kalani tomorrow, I can turn over whatever I find to her and see what she thinks.

I just wish I could get Sophia's opinion too. I miss her. I think I'll miss her everyday. It's been almost impossible to move on from losing my best friend, but over the years, I've just grown used to carrying the pain. I like to think that she's in heaven looking out for me. If that's the case, she must have been taking a nap when Callum's brothers were kidnapping me.

But that's okay. Maybe I have another reason for being here. Maybe there's some twisted cosmic reason for Callum and I to come together again. I search all the normal places in Callum's living room and only find a couple unloaded guns and cash, nothing too surprising since I know he's a mobster.

If Sophia were here, she would have also told me to search the couch again and make sure he wasn't lying about getting rid of all those stupid flags. I scramble over to the couch cushions and flip them over, finding absolutely nothing. His new house definitely has the vibe of a bachelor pad, but it's a lot more mature than Callum's last place.

Maybe he really did grow up. I want to believe that, but I just can't. Not until I search his place top to bottom and ensure he's telling the truth. The man had me kidnapped and forced me to marry him. I can't take his word for it that he's some good person.

But I don't find anything unusual in Callum's living room. The only unlocked room left is Callum's office. It's a little surprising that he has one and I want to tell myself that Callum the jock could never sit at a desk in front of a computer for hours a day, but I guess he was always going to get involved in one of his family businesses.

Callum's office is so... *him*. There's Red Sox paraphernalia everywhere. It's like a little boy got to decorate his dream office. A very rich little boy. The leather chair sits behind a solid oak desk. His office smells like sandalwood and there are even bookshelves... not something I typically associate with Callum.

I can't allow myself to romanticize him because he reads now. This ain't *Beauty & The Beast*. I scramble around the desk and yank the drawers open, hoping they aren't locked. They aren't. Callum went to great lengths to keep me trapped here and keep anything important out of sight, so I'm beginning to lose hope that he will have left anything out for me to find.

But right when I fling open the top drawer of Callum's desk, a folded stack of papers practically leaps out at me. Well, it leaps out once I move all the books on top of the stack of papers and open the envelope. It's hidden – and just hidden enough that Callum might not expect me to find it.

I glance at the door to his office, but at this point, I don't care if he walks in. We're married, right? That means he's stuck with me just as much as I'm stuck with him. I unfold the stack of papers and the text at the top catches my attention.

"AUTOPSY REPORT".

There's a case number beneath it and then "Decedent: Sophia Chung."

What the fuck? Why does Callum have this? I've (obviously) never seen this before, but Sophia's autopsy report would have been part of her police investigation, not public information. Not even her parents ever saw her autopsy report.

Autopsy Authorized by Dr. Rafferty.

I wonder if it matters that it's an Irish name. I know Callum has criminal connections and a large, wealthy family, but it can't be as bad as all this, can it? That ridiculous thought only lasts for a second. If there's one thing I know about Callum, it's that it really can be that bad.

Chapter Thirteen

I read through the age, race and sex before folding up the papers and quickly stuffing them in the giant sweatpants I borrowed before sneaking out of Callum's room.

The younger version of me would have been foolish enough to confront Callum, but he'll never let me out of here if I do that. He promised to take me to see Kalani tomorrow, so when he does that, I'll take this to her. Why does Callum have this? What does he know about Sophia's death?

A FINAL DARK thought enters my head. I know Callum has a dark side, a dark past and a dark fucking family. Maybe he had something to do with my best friend's death.

Chapter Fourteen
Callum

Then
One Year After Zariyah Leaves Boston

My father has no clue why I'm really in New York. He thinks I'm only here because of duty, but I have personal reasons for leaving Boston. I got a dog to keep me company in the apartment, a tiny basset hound puppy I named Queenie. She howls all fucking day and night, but I love having her with me. It's better than being alone all day obsessing over Zariyah.

I know her routine like the back of my hand now and even if she wants nothing to do with me, I can't help my fixation with keeping her safe. There's something fucked up happening in New York and dad wanted me out of Boston after my past year of screwing up. The only thing that has kept my fucking life together since Zariyah left Boston has been lifting weights.

And now, Queenie.

After taking Queenie for her evening walk, I get her down for a nap in the penthouse apartment I lease in Bushwick. There's someone in our family who's breaking the rules in New York. I don't mean my literal, biological family, but the mob family – the Irish folks who pledge loyalty and resources in return for protection from Padraig Murray.

There's someone breaking the rules by killing outside of Padraig's orders and they're killing young women in New York City. Before my father sent me on this investigation, I came here to make sure Zariyah wouldn't run into this unknown individual. I don't know why she would be in danger, but if there's any potential risk to Zariyah's life, I have to be there to keep her safe. With her brother playing football in the South, she needs someone looking out for her.

And anyway, I miss her. There won't be another woman for me. It's just Zariyah. Queenie falls asleep in her bed and I get dressed for an evening of grunt work. Our family connection in the criminal pathology lab, Dr. Rafferty, gave us all the information he could about the last three bodies in Brooklyn that were turned up by the police. Two of the women were black, one was mixed race. Like Zariyah.

There are so many missing people and so many murders in the city clamoring for attention. The press hasn't paid much attention to a few unknown women from Brooklyn who turned up dead. But I can't help noticing from the autopsy reports that the last body turned up by the NYPD was suspiciously close to Zariyah's bookstore. I don't want to leave this in anyone else's hands. Aiden comes in and out of the city on business, and if I need help, he'll be there for me, but aside from that, I don't need anyone else involved in this.

Dad's just happy I'm doing something aside from getting drunk and raising hell in Boston. It's not like I can tell him it's because a woman broke my heart. So I just keep doing what I know how to do – love her and keep her safe and hope one day she comes back to me. The only thing that could stop me from staying here is dad ordering me back home, but I'll find a way out of doing that until I can ensure Zariyah's safety.

With an active killer targeting young women in Zariyah's part of the city, she's not completely safe.

I dress in all black – joggers, black sneakers, a black long-sleeved t-shirt and a black hoodie. I pull the hoodie up over my hair. It's not easy for me to go incognito because of my height and sheer physical size, but I've grown so accustomed to watching Zariyah and stalking through her part of the city that it's become habitual to avoid her notice. She lives freely, like she's not afraid of anything.

I hope she can stay innocent like that forever.

Dad's instructions tonight conveniently take me close to the apartment Zariyah shares with her best friends, Kalani and Sophia. They all moved to New York together. Her friends are tough cookies, so it's some comfort that Zariyah isn't alone. But it's worrying that the man killing women keeps moving closer to the streets she walks down every day.

The killer has to be one of ours because of the weapons used and the signature he leaves on each girl's body – a brand with a four-leaf clover and a cursive 'M' in the center. It was enough for the doctor to reach out to my father, concerned that he ordered the killings and might run into trouble with the NYPD.

No fucking way. With the Vicari family Italians spreading their business through the city, the last thing my father would consider is risking a war with them. The Italians are brutal and they're just as territorial as we are. If this investigation gets too deep, we might have to let them know why we're here, although they probably have their suspicions.

Dad wants me to search a ten-block-by-ten-block grid again tonight. The center of this grid is the address where the NYPD recovered the last victim – a 21-year-old mixed race college student who was last seen by a cab driver three blocks away from where the police recovered her body. I'm looking for clues the cops won't bother searching for. Killers like this choose their victims because they understand the screwed up state of affairs in the city.

The cops don't give a fuck about women from Brooklyn or Queens. They don't give a shit about missing women who don't have the All-American look that gets more attention from the press. Even dad will admit it, although he doesn't think it's a bad thing. I walk around

Zariyah's neighborhood while she's safely locked in her apartment for the night. She luckily doesn't spend her nights in the city clubbing. That would make my job a lot harder.

Zariyah doesn't know I'm here but if this gets any closer to her, she might find out and then she's really going to lose her shit. She wouldn't approve of what I'm doing. She made it clear that she wants nothing to do with me and I've had to force myself to let her go. Mostly. I'm still technically stalking her, but I have a good reason for that. It's not like I think we have a chance anymore.

I start on the outermost streets, searching for clues, observing details about the streets I walked the nights before that I might have missed. Where and why might someone target a young woman? Does he find them at night? Why doesn't the bastard care where he leaves their bodies? Nobody around me seems particularly bothered that there's most likely a serial killer in their midst. If the media doesn't tell them to be afraid, they assume they're safe.

I suppose most people here are. The killer certainly has a type. Not white. My father doesn't have a problem with that part of things, he made that much explicit, but he definitely has a problem with someone killing in Vicari territory and potentially stirring up trouble with a family that's just as fucked up as ours.

This type of behavior could start a war.

After two hours of walking around and waiting for the sun to set and obscure my presence even more, I finally see something that could be useful. A woman-only club . I never noticed it before. It's exactly the sort of unassuming Brooklyn small business space that could be anything. But it's not just anything.

The Boss Ladies: A Feminist Women's Co-Working Space & Women's Club

I never noticed it before because… well… It's not exactly my thing and the building doesn't exactly stand out. I only notice it now because the door swings open, a bell rings, and a familiar face exits the building. I freeze, but she doesn't notice me and turns in the other direction.

It's Zariyah's best friend Sophia. I glance up at the building again, keeping her in my peripheral vision as I take a quick picture of the building with my cell phone and send it to my brother Aiden. He's in Long Island for business and officially on stand-by in case I need help with anything, dad's orders.

After sending him the picture, I follow up with a message.

Could this be where he's finding the girls?

I SHOVE my phone in my pocket and start following Sophia. Most women are pretty keen on when they're being followed. They're keener than men, so I know I have to be smart about it. For all I know, she could be meeting up with Zariyah right now and while I might slip past Zariyah's friends, I doubt I could slip past her. She's far too quick and she would be too attuned to my presence.

Zariyah has nearly caught me following her a couple times, even with my best disguises and all the skills I've learned about trailing people from doing business for my father. Her friend Sophia appears oblivious and it doesn't help that she has headphones in. I quickly glance at the map on my phone as Sophia turns right. We're still in my search radius and heading deeper into the circular shape marking the boundaries of the part of Brooklyn my father wants me to explore.

This feels more important.

I TEXT AIDEN AGAIN.

I might have a lead.

I FOLLOW Sophia for three more blocks before I have to hide behind a large rat-infested pile of trash bags to stay out of sight. She stops walking and looks at her phone, texting furiously. She turns to the building, checks the address and then looks around before furiously texting again. I guess that she's waiting to meet someone who isn't here. Wherever *here* is. I've been so intent on following her that I haven't bothered with tracking any landmarks or details about my location.

She turns around after sending her text messages and then she walks right up to the door behind her. It just looks like a normal Brooklyn brownstone. The door opens up and a man joins Sophia outside.

JESUS FUCKING CHRIST.

SOPHIA ISN'T SAFE. I want to run over to her, but I don't have time. I'm too far away and she doesn't even look terrified. She looks happy. Before I can take a single step forward, the man puts his hand on the small of Sophia's back and leads her into his apartment.

Even if I know it's too late, I tell myself that I at least have the advantage of the man not seeing me. The killer takes for granted that Padraig Murray has eyes everywhere. I run to the apartment door as fast as I can, even if I know it's locked and the man behind it can do what he needs to in seconds.

As I get to the door and yank on the door handle, I hear three gunshots in rapid succession. *I'm too late.* Holy fuck, I'm too late. Guilt floods through me first. If this were Zariyah, would I have been so slow to act?

I didn't think he would do it so quickly. I knew he could, but I didn't think he would. I still don't even know *why* this motherfucker is doing what he does.

I can't begin to understand why or how someone could be that fucking sick. I step away from the door, wishing I had more on me than a pistol. It's not like a pistol won't be enough against this guy, but I don't know what the hell he's got going on in there or why he would risk doing something like this against my father's orders. With my mind made up, I kick open the locked door.

I GO IN THERE and become one of the last people to see Sophia alive.

Part Two

Now

Chapter Fifteen
Zariyah

I make it back into Callum's bed without him noticing that I rifled through his things. I search for my phone and an escape route before I return to bed, but I don't find either. I can't even celebrate not finding anything racist in Callum's house because I found something worse than racism – evidence he knows more about Sophia's case than he's letting on.

Was he in New York back then? I don't want to believe that he could hide something this huge. When I slide back into bed, Callum doesn't even notice I'm gone. He drags me back into his deep cuddle and I keep the stolen autopsy report in the sweatpants. I know it's risky, but I don't want those papers out of my sight.

I let Callum think he wakes up first in the morning. He gets out of bed and heads straight for the shower while I'm pretending to sleep. As he hops into the shower, I rush out of bed. He only has three changes of clothes for me here, and I don't know where he got women's sweatpants or the scoop neck t-shirts. *Probably an ex-girlfriend.* I don't know why the thought bothers me, especially since Callum has sisters and he could have just as easily obtained the clothes from one of them.

I hope I get to keep the sweatpants. They make my butt look good.

I adjust the autopsy report so Callum can't find it and climb back into bed, sitting up and acting all innocent when Callum gets out of the shower.

He emerges from the bathroom with a towel wrapped around his waist. When I stuffed the autopsy report down my pants, I didn't anticipate keeping them on would be such a challenge but Callum gets out of the shower looking like a snack. It's been years since I've seen his body in broad daylight and as sunlight filters through the bedroom window, Callum's body looks amazing.

I don't know how he packed on even more muscle than he had before. His giant body oozes sex appeal, even if I'm a little bit terrified of just how large Callum is. I don't want to stare at him, but I can't help it. Callum's body has always aroused me. I never thought I would be that black woman who obsesses over white boys. I never obsessed over white boys as a concept but this one white boy has always just done it for me. He's not skinny and assless like a lot of white boys on television. Callum has thighs, a nice ass, big broad muscles like Dwayne "The Rock" Johnson and Callum's dick...

Callum has a dick that makes me throw my morals out the window.

"Like what you see?"

"I'm not even looking at you," I snap at him, even if I was clearly glancing at his towel hoping for a peek at Callum's dick. I don't want to give him the satisfaction of ogling his muscles.

"Fine. Get your ass in the shower then. I'll take you to your friend's place. But I'm sticking around and if you try anything... You don't want Aiden coming over to drag you back."

"As long as I can do my job and explain everything to my friend, I won't try to escape."

Now that I know Callum's ass has information I need, I'll stick very close to him. Kalani will definitely help with my plan once she hears the situation. Callum never told me that I have to keep our marriage a secret. I know Kalani will be surprised, but I can't exactly predict how she'll react to the news.

Chapter Fifteen

I walk into the bathroom fully dressed with a towel and a change of clothes so I can keep the stolen autopsy report out of Callum's hands. He never suspects a thing. Once I'm alone in the bathroom, I turn the shower on and read more of the report. I don't understand a damn word. I mean, I understand *some* of the words, but I don't know how it all fits together.

I don't know where Callum fits into this at all. Eventually, I have to actually shower to avoid rousing Callum's suspicions. Once I'm out of the shower, I pat my hair dry with a towel and twist my curls into a tight, high bun to keep them off my neck. My hair is cute most of the time, but it can also be a huge pain in the ass. I try not to take too long to get dressed, and then I stuff the autopsy report in my pants again before meeting Callum in his bedroom.

He sits on his bed waiting for me with a grin on his face. His smile makes me scowl instantly. What the hell does he have to be so happy about?

"You look beautiful. I don't know how you do that."

I roll my eyes.

"You could roll out of bed and you would still be the hottest girl I've ever seen. Blows my fucking mind."

"Whatever, Callum. I'm hungry."

His grin only gets wider. Does he not get the part where I don't want to be tethered to his annoying ass? I deepen my scowl hoping that he will eventually 'get it'.

"I always liked that you could eat," he says. "Don't worry, baby girl. I know you get hangry. I'll whip something up quick and then we can head out of here."

"Since when can you cook?" I grumble. Callum is so annoying. I don't think he's done anything for himself, but he seems confident in his cooking skills.

"That's nothing your sexy ass needs to worry about. Come on."

Callum feeds me breakfast that's disturbingly healthy and he eats about triple my portions. I finally understand how the hell he stays so damn big. He eats like a monster. He slides his prepared breakfast of eggs, a tomato and arugula salad, toast, baked beans and bacon. I normally have a coffee and the nearest, biggest serving of carbohydrates I can find.

I never cook. I've always wanted to have my own shit, not be some guy's 'wifey'. I don't see the point of cooking unless I really need to eat. Reluctantly, I take a bite of the breakfast Callum made me, expecting the eggs to taste like rubber, the toast to melt in my mouth and the baked beans to be sour.

But damn... from the first bite, I have to admit to myself: this shit tastes good. He clearly knows what he's doing in the kitchen, and the bedroom. I ignore the little voice in my head that says *hubby material* and shut it down completely by chugging the black coffee Callum prepares me in his French press. Judging by the old cups on his counter, he hasn't completely given up his Dunkin' addiction, but at least he also makes coffee like a grown-up.

I pretend Callum isn't watching me eat because although I don't want to give him the satisfaction of enjoying his meal too much, it tastes damn good and I'm hungry, especially from last night, so there's a limit to how much I can hide from him. I have to at least play along until Callum takes me to my best friend's place.

I finish eating way faster than Callum does. He has what I have in a much larger portion, plus a protein shake, a stack of four Eggo waffles coated in butter and maple syrup, and an extra sirloin steak. I watch him eat in fascination, even if I want to be completely disgusted by the beastly way the gigantic man eats. I gross myself out by thinking of how sexy Callum is when syrup drips from his lip into his beard.

Why am I turned on by his animalistic eating? Was it the sex? Ugh. The last thing I want to do is admit to even the slightest romantic attraction to Callum Murray. I will deny having feelings for him until my dying day. After the shit he put me through, I'm too proud to give him an inch of emotion.

I need more time before he convinces me that he's changed.

CALLUM AGREES to take me over to Kalani's place once I tell him the address.. He still won't let me have my cell phone and when I call him an abusive spouse he threatens to "abuse my pussy upstairs until I cum" if I don't get in the truck and leave it be. He drives a much more obnoxious vehicle than I remember – a lime green Dodge Ram 2500 with a diesel engine. I glare at him seethingly as I struggle to get into the truck.

He offers to help but I smack his hands away when he puts them on my waist. After the indignities of the day before, I can get my own ass into a truck. Even if it takes twice as long. Callum patiently waits for me to scramble into the passenger seat once he realizes I'm serious about him leaving my ass alone.

"What do you want on the radio?" he asks.

"I don't give a flying fuck."

He puts on *Holler Boys* by Ryan Upchurch and I regret not asking him to put on something from my R&B playlist once the man starts doing his thing. I stare out the window and try to reduce my intense scowling as much as possible. Callum might be annoying but in a few minutes, I'll be at Kalani's place and for the first time in years, I have something that could change our lives.

We can find out why the hell Callum has her autopsy report, and more importantly what actually happened to Sophia. He was too focused on me this morning to realize I'd gone through his office. I'll probably have to sneak it back in there if I can't come up with a better plan. That's where Kalani comes in.

Excitement builds up inside me as Callum parks his truck outside of Kalani's building. He takes up two parking spaces on purpose. This man must have more parking tickets than anyone in Massachusetts. It's not exactly like his garish monstrosity of a vehicle could go unnoticed. Nice leather seats inside, though. I'll give him that.

Callum rings the doorbell before I get to it.

"Do you have a plan for what you're gonna say to her?"

"Nope."

"Great. I'll handle it."

"'Preciate it," Callum grunts. I want to elbow him in the stomach, but I don't, because Kalani doesn't open the door to her apartment to greet us.

"What are you doing here?" I blurt out, taking a large step away from Callum so there's no question at all that there's absolutely nothing going on between the two of us.

My brother looks just as surprised to see me as I do to see him, and judging by the clothes he's wearing... he slept over here. What the actual fuck?

"Who's that by the door?" I hear Kalani calling from the other side of it. She doesn't sound surprised that my brother just answered her damn door. I feel like I got punched in the gut. Again. Is this what my life will be like now? Callum rolls in and now it's gonna be one problem after another.

"Did you ask Callum to give you a ride over here? If you would ever answer your texts, you would know I was in town," Lamonte says, never failing to give me a lecture about how bad I am at texting back. I glare at Callum because this time I have an excuse – that gigantic oaf took my cell phone.

I know Callum's ass isn't dumb enough to confess the truth to Lamonte right here, so I'm curious what the hell he's gonna say to appease my brother. I fold my arms and gaze up at him waiting for a response, playing the obedient wife for Callum and opting out of getting into this conversation with my brother.

I have a mission and they're the ones who are best friends. I don't need Lamonte getting all mad at me for thirsting over his best friend when I'm only here because Callum kidnapped me.

"Yup," Callum says, chuckling awkwardly. "She got lost like she didn't grow up here and called."

"So you had your phone on you?" Lamonte says, turning to me. I glare at Callum and don't even bother looking at my brother. In this situation, I'm perfectly content sitting back and letting my husband handle things. If that leads to him getting his ass beat, well, life is like that sometimes. They've fought before.

"No," Callum says quickly. "Right when I got there, she dropped it in a puddle and some dickhead kid on an eBike ran right over it."

Why the fuck is he adding all these unnecessary details? I swear Lamonte will see through the lie, but he honestly looks more nervous than concerned about what the hell I'm doing here. As the younger sibling, I learned one quick way to get out of trouble was to point out something bad Lamonte was doing to distract my parents. I have to use the same tactic.

"Why are you at my best friend's house in your pajamas?" I say to him, raising my voice in a tone positively dripping with sanctimony to really sell it. Me? I would *never* sleep with my sibling's best friend.

Kalani finally pops up behind my brother, but she doesn't exactly look like they're romantically involved. She's fully dressed for work. Since we open in a couple days, she's finishing up the inventory ahead of time and handling the arrival of our last shipment of books salvaged from our Brooklyn store.

"Where the hell have you been?!" she says to me. "Your brother shows up to hide out from the paparazzi who showed up at his hotel and his ass begs me to stay here, so I say fine. This big ass nigga starts eating me out of hearth and home…"

Yes, Kalani launches into her complaints without a care in the world for the awkwardness of the situation. We all have to stand around and listen to her. Callum flinches when she says the n-word, but she continues.

"He has eaten every damn thing in this house! I get up and I can't find a single egg to crack for breakfast. Lamonte, what the hell? I have to get to the bookstore, your sister's showing up dressed like a scrub and for some damn reason, she brought a big ass white boy with her who I haven't seen in years…"

As Kalani narrates all her frustrations in life, I can see that it eventually dawns on her that something is going on here. Something she wants to pay attention to.

"Hold on," she says. "What the fuck? Can y'all get y'all asses inside? Actually, Lamonte, white boy, y'all go get breakfast. I'll hold onto Zariyah here."

Callum gives me a nervous look, but he doesn't have much of a choice, does he? *I'll have a chance at escape.*

"No problem," Callum says, flashing me a quick threatening glare that no one else notices. He made himself clear before. I try running away, he'll get one of his creepy mega-racist brothers to drag my ass back to his apartment. I heard him loud and clear but... I don't give a crap.

I smile compliantly as Kalani shoves my brother out the door in his pajamas with Callum. She drags me inside and then reaches behind her to the kitchen counter where apparently my brother left his Gucci wallet with the snake pattern on it – that tacky shit he bought with his first NFL paycheck. She throws it after him and slams the door.

"I want a bagel!" she calls out. "Hurry up!"

We hear male voices grumbling in frustration and confusion outside and then footsteps. They're really doing it. They're really walking away. Kalani could always handle herself around men, but the way she handles those giant idiots makes me smile. Wait, no smiling. We're finally alone and it's time to get down to business.

"HOLY SHIT GIRL, I have so much to tell you," I blurt out.

"I do too," Kalani says, her eyes lighting up. "Your brother is *fine* and if you don't mind, I'm going to do everything in my power to get that mixed nigga in my bed."

I want to throw up. Kalani's confession momentarily distracts me from everything. But I don't want to be a hypocrite and demonstrate my disgust. It's just a natural feeling when anyone brings up thinking of your sibling in that way. Yuck. But I'm not exactly in a position to judge her.

"Kalani..."

"What? He's fine. I saw the naked Sports Illustrated shoot he did last year. Yummy."

"Ew! Kalani, that's my brother we're talking about. And I have way more important things to talk about than that."

"So I have your permission?" Kalani asks gleefully. Just because I'm not visibly throwing up in front of her, she thinks I'm okay with this. *Sigh.*

"I did *not* say that. Lamonte is a green-eyed biracial man who spent the past several years drowning in women. He's been ran through. He's basically a hoe."

"Yeah, and now I want a turn," Kalani says, genuine lust lighting up her face. Is the dating market in Boston that bad that she suddenly wants a wealthy, six-foot-tall, biracial ex-NFL player? Couldn't be me.

"Ew."

"Whatever," Kalani says. "Not saying no is basically yes."

I don't want to argue with her about that viewpoint, although I find it deeply concerning. We still have more pressing issues.

"Yeah…"

"What the hell happened to you?" Kalani asks. "I've been blowing up your phone since last night and I don't believe the bullshit story that came out of that big ass white boy's mouth for a second."

I don't know how to tell her, so I just blurt it out, even if it sounds stupid.

"HE'S MY HUSBAND. We got married last night."

YOU CAN NEVER REALLY KNOW what to expect when you drop a bomb like that, but Kalani's reaction is the opposite of what I expected.

"YES! FINALLY!"

"What? Kalani! You do know who was just at your door, right?"

"Duh. Do you seriously think *anyone* could forget Callum Murray? He's the only giant I know in real life."

She is getting the complete wrong message from this.

"He's evil," I remind her. "And he forced me to marry him last night. I am legally his *wife*. Do you not get how fucked up this is?"

She grins. "Did you consummate the marriage? You look like you got a little sex glow going on."

"I did what I had to do."

Kalani laughs. "Yeah I bet you did. Tricks on the dick and all that…"

"Kalani, ew…"

I don't want to relive last night and allow myself to recall even for an instant the way Callum's dick made me feel. I can't allow any positive feelings about that monster to linger for long. It doesn't matter how hot he is, or how he treats me. The man is rotten to his core. He had our best friend's autopsy report secretly stowed away.

I mean… He has to be evil.

"Girl, why are you tripping? If I remember correctly, the Murray family is a multimillionaire Irish family and the racist old man died, according to your brother, so if that white boy wants to blow your back out and spend his racist daddy's money on you, I don't see the issue."

She just doesn't get it. Kalani saunters towards her fridge, opens it and closes it again once she remembers there's no damn food inside.

"He kidnapped me and forced me to marry him!" I impress upon her the seriousness of the issue at hand, but she remains nonchalant.

"He was your childhood crush," Kalani says, as if that justifies the several felonies committed to get me down the aisle with Callum.

"You won't romanticize him so much when I show you this!"

I delay my big reveal when I have to scooch around like an injured bug to get the autopsy report out of my pants. Kalani raises an eyebrow until I produce it and smack it on the counter in my big gotcha moment. She picks it up carefully and reads it for a few minutes.

I wait patiently for her to finish reading. Well, not that patiently since Callum and my brother could return at every minute. I pace furiously while she reads. Kalani is used to my anxious ways, so she doesn't rush. When she's done, she puts the autopsy report down, her tone finally more serious.

"That's what happened? Some guy shot her and then stabbed her a couple times? It doesn't say why he left her in an alleyway though."

"Well it wouldn't say that," I said. "It's just an autopsy report. We need to investigate." I can tell that she disagrees. I *know* that she disagrees because she's my best friend and we argued about Sophia and what happened to her all the time.

Chapter Fifteen

Kalani has acted tough and together about losing Sophia ever since it happened. She does a better job than me of keeping it together most of the time, but that doesn't mean she doesn't feel pain.

"Callum had this in his office. It's suspicious."

Kalani shakes her head and rolls her eyes. "Come on, Zariyah. That man is in love with you. He didn't hurt Sophia. I'm not saying he isn't hiding something, but why don't you give him a chance?"

"Did something happen to you between yesterday and today?" I ask her. "It's not suddenly okay that a racist white guy from my past pops up, kidnaps me, marries me and then hides important information about my best friend's death in his office. I have a right to be concerned."

"That man loves your crazy ass and in all the years I've known you… well… when has there been anyone else?"

"I'm meant to be single, Kalani. I'm meant to die alone. I already accepted that years ago when my high school crush ended up being racist."

"Clearly you aren't meant to be single if you're married," Kalani says, not taking me seriously at all. "Why don't you trust him? He pops up out of the blue after all those years… maybe he has good intentions."

"We are talking about a man, right?"

"Yes. A big sexy man, who blew your back out last night."

"I never said that."

"Your glowing face says it," Kalani says.

"Aren't you going to help me at all?" I huff at her. "I told you he kidnapped me. Help me escape. I could run away to Charleston. No one would *ever* think I'd end up in Charleston."

Kalani laughs. "Girl, I'm not sending your stupid ass to South Carolina and I'm definitely not helping you escape the best dick of your life. Callum is rich, muscular, and crazy about you. I'm sure he has a good reason for hiding this. Tell him you went snooping through his stuff and see what he says."

Kalani can be so frustrating sometimes.

"What about Sophia? Wouldn't she want us to find out what happened to her? She would want us to investigate this."

Kalani's face gets all sad and then a little frustrated. "She's dead, Zariyah. It hurts me too, but it doesn't matter if we find out what happened to her. She's gone. We have to cling to the life we have for her."

It's not that I think Kalani's wrong, it's just that... I can't trust Callum that easily. We didn't exactly fall back into each other's lives under the best circumstances. But clearly, I can't budge Kalani and she won't help me escape.

"If I can't come to work, just assume that giant idiot has me tied up in his bedroom."

"If you need a few weeks to get used to married life, I'll hire someone part time to help me. Just settle into Boston, girl. The bookstore will be fine."

"I can't believe you are completely unbothered by the fact that a racist mobster kidnapped me and forced me to marry him. You're giving me time off to cope instead of planning to end his life."

"Girl, I stay unbothered. And I'm not messing with no damn mobster. Callum has a big bad family that could take my ass out. Lucky for you, he's fucking crazy about you and wants you. Bad."

"What kind of best friend are you?"

"The best kind," Kalani says. "Now look, take that autopsy report, put it back in your coochie or wherever it was and do whatever it takes to make that man happy."

"This is the least feminist conversation we have *ever* had."

"And I'm *not* sorry," Kalani says. "Do you know how badly I want my back blown out? Shit. I won't have you taking it for granted."

I throw her a dark glare, but Kalani only responds with a smug smile. I hold onto the autopsy report and consider hitting her with it, but I hear male voices in the hallway. It's Callum and Lamonte coming back with breakfast. I only have a couple minutes to act and apparently, I'm on my own here.

My own damn best friend sides with Callum. I stuff the autopsy report back down my pants just as Lamonte pushes the door open.

Chapter Fifteen

Kalani meets him at the door, lecturing him about inviting himself into her place without knocking first.

Callum clearly didn't tell him the truth since they're laughing together and talking baseball scores again. Even if they both played football, we all grew up Red Sox fans. Lamonte isn't acting any differently, so clearly he doesn't know or suspect anything.

I hear Kalani cackling flirtatiously with my brother from the front door. Ugh. She had better *not* see anything in Lamonte. She has been single for way too long if she does. She keeps cackling and I hear my brother chuckle, which he never does.

Great. I'm definitely on my own here. I glance around the kitchen before they break around the corner where they can see me. There has to be something here that can help me and I only have seconds to find it. Callum grumbles something that probably has to do with breakfast. I act impulsively, scanning Kalani's counter for something useful.

Score. I spot a small bottle on the counter with something that will definitely help and I slip it into my pocket.

If Kalani won't help me handle Callum, I'll have to interrogate him my way…

And he definitely won't like it.

Chapter Sixteen
Callum

Zariyah smiles at me sweetly as I return with her brother to her best friend's apartment. Talking sports with Lamonte was the only thing that could keep us safely away from the topic of marriage and I suppose Zariyah approves of my ability not to piss her brother off. Wow. This is all it took to impress her. She's barely given me a kind look since last night and I want to do everything I can to get her to just... fucking look at me.

I missed her soft brown eyes.

"I'm glad you're back," she says and her voice almost sounds like she's purring. I give her a suspicious look and she rolls her eyes.

"I'm starving," Zariyah adds quickly as if she doesn't want me getting the wrong idea. She grabs her food and takes a sip of the latte I got her – I still remember her order from highschool (soy latte with sugar free vanilla syrup) – but I'm not willing to sit around here for long and risk Lamonte getting wise to my bullshit.

By the looks of it, Kalani wants his attention more than I do. She leans over the counter with her boobs squeezed together, hanging onto Lamonte's every word about the recent Red Sox trade – something no woman alive gives a fuck about. Zariyah likes baseball just fine and even she doesn't give a crap.

"We'd better get moving," I announce. "I gotta get to work and uh… Zariyah wanted me to take her to get a new phone."

Zariyah doesn't protest, even if we both know what I just said is a downright lie. I'm taking her back to my place where she can't escape or get into any other sort of trouble. I'm sure if I left her here any longer, she would have hoofed it out the fucking window. "He's right. I'll eat on the go. Bye Lamonte. Bye Kalani."

I wonder if she's almost too willing to leave, but when I notice the confused expression on Lamonte's face, I decide not to linger too long to give him time to work it out.

"I don't want him to be late," Zariyah says. "I've wasted enough of this old man's time…"

Okay, I'd better get her ass out of here before she says something even more suspicious than that. We say our goodbyes and I help Zariyah's ass into the truck. She's too busy eating to protest and apparently, she's in great spirits.

"Should I be suspicious?" I grumble as she takes a delighted sip of her latte.

"Suspicious of what?" she asks with a snappy tone. "I'm adjusting to this horrific situation because Kalani won't help me escape from you."

"Wow."

"Yeah, don't think I've gone soft all of a sudden."

Hm. I could never be stupid enough to think *anything* could soften Zariyah. She's always had to be a tough cookie. I like that side of her. She's all fiery and spicy and everything regular Boston girls weren't. *I want her to get used to this, but I want more than that too. I want her to feel something for me. I'll keep trying until she does.*

"I could never think that, baby girl."

She gives me the meanest side-eye she can muster up. It's so damn easy for me to piss her off.

Zariyah stiffens in her seat and says haughtily, "I just recognize there's no chance of escape, so even though I will never have feelings for you again for the rest of my life, we can be roommates and continue this marriage contract until your brothers give us permission to have an amicable divorce."

Divorce? She must be out of her fucking mind. This didn't happen the way I thought it would, but there's no way I'm letting Kalani out of my grasp.

"What if Aiden never gives permission for us to get divorced?"

"We will live as collaborative partners," she says. It doesn't sound like I'll be getting a lot of pussy with this "collaborative partners" arrangement. Her stubborn ass won't even admit that we could be friends. That we *were* friends. I know I was a shitty guy back then but... I've changed. I really have.

I stifle my desire to scoff and instead nod along as if I agree with her.

"I see. Do collaborative partners have sex?"

Zariyah rolls her eyes, but she doesn't seem completely unhappy. "Your mind is only in one place."

I shrug. "I won't apologize for wanting to fuck my wife."

"You're right," she says. "Don't apologize."

Okay. Something is definitely up with her. I can't figure out what. Her face betrays nothing except maybe that she's a little annoyed with me. Zariyah is always a little annoyed with me, so that doesn't help in the slightest. I keep quiet until we get home. Observing her. She gives me very little to observe and when we get inside, she sighs and turns to me with an expression on her face that's almost warm. She gives Queenie a nice long pet and then I give Queenie a few treats while Zariyah cracks a few jokes about Queenie's lust for food.

It's nice. It's *almost* like I'm getting through to her. Fuck, maybe I am making progress with her stubborn ass.

Maybe she's had a change of heart. Her best friend has a good head on her shoulders and probably talked some sense into Zariyah. That would explain the change in her attitude perfectly.

"I'm sorry for being off the rails, Callum. This is a big change for me and... well... I just never expected to see you again."

"I didn't expect to see you either. My brothers... I think they thought I would want this."

Chapter Sixteen

"Do you want this?"

"I didn't want *this*. But I have always wanted you, Zariyah. The first night I held you in my arms... You were just different. You were perfect. I knew I never wanted to let you go. If I knew how much my actions and beliefs would have hurt you, I would have been a better man."

"Wow," she says. I don't know what to make of her reaction, but I know I want to close the distance between us. We're inches away from my couch and I can think of a lot of ways I'd like to spend the morning. First, I have to lock everything up. I lock us inside and put the key to the deadbolt in my front door safe, bolted to the wall and activated only by my fingerprint.

There's no way I'm letting Zariyah out of here for the rest of the day. With her brother in town, there's too much at risk. If her best friend supports our new relationship, she'll eventually come around. I can tell she's coming around already because she doesn't even scowl at me for locking the door and double locking away the key. Queenie bounds up to us with a wagging tail, and whines in frustration when I don't give her any treats.

"I know you're all pissed off at me, but I don't have any more secrets. I got forced into this the same way you did. There are probably a hundred women in Boston mourning my marriage right now," I respond to Zariyah, patting Queenie on the head.

Zariyah rolls her eyes. "Puh-leez. You are so annoying."

Queenie loses interest in me and wanders over to Zariyah, sniffing her fingers for remnants of anything tasty. She offers Zariyah's fingers a gentle lick, but loses interest, waddling over to her favorite spot near the couch. Zariyah and I don't take our eyes off each other.

"Yup. But I'm also yours," I tell her, hoping she can see how goddamn serious I am. "Now. Forever. From the first time I held you."

I close the distance between us, hoping to get us closer to the couch where I can convince Zariyah to get into all types of marriage celebrations. We both need time to get used to this. And I need to keep her out of sight so her brother doesn't catch on. I found out he won't be in town for long, so we can definitely keep this under wraps... at least for a while longer.

Zariyah allows my fingers to touch her hips and electricity shoots straight through me the second I hold onto her. This strong, possessive impulse overwhelms me every time I touch this woman. My grasp on her tightens instinctively and I pull her against me so our bodies touch.

She looks up at me, finally giving me her complete attention. I don't know what exactly I've done differently to earn it, but I know I have her now. Here. Stuck with me.

"We're going to stay here for the rest of the day. Get used to this new arrangement."

"I didn't get *anything* from Kalani and I didn't get my shit from my apartment," she says. "We can't stay cooped up in here all day."

"With your brother in town, I'm not letting your ass run all over the place. My brother Odhran will pick your stuff up."

"Who?" she asks, looking confused, but not reluctant. *She wants to be here.*

"Black hair. Played the organ at our wedding."

"I guess," she says. "The music was the last thing on my mind."

"Yeah," I murmur. "Same here. I was thinking about how much of a fucking bombshell you still are."

"Shut up, Callum."

"I'm serious," I whisper. "You're just... everything."

"I guess we're stuck with each other," she answers in a soft voice, giving me a look with those brown eyes that makes me totally weak. *Yes. Yes, baby. I want her to want me and right now, she's looking at me like she wants me and I'm rock hard just from looking at her.*

"Yeah. I guess so."

"Does that mean you're gonna want me to get used to my wifely duties?"

Her words hit me like a smack in the face. She *has* come to terms with this and now I get it. Sex. I did an excellent job at working her in the bedroom and now, she's finally coming to terms with our future together. I bet getting some food in her helped too.

Chapter Sixteen

I break out into a broad grin. "I'll always appreciate any wifely duties if that's what you're hinting at."

Zariyah smirks and reaches for my dick, cupping it through the outside of my pants. I stop thinking straight. Fuck, I probably stopped thinking straight the second she locked eyes with me. She rubs her hands slowly over my bulge, which only gets bigger as she fondles me through my pants.

This is a dream come true…

"I'm hinting at a blowjob," she says. "Then I'll make you some lunch."

Holy shit. What an incredible change of heart. I must be the luckiest motherfucker alive. Irish heritage does make me luckier than most. I think.

"Didn't we just have breakfast?" I ask her, tilting my head to the side. Zariyah doesn't strike me as the type to chase her breakfast with a second breakfast. But she just smiles sweetly, melting away all my concerns and suspicions.

"You're the size of a train, Callum. I know you're already hungry again."

Damn, she's right. And she appreciates my size, which means she notices the hard work I put into my muscles. Fuck yeah. This woman is beyond made for me. She's perfect. She's even more perfect than I thought now that she's not scowling at me like she wants to bite my head off.

"Okay. Blowjob and lunch. I can't argue with that."

If I knew this is what marriage was gonna be like, I would have done this a long time ago.

"WHY DON'T you sit down at the kitchen table," Zariyah offers. "Head for the head of the household…"

Her voice is like butter and I don't need her to tell me to get my ass in the chair twice. Just last week I was a bachelor forced to handle all my sexual urges with my hand. Now, I have my dream woman offering to get on her knees. I don't question a fucking thing. I slam my ass in the chair and spread my legs as Zariyah seems to saunter between them.

I can't take my eyes off her as she drops to her knees. She squeezes her sexy ass legs together as she eases forward, fully clothed. Before I can ask her to take her clothes off, she greedily reaches for my belt buckle.

My hips thrust forward enthusiastically as Zariyah rips my belt open. My zipper flies down, seemingly of its own volition and my cock nearly bursts through the fabric on my underwear.

"You have such a big dick," Zariyah says with genuine awe in her voice. It's almost enough for me to burst on the spot. My eagerness for her mouth is the only thing holding me back from instant release. I help Zariyah drag my pants and underwear over my ass and pretend not to notice how her hands linger over my butt cheeks.

She likes to pretend she doesn't appreciate my ass, but I've caught her checking it out before. She kisses the patch of hair above my cock and then plants soft kisses along the length of my shaft, forcing precum to ooze out of the tip of my cock in eager anticipation of her lips. *Fuck, her lips are so soft.*

"I want you so bad," I growl.

"Yes, Callum," she whispers, teasing me more by kissing the tops of my thighs. "I want you too. I want you so bad…"

I don't question her desire for me for a second. Zariyah's full lips feel so fucking soft. After her, I didn't bother with other women. I knew I'd lost the only woman I wanted. This is fucking heaven. Her hands wrap around the base of my cock and Zariyah squeezes me with just the right amount of pressure.

She runs her tongue over her lips to get them ready for my dick and just watching her is enough to push me close to the edge. The muscles in my legs tighten as I fight the urge to cum before she even puts her lips around my dick.

Zariyah gives my dick a nervous look before stretching her mouth wide around the head of my cock. She presses her free palm to the top of my thigh as her lips touch my cock for the first time. I suppress a groan as her tongue slides out beneath the head of my cock and Zariyah swirls her tongue around the sensitive head.

Holy fuck.

I don't remember the last time I had a woman's mouth on my cock. I forgot how incredible it feels to sit back and just *feel*. Zariyah moves her lips to take more of my shaft down her throat. Just when I think she'll stop because my cock is too big, she inhales sharply through her nostrils and then pushes herself to take my dick deeper.

The head of my cock brushes the back of her throat and I groan as my dick fills her mouth to capacity. Just touching the back of her throat makes me explode. My fingers slide through Zariyah's thick dark curls as I cum. Instinct takes over and I need every last drop of my cum to slide down her throat.

She patiently sits back on her heels and doesn't move as I release down her throat. I feel her tongue jut out and stroke the underside of my shaft as I cum, which draws more of my cum out. Shit... This is the best head I've ever had.

I could get used to marriage. I'm sure this is just as incredible for Zariyah as it is for me considering the smile on her face as I slide my cock out of her mouth. She even licks her lips. *This is love. She loves me.* My heart skips. She doesn't have to say it. Fuck, I don't care if she verbally spars with me the rest of our life together. Her lips said enough.

A blowjob as good at this one has to come from the heart.

"Fuck, that was good."

Zariyah nods. "Uh huh. Now let me get you something to eat."

"Is there a reason you're doing all of this?"

"I already told you. Kalani won't help me escape. I'm accepting my circumstances," Zariyah says, standing up and hurrying over to the kitchen. I stay planted in the chair with my pants around my ankles and spit in all my nooks and crannies.

"I'll take a shower before this *very* early lunch you're preparing."

"Take your time," Zariyah says. "I don't need you standing over me while I cook."

"I don't know. You have a way of getting into trouble," I say to her. I'm so fucking stunned from the good head that I'm practically slurring. I feel like a damn virgin.

"I'm not getting into trouble. Just calm down," Zariyah says reassuringly and with her typical frustration with me. Okay. I get up feeling all weak and pull my pants up. I need a shower badly to get my mind right. This woman... Where the hell did she get those tricks from? I'll have to ask her later when I get her in bed again.

I am *definitely* getting Zariyah's ass in bed again today after the shit she pulled on me.

It's hard not to jack myself off when I'm in the shower. I can't stop fantasizing about Zariyah's lips and about all my favorite parts of her. She's always been convinced that her ass isn't much to look at, but her butt is so fucking cute. I love grabbing those little cheeks and pulling her close to me. I love her boobs. *Fuck, I love her boobs.*

I spend my entire shower thinking of Zariyah without touching myself and after I dress for lunch, I still have a stiffie. I don't know what the hell she's thinking with all this cooking me lunch early, but she's right that I'm hungry. I normally eat *way* more than I did this morning. I just wanted to get the fuck out of Kalani's place before Lamonte pieced this shit together.

Zariyah has a steaming plate of my favorite food – corned beef and mashed potatoes with green beans – ready at the head of the table by the time I head out there. It's healthy and fits right along with my nutrition program for lifting. I'll have to bring Zariyah along to the gym tomorrow, but we'll discuss that after I dig into this delicious corned beef. I lose so much sodium on my heavy lifting days that I need the salt.

"This smells fucking good," I tell her, ready to dig in and hopefully get some dessert by dragging Zariyah off to bed. She gives me a big warm smile. *She wants to make me happy.*

I pull out the chair and ask her if she plans on eating anything.

"Nope. This is just for you, Callum. All yours."

Chapter Sixteen

This is definitely a change of heart.

"Thanks, babygirl."

"No problem, Mister Murray," Zariyah says sweetly. Respectfully. Finally, she's coming around to this. I feel like I've won a goddamn prize.

I sit down and dig in. *Fuck,* this tastes delicious.

Chapter Seventeen
Zariyah

I smile sweetly at Callum as he eats the lunch I drugged with the sleeping pills I stole from Kalani's apartment. I love handling things my way. I don't know when the pills will kick in, but I crushed in enough to hopefully knock out a man Callum's size. He's roughly the size of a rhinoceros with those gigantic shoulders and his ridiculously built chest. Who even needs that much muscle?

"This is damn good," Callum grunts as he scarfs down the food eagerly. My fake smile turns genuine as I watch my plan working. I make conversation with him about the Red Sox for fifteen minutes before Callum starts getting groggy and talking about the batter's touchdowns.

Maybe I went a little too hard on the sleeping pills. He's going down fast. I nod along and pretend everything is normal until he slumps over in his chair completely unconscious. I suppress the pang of guilt that emerges at the sight of Callum's unconscious body. I *almost* sympathize with him. When he's unconscious, he's not saying or doing anything to piss me off and I can appreciate how handsome he is.

I only give myself thirty seconds to appreciate him before I get to work tying his ass up. This will be the hardest part considering

Callum is a freaking giant. I race to his bedroom and grab every piece of relevant fabric I can find – mostly neckties, bedsheets and belts.

I use the belts to strap Callum's legs to the chair and then move his meaty arms behind his back. Just moving Callum's arms takes considerable effort, and I break out in a sweat by the time I finally have his arms tied together. Why the hell are his shoulders the size of fucking hams? I mean, he's hot as hell, don't get me wrong. But he's a bitch to tie up.

Thankfully, he's out cold, although I don't know when he'll wake up. He's still breathing too, which is good. I don't want to kill him.

Not yet, at least…

I use everything I have to tie Callum up to the point where he's basically mummified. I search the house for additional defenses and come up with a steak knife and a nine-inch cast-iron pan, which I rest on the dining table, out of Callum's reach in case he gets free. I set the autopsy report near the cast-iron pan and get the rest of my torture instruments.

It's nothing too crazy – a bowl I fill with water from his kitchen sink and *one* loose leather belt in case I have to hit him. I know it sounds extreme but… I'm on my own here and I desperately want answers. If I have to whup Callum, I'll steel myself to his screams and get the job done. I consider getting a filet knife from his kitchen, but I don't know if I can handle making him bleed like that.

Hell, maybe I'll even get him to unlock the freaking deadbolt that I can't find the key to and let me *go*. The inside lock does nothing to release me from my prison without the deadbolt key. *Asshole.* He really did prepare for everything.

Callum makes a sleepy snoring sound which makes me jump. *Damn.* I look over at him and even push on his tattooed shoulder, but he doesn't budge. He looks so sweet asleep that it almost makes me believe all the smooth, buttery words that spilled out of his mouth earlier.

I have always wanted you, Zariyah.

I can't believe he would say something so stupid. Callum slept with me because I was easy, tipsy, and eighteen-years-old. What he loves about me is sex, plain and simple. I can't let him fool me. I have to stay focused.

Before pity creeps into my heart again, I spend more time searching Callum's row house for clues. I don't find any clues but I find my cell phone in one of the kitchen drawers underneath a wooden cutting board. *Score.* I read through all my text messages and scan my missed calls.

I consider texting Lamonte about the situation I've found myself in, but I don't know what exactly I expect him to do. He would just take it as an affront to his own ego and blow up in some completely unproductive way.

I'm *legally* married to Callum Murray, I live here now, and Callum's entire mob family held me at gunpoint to get me to this point. Lamonte won't be able to get me out of this easily.

Instead, I open my chat with Kalani and read her three latest messages.

KALANI: Did you take something from my apartment?
Kalani: Your brother is taking a shower. OMG.
Kalani: How is Callum?

SHE IS COMPLETELY unbothered by my predicament. I don't see the point in replying to her either. I scroll through Pinterest on my phone for a while after deleting my dream wedding board. There's no point in *that* anymore.I set my phone on the kitchen counter in case I need to grab it on the way out. I'm assuming I'll find a way out. I need to give the sleeping pills time to work through Callum's system.

I make myself lunch, clean the kitchen and then keep scrolling until just before sundown. I won't lie, it's a bit boring, so I do break up my scrolling by idly going through Callum's things. Queenie follows me around sniffing everything. I have nothing against Queenie and supplying her with treats immediately endears me to her.

She's the perfect accomplice as I search through Callum's stuff, way more loyal to her nose and tummy than to Callum. *Smart choice, Queenie.*

He's cleaned up his act a lot since I was eighteen. He doesn't have racist paraphernalia hanging around. Most of his clothes are gym clothes, specifically clothing designed for powerlifters. There are puns about deadlifts, giant muscular animals, and what seems like a hundred different hoodies.

They all smell like him. I hate that I want to put one on when I should be plotting how to torture Callum and get exactly what I want. I need a list of demands, but instead I'm pressing Callum's hoodies to my nose and taking him all in.

Did he really mean it when he said, "I knew I never wanted to let you go"?

Ugh. I shouldn't even give that a moment of thought. He obviously didn't mean it, because he let me go. Sure, technically I walked away, but Callum didn't press me and as far as I can tell, I'm not really the reason he changed.

He just grew up and realized how bad it looked, but I don't think he's truly any different. I don't know. I guess I'm having doubts now. It's probably because he's asleep and there's a limit to how much he can annoy the crap out of me when he's unconscious.

He looked like he meant it though. I was the one faking everything. Callum was being real and he's been real since the second he dragged me through his front door. He might not have chosen this directly, but he's not unhappy with the arrangement. Judging by the big grin that was on his dopey ass face after I gave him head, he was downright euphoric.

I don't feel too guilty to change my course of action. I grab my bowl of water, which admittedly isn't cold anymore, and fling it over Callum. Queenie barks from the other room and comes sprinting over, lapping the water off the ground around me as Callum lets out a loud groan.

It worked. My heart pounds like crazy. Out of all the shenanigans I've stumbled into, I've never done something this crazy. Callum groans again and I consider getting more water when his eyes flutter open, sending droplets of water flying over his soaked face. His strawberry blond hair sticks to his neck and he looks confused as hell.

Maybe I should go put some coffee on. We could be here a while if my binds hold. Watching him regain consciousness makes me want to savor this rare opportunity. Callum always seems to have ultimate control. Now, it's my turn to take the reins.

"What the fuck?" Callum grunts and I decide against turning my back on him. He could lash out like an angry beast or break free like *The Hulk*. I grab my belt and hold the buckle and the end together so I can whip him properly if I have to.

"Hello, Callum. The tables have turned," I say seriously. I want to sound like a super-villain, but I sound like I don't know what the hell I'm doing.

"Zariyah…" he groans. "Are you fucking kidding me?"

He attempts to pull his arms away from the chair, but apparently I did a damn good job of tying his ass up. Neither Callum's arms, nor his legs move at all. He's securely tied to that chair and the more he struggles, the more confident I become that I secured the damn giant.

Perfect. His gaze snaps to mine and for the first time since he brought me here, Callum is genuinely pissed off. I fucking love to see it and I don't even bother hiding the smirk on my face.

"Zariyah what the fuck are you doing? How did I get here?"

"You don't need to worry about that, Callum. You need to worry about answering my questions."

Callum's face turns red. I love that about white men. I'll admit it. The way his cheeks show when and how bothered he gets. I know Callum has a temper buried underneath his strong, silent exterior. Now that he's tied up, I don't mind pissing his ass off and giving him a taste of his own medicine.

"This is not a joke, Zariyah," he says, straining fruitlessly against his binds while I smirk at his pain. "Odhran will be here with your things any minute. He was supposed to come tonight and I don't even know what time it is… If he walks in here and sees this…"

I don't believe his ass for a second. It's the dumbest lie. Like he said, he doesn't even know what time it is.

"What?" I interrupt. "He's going to kidnap me and make me marry my worst enemy?"

"Don't be so goddamn dramatic," Callum spits. I love that he's totally lost his cool. "I am not your worst enemy. You certainly didn't suck my cock like my worst enemy."

"I only did that to trick you into a false sense of security," I hiss at him. "And clearly, it worked."

Callum chuckles. "There was nothing false about what you did to me."

"We are *not* talking about sex," I yell at him, snatching Sophia's autopsy report off the table and rolling it up. "We're talking about this."

I smack Callum's shoulder with the rolled up paper. He doesn't budge or sound like it's really hurting him, so I give it up and just glare at him instead.

"Are those my tax returns?" he asks stupidly.

"No. This is my best friend's autopsy report," I yell at him. I don't really mean to yell, but I honestly lose my cool. There's too much adrenaline flooding through me and my emotions are all over the place. I'm sad. I'm furious. I loathe Callum, but even calling him my "worst enemy" out loud feels wrong. I want to trust him, but this stops me from giving him even an inch...

"Oh," Callum says, the scowl falling from his face. He doesn't even look nervous anymore. His emotions just fade away and he relaxes, as if he has nothing to hide. As if he completely understands.

"That's all you have to say for yourself? What did you do, Callum? Did you kill my best friend?"

That brings out his outrage instantly. "How the fuck could you ask me that, Zariyah?"

"I know you're shady, you're racist, and you had this completely hidden away, just like a criminal would."

I can tell he's trying to hold back his anger. Part of me wants to push him to his limit. I'm just so furious with him. *For everything.*

"I might be a criminal, but it's not what you think. I didn't kill Sophia, but I killed the man who did. And I fucked up real bad, left a shit ton of evidence. My brother used his connections to help cover it up. Your best friend's murder had to go unsolved, but I made sure the man who hurt her didn't hurt anyone else."

Callum hits me with so much information at once, that I don't know what to focus on first. I gape at him for a few seconds before I blurt out the first thing to pop into my head.

"How the hell did you know who killed her?"

Callum's response is an immediate wall. "Has it ever occurred to you that I keep certain things from you to protect you?"

"I'm not a baby, Callum. I am a grown ass woman and I don't need some caveman trying to protect me when I'm perfectly capable of handling myself."

"You have no idea the type of shit I deal with, Zariyah. You have no idea how fucking far I've gone to keep your ass out of trouble."

"I never asked you to do that," I snap at him, but honestly, I have no idea what Callum means. I haven't seen him once since I walked away from him all those years ago, but according to his confession, he was in New York City.

What the hell was he doing there?

"You don't have to ask a real man to protect his woman. He just fucking does it."

Callum makes my fucking head spin. I'm torn between diagnosing the words out of his mouth with toxic masculinity and wanting him to peel my panties off for being so damn into me. I'm used to fighting my body's irrational desires for Callum's brutish ways.

"How the hell were you protecting me? What were you doing in New York? And if you were so damn close to this, why didn't you save my best friend?"

Again, I don't mean to scream at him, but I've definitely gone off the rails. If Kalani could see this, she definitely wouldn't approve. But the eighteen-year-old version of my friend Sophia would. She would at least understand why I couldn't let this go.

Callum's facial expression softens and he doesn't take his eyes off me. I hate that his eyes are so intense and that they make his other-

Chapter Seventeen

wise cruel looking face so goddamn handsome. You tell yourself that a man with such beautiful eyes could never truly be a beast.

"I wanted to save her," he says. "But I was too late. So I broke every rule my family has to make sure a bastard targeting women like you never hurt anyone else. I could go to prison for the rest of my life for what I did. They have my blood, my hair, and my skin fragments in a lab somewhere and if my family didn't intervene... I would be in prison."

I feel the type of shock you feel when your idiot brother flings a football a little too hard at your head. My ears even ring the same way and I know my mouth is hanging open almost cartoonishly. Callum's murder confession contains more layers than I can handle all at once.

I don't know where to start.

"Explain yourself," I say to Callum in a shrill voice. He doesn't react to my shrillness with anything aside from his typical cool. I feel unhinged in comparison to him, which is crazy because he's the one who just confessed to murder.

"I'll explain myself if you untie me," Callum says, his request making his eerie calm more annoying because of its inherent cockiness. Does he really think learning that he's a murderer will inspire me to set him free? He's already too big for me to subdue without copious amounts of drugs.

"There's no way in hell I'm untying you. So talk."

"Zariyah..." he grunts, attempting to pull free again. I watch him fail with smug pride as he struggles against his binds. Thankfully, he gives up quickly, wrongly guessing that he'll have better luck convincing me to set him free by holding this information over my head.

"If you don't want to tell me voluntarily, I can always torture you."

"You wouldn't do something like that," Callum growls. "You're Lamonte's innocent little sister, not a guard at Guantanamo Bay."

"I don't need experience when I have the internet," I tell Callum. He might think he's hot shit because he's in the mob, but anyone with the internet can learn how to become a master criminal.

"You're not going to torture me," Callum says like he's commanding me on what to do.

"You have *no* idea what I have planned for you. I'm going to cut your skin into tiny little pieces unless you tell me the truth."

Callum raises a skeptical eyebrow. "Go ahead, then. Cut me."

"I'll do it."

"Go ahead," Callum says. "If you're going to torture your husband for information, let's get to it."

My husband. I ignore the way my stomach flips. I don't want him using emotions to manipulate me unless I have *all* the answers that I want.

I shoot back at him instantly, "Don't pull that shit with me. You're not my real husband. This isn't a real relationship."

I feel a sense of smug satisfaction that my words clearly hurt him and for once between the two of us, I have the upper hand.

Callum snaps back immediately, "Say that again and I'll tie your ass to the bed once you set me free."

"What great motivation to let you go," I respond to him, getting the steak knife and walking over to Callum, who doesn't even flinch. Is he really going to make me do this? I honestly hoped he would crack before this, but Callum keeps his unnerving gaze fixed on me.

His hair and skin is still wet and his muscular chest heaves with slow, deep breaths. If he's nervous, he doesn't show it. Sure, I'm scared to act on my threats, but he's wrong if he thinks I won't.

I take the knife and press it against Callum's skin, right against his chest. My hand shakes and we can both tell.

"Go on, Zariyah."

"I will if you don't talk."

He starts to say something, but I get too eager and I press the knife into his skin, slicing a little until blood seeps out. It's just a little, but my stomach churns instantly and I feel sick from what I've done. That's way more blood than I thought would come out.

I gasp as Callum makes an annoyed grunt and I drop the knife on the floor. Queenie barks and comes running back into the room, assuming that anything falling on the ground must be a treat for her.

Chapter Seventeen

She sniffs around the bloody knife, but neither Callum or I pay her much mind because we're glaring at each other.

"Seriously, Zariyah?"

"I told you to talk," I snap at him. "So talk."

"That hurt like hell you little demon," he grunts, pulling against his binds again. He seems more angry than pained, but he's definitely red in the face, which heightens my satisfaction. He deserves to feel a little pain for what he has put me through. I flinch as Callum's right wrist nearly gets free. That would be a goddamn disaster, but thankfully, my binds hold.

"Good," I hiss at Callum. The blood dribbles down Callum's bare arm. I definitely hurt him and I didn't mean to cut him that hard. But it's too late. I'm committed to the thug life now and I have to see this through.

"You have to untie me, Zariyah. Odhran will be here at any minute, and you don't want anyone in my family to find us in this position."

"If they were going to kill me, they would've done it instead of forcing me to marry your ass."

"You're messing with shit you don't understand, Zariyah. And if you breathed a fucking word about that autopsy report to anyone–"

"Well, I obviously told Kalani."

"Christ…" Callum growls, throwing his head back in frustration. His ability to make me seem like the bad guy is out of control. He's the one who kidnapped me. He's the one hiding his involvement in a murder.

"You never tell me the truth. If you told me the truth, I wouldn't have to conduct FBI level investigations to get to know who you really are."

"You know who I really am. If you would trust me for one goddamn minute, you could see quite clearly exactly who I am and exactly where I stand with your annoying ass."

"Really, Callum? Because I didn't know you were racist until I dug through your things. I didn't know that you killed someone until I stole this autopsy report. So far, my investigations have worked."

"The only thing you've done is get your ass into boatloads of trouble," Callum says, attempting to hide how he winces as sweat drips into the slice on his arm. He still isn't talking and I'm considering cutting him again. I didn't like how it felt and I definitely don't like how he looks with blood dripping down his arm but... *I need more information.*

"I am *not* in boatloads of trouble," I reply antagonistically. "I am in complete and total control here. You hate that."

"What I hate is being head over heels in love with a madwoman."

I raise my eyebrows and focus on the madwoman part because if I have to think about Callum saying he's "head over heels" in love with me, I might yield. He's practically shouting as he says it and for a man who speaks primarily in farts, grunts and growling commands, this is more than I've heard Callum say in a while.

He's really motivating me to keep torturing him.

"I see."

"Yes," Callum growls. "Good. So begin untying me at once."

"I still don't see why I should do that though."

"My brother," Callum growls. "And you hinted to someone that I committed a murder, Zariyah. It doesn't matter that it's your best friend. You've put both of us in serious danger."

"Don't be so dramatic."

"You can't keep me tied up forever. You got what you wanted."

Callum sounds a little desperate, but I don't want to give up my upper hand so quickly. I can use this position to negotiate some benefits for myself in this situation.

"I got information. You don't know if I got what I wanted yet," I say to him before bending down to retrieve my knife before beginning to pace back and forth with somewhat renewed vigor. Sure, Callum looks like he's in pain, but he's handling it well, which means he could probably handle another slice or two.

. . .

I APPROACH him and press the knife to his other arm as Callum glowers at me.

"Are you fucking kidding me?" he growls. "Zariyah... stop this at once..."

His firm command makes me hesitate. At what point is slicing up my husband unnecessarily cruel?

"Are you telling me the truth?"

"Yes. I killed your best friend's killer. I was in New York because I was worried about you. I never came to your apartment because I respected your decision to want to stay away from me. I have done *everything* to keep your ass safe that I could. I've kept tabs on you."

"Bullshit."

"It's not bullshit."

"Are you telling the truth about the other stuff?"

"What other stuff?"

"The being in love with me stuff?"

"Yes," Callum growls, his brows pinching together angrily. "Although I'm beginning to think I'm fucked up for caring."

"You aren't," I tell him. "I just..."

I'm hovering on the edge of a choice. Cutting him up or cutting him loose. *He loves me.* I know that shouldn't be enough to move me, but I can't help thinking that Kalani was right. Callum didn't kill my best friend and I feel a little stupid for thinking he could. Even now, he looks pissed off, but he doesn't look like he wants to kill me.

It's terrifying, though. What if I'm just too naive to know? What if he really is a dangerous person?

"Why is it so goddamned hard for you to trust me?"

"Because the first guy I ever liked, the first guy I ever trusted broke my heart in the worst way. He made me feel like he disrespected everything about my heritage and who I was."

I pull the knife away from Callum's skin. There's enough hurt between the two of us and I don't want to cause anymore. Just saying that to him was hard enough. I don't know if I can stomach cutting him again too, despite the temptation.

Zariyah

"I know I hurt you," he says. There it is. I think he's finally beginning to understand.

"Yes."

"If you let me go, I'll make it better," Callum says, hypnotizing me with those pretty ass eyes of his.

"You aren't mad?" I ask suspiciously. He seemed pretty mad before, but the energy between us has definitely calmed down.

"I just want you to untie me so you don't get your ass in more trouble with my brothers. If you had just asked me for answers, I would have told you the truth. I'm not the same stupid kid I was when you left town."

It's tempting to believe him. Oh so damn tempting...

Chapter Eighteen
Callum

I'm holding my breath waiting for Zariyah to respond. I'm mostly honest about my intentions with her once she sets me free, but I definitely cannot allow this unhinged and feral behavior to slide. I love this biracial woman with all my heart, but her crazy ass cannot go unpunished for drugging me and tying my ass up. No way in hell.

I keep my eyes trained on her, having learned the hardest way possible not to underestimate this sexy ass woman. She is *nuts* and right now, her fierce stare is getting me rock hard. I'm not ashamed. There's something about her sneaking, her plotting, her bratty fucking behavior that makes me want to show her I'm the boss.

Patience, Callum.

She yields just enough. Fuck, my arm hurts. Before I sink my claws into her, I'll need her to tend to that. Zariyah should know better than to just go slicing into people's arms. It's not a big cut, but it could easily get infected. I should know, I've tortured people before but I didn't do such a sorry ass job of it, I'll tell you that. But I act appropriately tortured, wincing dramatically as she prowls in front of me.

"Okay," Zariyah says. "I'll let you go. But only because your brother will probably pop up and I don't want him killing me on the spot."

"Give my brothers credit. They're a lot different than they were when we were kids."

I nearly lose my chance at freedom for *that* idiotic comment. Zariyah lectures me about how my brothers held her at gunpoint and forced her to marry me which proves her point that they're the "same old assholes" as before. At least she unties me as she rants, so I quietly allow her to proceed, not wanting to stumble into more trouble than I already have.

When my arms and legs are free, I wait patiently before acting. I need to establish a false sense of security in Zariyah. I groan and glance pitifully at my arm.

"You *hurt* me."

"Yes. You deserved it," she says.

"Didn't I just prove that I wasn't the wicked bastard you accused me of? I have never killed a woman. I wanted to stop what happened to your friend. I thought... I just want the world to be a safe place for you."

"Hm," she says, glancing at my wound. "Where is your first-aid stuff? I'll clean that up. I guess."

I direct her to the first-aid and use my newfound freedom to get my phone out of my pocket and establish my brother's whereabouts. He's late, naturally. As the youngest son, Odhran has always been the most spoiled. There are occasions where you can count on him and others where he needs a good kick in the ass to get going.

After I text him angrily, he messages back that he's thirty minutes away and adds a selfie of himself holding a baggie of marijuana. We don't have a huge age difference, but Odhran is from an entirely different generation. I send back an emoji and quickly shove my phone in my pocket. Thirty minutes is plenty of time for me to get what I want. Zariyah returns with the first-aid kit and I don't bother updating her on my brother's arrival time.

I'm still a little groggy and she has such an advantage on me that I don't want to yield more than I already have. She moves my arm gently and gets to work nursing me. For a woman who was so harsh moments before, Zariyah acts downright maternal when she wipes the blood away.

"This is gonna hurt," she says, the gleeful mischievous tone returning to her voice as she cleans the wound with iodine. I give her the pleasure of watching me wince. She's a little bit of both – a little bit baby mama material and a little bit crazy. I fucking love her.

She cleans me up, puts on some gauze and bandages me up. Once she's done, Zariyah throws her hands on her hips and gives me a concerned look.

"Great," she says. "You're all better."

I grunt and try to stand up. My legs are completely fucking stiff, so it takes considerable effort and I have to brace myself against the table. Once I stand, I feel my power returning. I glance over at Zariyah, who doesn't look the slightest bit nervous.

"Odhran will be here soon," I tell her.

"Yeah," she says, looking at me nervously.

"We all good?" she asks.

We will be. I nod and then close the distance between us. She doesn't suspect a thing. *Good.* I lean over and wrap my arms around Zariyah's waist, quickly hoisting her ass over my shoulder before she knows what hit her.

"CALLUM!" she screeches, beating her fists into my muscular back as hard as humanly possible. "CALLUM, YOU SAID WE WERE GOOD!"

She keeps screeching as I carry her to my bedroom, ignoring her yells. Queenie opens a lazy eyelid as we walk past her and determining that neither of us are screaming about snacks, she returns to her nap.

Zariyah keeps up her hollering until I shut my bedroom door behind me and quickly toss her on the bed, flipping her over so she's lying ass up. She knows something absolutely fucked up is about to happen, so Zariyah tries to scramble away, but our size difference makes it extremely easy to drag her ass back right where I want her.

I'm blind to the pain from my cut as I indulge the fantasies I entertained the entire time this fierce woman had my ass tied up. As

Zariyah screams, I pin her hips down. I'm too strong for her to properly fight back. She kicks her legs and thrashes like a bug, whipping her neck around in a strong effort to sink her teeth into my arm.

Holding her down with one arm, I use my other arm to rip away Zariyah's pants and underwear in one swift motion. She cries out loudly enough to wake the neighbors, but I'm lost in zeal as I expose her pale caramel ass to the cold air in my bedroom and watch goosebumps break out against Zariyah's sexy butt.

I can't believe she thinks this ass isn't perfect.

I raise my palm over Zariyah's butt and give her a hard swat that reverberates through her ass cheeks. She yelps loudly, screaming my name and calling me a very unkind name in return. I don't give a flying fuck if she's mad. She went too far and she pushed my patience this time.

"Callum!" she shrieks. "Callum, this is abuse!"

"I don't give a flying fuck," I growl, enjoying Zariyah's vulnerable position in front of me. For once, I've found a way of getting her ass quiet and under control. Tying me up was completely unacceptable, and she needs to learn that there's no fucking way she's getting away with this again.

I run my hand over Zariyah's smooth butt cheek, planning exactly where I'll hit her again. She shrieks and squirms, desperate to get away, but I smack her ass again. This time, Zariyah yelps even louder. My cock stiffens as I watch her perfect ass jiggle.

"I'll stop when you've learned your lesson," I growl. "Or when I turn that caramel ass red as a goddamn tomato."

"Fuck off, Callum!" she yells. Her ass is already turning a rusty-bronze color from two slaps. She's got under my skin so damn bad, I could smack those soft ass cheeks until she can't sit for a week. But watching that perfect ass of hers jiggle is getting in my head, distracting the fuck out of me.

I smack her again. And again. She cries out again. My dick gets impossibly hard and I stop after eight, keeping Zariyah pinned down. She trembles with pain, her ass completely covered in welts. This woman riles me up and turns me into a fucking beast. Her ass is redder than I've ever seen it before and the coloring makes me wonder if she'll be nice and bruised tomorrow.

Fuck, she looks hot like this. But I really did hurt her. And I got off on it. The guilt and the excitement swirl into a delicious blend of uncontrolled emotion. I bend over and kiss Zariyah's bare ass cheek, like I'm apologizing directly to the spot I spanked. She shivers and then squirms stubbornly, as if she stands a fucking chance of getting away from me.

I kiss her other ass cheek, provoking the same reaction from her. She shudders and I dip my fingers between her legs, finding soaked lower lips between Zariyah's thick, caramel thighs. She is so fucking wet. My fingers probe deeper, pushing past her thick outer lips to an even gooier center.

Zariyah makes a noise somewhere between an impatient grunt and a moan. Fuck, I don't feel like I'm in control around her in this state. This started off as wanting to punish her but my fury melts away into an overpowering desire to make love to her with just as much energy as I smacked her gorgeous behind.

She doesn't say anything after I touch her pussy and feel how wet she is. Normally, she knows exactly what to say, so it seems like I finally got the sass out of her for the time being.

"You arc soaked. Fuck, that little pussy is so wet..."

I run my finger over the length of her slit and my cock jerks hard against my pants, desperate for release. Not yet. Holding Zariyah's subdued body, I maneuver her so she's bent over the bed and I get on my knees, holding her hips in place so I can assess her ass and pussy from behind.

"Callum..." she pleads as I kiss every inch of her from the backs of her knees all the way up her gorgeous thighs and all over her welted ass. I caress her ass with kisses and she doesn't stop me. Pussy juices dribble from between Zariyah's thighs as I keep teasing her with my tongue.

Her thighs are fucking gorgeous and I could spend all night lavishing her with kisses. But that pussy smells delicious and drips with desire for me. After softly kissing Zariyah's ass, I push my tongue between her lower lips, her scent enveloping me as my face presses against her sex.

She moans with pleasure as my tongue slides over her clit. That woman tastes so fucking incredible. I grunt with desire as her juices first coat my tongue and then I tease Zariyah's outer folds with my tongue until she squeezes her thighs together and I feel her body moving towards an intense climax.

While I kiss and tease her pussy lips, I bring a finger to her clit and start rubbing her nub in slow little circles as I push her to the edge. She gasps for breath and whimpers my name before finally relenting to an intense climax.

Her body quakes with pleasure as she cums. Her curls spill around her head in a gorgeous, sexy mess of hair. I grab onto as much of it as I can, wrapping her curls around my hand and tilting her head back as I eat her pussy. My tongue teases her back door every few strokes and that forbidden pleasure makes Zariyah cum again quickly.

I am fucking addicted to watching her cum. Holy shit. I want her so damn bad. I keep eating her pussy until her thighs are drenched with her juices. Keeping a firm grasp on her long curly hair, I rise to my full height behind Zariyah and drop both my trousers and my boxers at once.

They both hit the ground with a thud and Zariyah flinches, sensitive to all sound and movement due to her well-deserved spanking. Tilting her head back and taking full control of my woman's body, I rub the head of my dick along her entrance, teasing her slowly. Zariyah yelps but against her own higher thinking, her ass moves back, causing her delicious pussy entrance to tease my cock.

I could slide inside her tight ass pussy with one swift motion, but I want to take my time. I want to feel this woman's pussy clenching around my dick.

My woman…

I ease the large head of my cock into her until she cries out. I only take a break when Zariyah moans in pleasure and then I continue entering her one painfully slow inch at a time. Her pussy grips my dick hard and it's tough to work my way inside her, even if she's wet and deliciously soft, primed for entry by my tongue.

"You are so fucking tight…"

My grasp on her hair tightens and as Zariyah moans again, I lose myself in my desire for her. I push more inches inside her than before and as my thick girth stretches her completely, her cries become impatient.

I nearly burst watching my cock disappear inside her, but I keep pushing into her until I fill Zariyah all the way to the hilt. That's when her pussy clamps down on me hard and it takes everything I've got not to let her milk me for every drop of my cum before I take a single stroke.

She might be a pain in my ass, but damn this woman was made for me. Her pussy is perfect for my cock and I can't hold myself back from exactly what I want now that I have my dick all the way inside her. I grab her hips and thrust into her from behind, recklessly pumping my cock into her hard and deep.

Zariyah has all the orgasms she needs and with all the tension she fires up in me, I'm desperate for my own release. I grit my teeth, wanting to go easy on her but pounding into her with animalistic desire. She moans with each thrust, yielding to my rough invasion of her tightness. I can feel her getting wetter as I pound her into the bed.

She likes this. Fuck yeah, she likes this.

Knowing that she enjoys taking my cock hard and deep like this drives me wild. I pump into her harder and reach around for Zariyah's clit to tease her as I get ready to fill her with my cum. An orgasm isn't even the best part, it's watching her lying there with my cum inside her and knowing that nobody else gets to do that. *She's mine.*

It's possessive, protective and utterly primal. Zariyah responds with instant pleasure once I begin teasing her clit. She cums hard and once her pussy tightens around my dick again, I let loose. My climax hits me hard as fuck and a gush of my cum erupts between Zariyah's legs.

The burst of pleasure that we both share forces our bodies tighter together. I lean over her and kiss the back of her neck and then her ear lobes, keeping my dick buried deep between her legs.

"You might be a very disobedient woman," I murmur into her ear as I keep nibbling and kissing her. "But fuck, you are made for me."

"Asshole," Zariyah gasps, but she doesn't sound like she means it this time. I smirk with satisfaction and pull out of her slowly. I give her ass an obligatory slap which makes her cry out and turn around to give me a brown-eyed glare.

"You drugged me and tied me up," I grunt as I search for a towel. I'm not even sure I'm done with her ass. I definitely need a shower to wake up before my damn brother gets here.

She lies there with her ass exposed and her gorgeous pussy gaping. I love how her caramel and dark brown folds fade into a juicy pink center. *Fuck,* there's something sexy about how she looks right now with my cum dripping out of her.

I want to smack her ass all over again, but it's too red for that. Zariyah moves on the bed, changing my entire view. Damn, I would have paid to watch her like that for hours.

"You deserved it."

"For what?" I grumble. "My brothers surprised me just as much as they surprised you. Since you've come here, I've been nothing but kind to you."

She hops off her bed and glances behind her to scope out the damage to her ass. Zariyah points to her bruised behind with a quizzical look on her face.

"That's you, Callum, filled with the milk of human kindness. My ass is *red.* I'm black. My ass isn't supposed to get red."

I'm smart enough to know now that I shouldn't mention that she ain't exactly black all the way, so she can still expect welts to show up on her latte colored skin.

"Your ass is damn fine."

"I won't be able to sit tomorrow."

She wanders over to my full-length mirror with my cum dripping down her thighs. Watching her perfect ass jiggle over there turns me into a goddamn caveman. But making love to her again wasn't meant

Chapter Eighteen

to be, because Odhran shows up at the door with Zariyah's possessions – and bad news.

Zariyah stays in my bedroom when I meet Odhran. I don't know how the little shit finds time to maintain so much muscle considering he spends most of his time gaming and indoors. The only person as pale as Odhran is Rian, and he was forced to spend time indoors because of all his damn jail sentences.

Odhran is different. He's always been different. And he makes me very uneasy to be around, because you never know when he's going to do something completely fucked up. Our mom eventually trained him to stop hurting animals but… even Queenie doesn't like him. He stands in my kitchen with three large duffel bags which he drops on the ground.

He doesn't look at me at all and his eyes are obscured beneath a thick crop of straight black hair. He's naturally blond but to piss everyone off – especially our traditional Irish Catholic mother – he's been dying his hair black and on occasion platinum blond. Now, he's black-haired again and it makes him look like more of a killer.

He's staring more than usual.

"Your wife is here," Odhran says in his deep, slow voice. He gazes up at me finally, wide blue eyes surrounded by thick blond lashes.

"Yes. Thank you for dropping off her things."

"Yes."

He stands there staring. I try not to show him that he makes me uneasy. Odhran enjoys that.

"Are you done?"

"No."

"Then speak."

"Can I see her?" he asks, tilting his head to the side.

"No. You can't. What the fuck do you want, Odhran? I don't have time for this."

Odhran runs his hands over his chin and finally speaks. He never hurries anything and it drives me fucking nuts.

Callum

"There's a big problem happening in Boston now," Odhran says. "They've already taken over all of Cambridge and chased off fourteen families before Aiden found out. He's been distracted by family concerns."

Odhran doesn't bother hiding the judgment in his voice. He might be nineteen now, but he's still just a kid. His biggest concerns are football, gaming and the occasional orders from Aiden. Unlike our father, Aiden doesn't believe in cultivating Odhran's dark tendencies. Unlike Rian, Odhran completely lacks control over himself and his emotions. He's a dangerous weapon, but some weapons are too dangerous for us to use.

Chapter Nineteen
Zariyah

Three Months Later – a Friday

It's been three months since Callum got the bad news from Odhran about the "big problem" happening in Boston. He claims we aren't safe and that everything is different now, even if it doesn't feel different. I'm still just stuck in the apartment with Callum.

But apparently in the mob, everything either moves fast as hell, or slow as molasses. Three months ago, we find out that Callum has a new problem and we can't make a damn move without a battalion of irritating Irish guys from Boston trailing us everywhere.

Callum breaks his promise to me and bans me from going to the bookstore. The only reason I forgive him is because Kalani says she doesn't mind and that she has "hired help". When I ask her who the hell she's hiring, she tells me not to worry about it and that I need to "enjoy Callum's big dick".

I don't have a choice. We barely leave the goddamn apartment as it is and Callum is addicted to sex, I swear. I don't want to sound like

I'm complaining. I'm not. Everything between my thighs hurts – my body is the one complaining. Callum's liking for spanking hasn't ended either. Ever since he got "revenge" on me, he's been obsessed with conjuring reasons to accuse me of being "sassy" and spanking me crazy.

I would complain more but the sex that comes after the spankings is so intense that I don't feel justified complaining about it. I dream about these orgasms, they're so powerful.

I've spent a lot of time with Callum and Queenie over the last three months, enough that Queenie is just as much my dog as Callum's. She won't go for walks unless I'm holding the leash and she only attempts stealing food off Callum's plate. She curls up next to me on the couch when Callum leaves to work for his brother and she puts her head on my lap, staring up at me with her cute basset eyes when I text Kalani.

She's my main lifeline to the outside world, although she seems to think I'm living a dream come true. Whenever I point out that I want to help with the bookstore, she hushes me and reminds me that I still collect my monthly check. I don't just care about the check. The bookstore reminds me of Sophia and our dreams of spreading knowledge to the world.

I can't spread knowledge holed up in Callum's apartment, even if it's so easy to forget the outside world exists when we're together. After our expenses, my income from the bookstore is nothing too crazy, but $3,250 a month goes a long way with Callum looking after me. He insists on paying the rent for my apartment since he's the one keeping me here and I refuse to give up my lease. He had my clothes and toiletries moved over, but all my furniture is still there and I don't want to move it. I don't argue when he offers to pay my rent because I could really use the savings after New York. I won't always have Callum looking after me. Once he gets tired of the sex stuff, he'll remember that he doesn't have much consideration for women of my skin tone. I have to be ready for that.

I have other problems too. My brother is apparently still in town. Since he's a public figure, he can't stay hidden for long. He didn't tell me that he planned on staying this long and when I text him about whether he's still staying with Kalani, he's evasive. After so much time in the limelight, he's ridiculously private about his personal life – even with me. I ask Kalani, but she's no better than he is. She always finds a way to turn the subject back to Callum.

In her opinion, I should have his baby. My best friend is crazy as hell, but I can't act like I haven't thought it could happen. Callum has never once used protection, claiming his dick is too big for condoms and that he finds it "ridiculous" not to cum in his own wife. When I argue that it's my body and therefore my choice, he claims the same thing.

Arguing with him is like arguing with a donkey. He calls *me* stubborn, but he's the one who only thinks with his dick. My dick-wielding donkey walks through the front door after a difficult session at the gym. I can tell by how red he is, and by the way he's dripping in sweat. It's not fair that the only exception to our "lockdown" is the stupid gym. Callum apparently had an argument with his brother about his muscles that nearly escalated to a gunfight, so he gets to pump iron while I'm trapped inside like a pet canary. He has to go with *two* of his brothers – Rian and Odhran – so he has "security", but I don't see why I can't tag along.

Even if Callum annoys the hell out of me with his muscle obsession, I get just as excited as Queenie when Callum walks through the door in his gross, sweaty and incredibly sexy gym clothes clinging to his hefty body. I love when he dresses like this. He hasn't cut his hair since Aiden put us on lock down and the shaggy, strawberry blond hair sits in a sexy mess covered by a goldenrod beanie with the Carhartt logo on the front. His hair looks almost curly, it's so messy and wet from sweat. *He smells delicious.*

I jump away from the book I'm reading, instantly rushing over to the door. After three months of fighting and fucking, there's no more pretending that I'm not excited to see him when he comes home.

He enjoys joking that his spankings "tamed" me, but it wasn't that. I'd warmed to him before his beastly ass dragged me to the bedroom to spank my ass until it turned a rusty purple color. I don't know why I'm attracted to this asshole. Is it his hair? His well-built legs? The fact that he has a big butt for a white guy and a huge dick? Ugh. I hate that I'm staring at him like this.

Callum grins as he walks through the door. The weather has been getting colder, so he's been living in beanies and hoodies.

I don't even care that his gray gym hoodie is darkened by patches of sweat. I run over to him and give him a big hug. Callum wraps his arms around me and I can almost forget that I'm virtually a prisoner here. He makes the rest of the world and the rest of my concerns melt away.

"How long do we have to live like this?" I grumble as I bury my nose into his neck. I don't even care that he smells like sweat. He also smells like deodorant and a sexy, natural man scent that turns me on far more than I would care to admit.

I know I'm not in this alone. Even Callum has to hang out with mobsters watching his every move. Luckily, that means he gets to hang out with his brothers and cousins all day, not complete strangers covered in terrifying tattoos. I don't exactly like the idea of a bunch of men following me everywhere I go, so I've become a couch potato.

But I yearn to go out there and reconnect with old friends, see Kalani and hang out with my brother who apparently still spends plenty of time in town. I just hate feeling trapped. Since Callum has spent some time in jail, I expect him to be somewhat sympathetic, but he just stiffens his body and pulls away from me.

"I don't want your ass trying to escape again."

"Who said anything about escape?"

Callum's face grows even more stern and I get the funny sense that he's trying to give me bad news. Shit. I step away from him and look at his face to see if I can determine what he might say. I'm not psychic, though, so I just have to wait.

"You might when you hear this."

He doesn't even have to say anything for me to feel an instant sense of anger and betrayal. I grit my teeth, preparing for another disagreement. Callum had better not try to deflect from all of this by spanking me, kissing me, or trying to drag me off to the bedroom.

"What is it?" I snap impatiently. I've been waiting here for him all day. I want to sit on the couch with him and run my fingers through his hair, not fight with him. I can feel his energy shifting right along with mine. But I'm fucking ready for a fight. I've put up with enough of Callum disappearing in the middle of the night and showing up at all hours of the morning. I haven't questioned him when he's come home with a bloody nose or bloody fists. His stash of ammunition has diminished steadily over the course of the last three months, and I haven't brought that up either.

I haven't even brought up everything I've noticed on the news the past three months. Missing people. Unsolved murders. Drive-by shootings. He doesn't say a fucking word about what he does when we're not together, but he expects me to be an open book. He expects me to belong to him completely. He must be involved in at least *some* of these crimes. He's no angel. But how much of the devil is left in him?

He walks past me without saying anything. My blood boils.

"Hello? I asked you a damn question," I snap at him, searching for any objects nearby that might make good projectiles.

"Can I walk through the damn door before you start pestering me?" Callum growls, his face suddenly fierce and mean. The romantic moment between us vanquished by cold reality.

I snap back. "Absolutely not."

"Aiden wants me to send you away," Callum says calmly. "And he's the boss, so it's happening. You're going back to New York."

He announces it like it's his right to tell me what to do and where to go when he doesn't share half as much with me. His little comment about escape makes so much more sense.

"I can't go back to New York City. I burned every bridge in that city," I say to him.

"I never said New York City. You're going somewhere no one will find you, far upstate."

"What? Upstate? Callum, I can't go upstate. I'm a city girl. I don't want to be upstate by myself."

My tone gets more frantic because I realize at this point, these people can make me do anything. Callum has ultimate control over my life. He wonders why I haven't said *I love you* yet, but it's the only thing I can control in the roller coaster of emotions that involve being tethered to him in this arrangement.

It's not like I don't love him. I just don't want to love a monster again, especially since he was my first monster, my first heartbreak, the first person that ever made me fear love, which was supposed to just be beautiful.

Callum is still unreasonably gruff, "You aren't going by yourself. Valentina, Heavyn, and Kamari will be with you."

He says those names like I'm supposed to know who the hell he's talking about. Are those his imaginary friends? A new girl group like *Little Mix?* Maybe they finally released some new Kardashians...

"Who the hell are those people?"

Callum becomes visibly annoyed, as if I don't have a right to question his ass. White men have a way of acting all funny when you talk back to them, but that doesn't bother me. I fold my arms to let Callum know I'm ready for a fight, which he probably already suspected.

"Valentina is Aiden's wife," Callum says. "She grew up in Idaho."

Why am I not surprised?

"I don't want to be stuck with some blond woman who rides horses all day."

Those are the only stereotypes I know about people from Idaho and I feel incredibly stupid as I argue with Callum for the sake of arguing.

"She's black," he says. "And so is Heavyn, who married my brother Rian."

I can't believe what I'm hearing. The terrifying monster who forced me into a wedding dress and *extremely* uncomfortable thong has a wife? Not just any wife, but a black wife.

"Did your brothers hold their wives at gunpoint too? Is that the new racist trend? Kidnapping a wife of a different race?"

Callum doesn't react to my increasing anxiety. He has too many endorphins from that damn gym, but the only hormones in my body are the ones that makes you stressed as fuck.

Chapter Nineteen

"No, it is *not* a racist trend. Hopefully, with a name like Kamari, I don't have to explain that Darragh's wife is also black. That's Kamari."

"Wow. So a white girl can't have the name Kamari?"

"I don't know," Callum says. "It would be weird."

"Interesting."

"It's not racist to recognize that some names are African American and others are not. My name is Irish. Your name is... I don't know. Zambian."

"Zambian? Where the fuck did you get that from?"

"Starts with 'Z'."

Unfortunately for me, he looks dead serious.

I roll my eyes and explain to Callum slowly, in case he lost a few brain cells at that damned gym, "It's an Arabic name that means 'scattering wind', and my mom chose it because she liked it, not because she was trying to match my name to my race."

"Lesson learned," Callum says gruffly, with a hint of sarcasm. "Now that we cleared that up, you won't be alone, you will be staying with my brothers' wives. I'm sure you'll get along fine. I'm done arguing about it."

"How are you so sure we'll get along? Is it because we're black?" I ask Callum, continuing to provoke him, pushing him harder because he seems so firm and I can tell he won't change his mind, even if it's what I'm most desperate for him to do.

"I can't believe you're just telling me where to go like I don't get a say," I complain to him, unsure of how I'm going to get out of Callum sending me off to God-knows-where.

"You don't get a say," Callum responds bluntly, with absolutely no sympathy in his tone. "You're my wife and protecting you is my duty."

I bristle when he brings up our marriage again. His family arranged that marriage between us, so it hardly holds the same weight. Except, it definitely feels like we're married these days, we fight so damn much. And we make love like we're married too. We even laugh like we're married, which makes this hard. I was convincing myself that our relationship was changing. That Callum had respect for me and maybe something good could come out of this.

I don't want to give that up when things between us were starting to feel stable and normal. I don't want to leave him and wake up alone in a bed miles away from home. This has been hard enough with Callum Murray, I don't want to live without him.

"I don't care if protecting you is my duty. I should get a say on where I spend my time. I don't even know these people, Callum."

For a brief moment, it's almost like he sympathizes with me. But then the emotion disappears from his face and he replies stonily, "You will get to know them."

It's useless. He'll do whatever he wants with me and it's always going to be this way, isn't it? My life changed forever when his brothers shoved me into that trunk and all I have is resisting Callum in the smallest ways, the ways that he'll allow.

"Whatever," I respond with annoyance. "Then I'm not going without my phone."

"That works perfectly," Callum says. "I'll need you on that phone so I can call you whenever I need to make sure you haven't put yourself in danger or done anything foolish."

"What danger? I've been basically trapped in this freaking house for three months. The greatest danger I face on a daily basis is walking past Queenie after she farts."

"Haven't you been watching the news?" Callum says, raising his voice. "This city has been on fire. We have a record number of murders. I stay up every fucking night working and then I go work out, so I can be strong enough to protect you. I am tired of you pushing me, and arguing with me and treating me like I'm an asshole for trying to take care of you."

"I'm not treating you like an asshole. I'm asking you to treat me like I'm an adult, not your possession and not some kid. You say you love me, but if you really love me, how could you go through with this? How could you send me away when this is the closest we've been?"

"I do treat you like an adult," Callum says. "You're not the only one who has to follow orders around here. We can live like this because I was brought up according to a set of rules that I still have to follow."

I don't want to think about how Callum was brought up. I know it involved a lot of racism and right now, I don't want to leave him. This isn't what I meant when I wanted out of the house. Just because I want freedom doesn't mean I want to be away from him. Despite everything that brought us here and despite how much Callum pisses me off, I still like being with him. He's a big, safe teddy bear when he's not being a complete dickhead.

"All we do is fight," Callum grumbles. "And after all of this, you still don't share my feelings. Maybe it's for the best if you take some time away from me. I promise, you will enjoy spending time with these women."

"We fight because you don't listen to my concerns."

Callum sighs and gives way just a bit. I'm surprised I managed to push through his stubbornness.

"What concerns, then? Because my only concern is taking care of you."

I want to pretend that what he says doesn't tug on my heartstrings, just a bit. I fold my arms and look away from him.

"I don't want you to send me away."

"Doesn't matter, baby girl," Callum says. "I have orders to keep you safe."

"You want me to love you, Callum, but you never let me into your world. Maybe that's what hurt so much all those years ago. It wasn't just that you hid beliefs that hurt me deeply, it's that you could hide so much of yourself from me. I want to love someone who gives me everything."

His face softens. I want to move closer to him, but something freezes me in place. *No, Zariyah. Let him come to you.* Callum takes a step closer.

"I will give you everything," he says, taking another step closer to me. I can smell his sweat again. It's gross to admit, but impossible to ignore how good his sweat smells to me. "For the rest of our lives together. You are my wife, Zariyah. I didn't choose how it happened, but I can choose how this ends."

"And how does it end?"

"You and me, together. Forever."

My heart drops to my stomach. How can he say this to me and then send me away? It feels cruel. But I've always been drawn to Callum for his cruelty as much as his gentleness. I'm fascinated and repulsed by how the two live inside him. Falling for him over time makes the combination of emotions more complicated and more intense.

He puts his hand on my cheek. It's so large and strong. His touch always sends shivers straight through me. I still don't want to look at him. I don't want to leave and I don't want to be trapped anywhere.

"How can you live following other people's orders?"

"Look at me," he says commandingly. I want to be stubborn. I refuse to look at him, making Callum command me in an even sterner voice.

"Zariyah, look at me."

My gaze flutters up to Callum's face. I don't know if everyone would consider his face handsome because of the freckles and the rough cuts and scars from his life of fighting and getting into trouble. But I don't care. I think he's fucking beautiful.

It's like his touch melts away how much I want to smack the shit out of him. My tongue feels like cotton in my mouth and my heart races, both wanting him to kiss me and wanting him to take me seriously. Emotions are always so damn complicated with him.

"I live like this because I trust my brother, even more than I trusted my father. He wants what I want out of life, peace and safety to have a family. But when you have this much influence, people come for it. No one out there will stand up for us. I think about your friend and what happened to her... I couldn't let that bastard live. There's no justice unless you take it."

"So you're always going to put your family first?"

"You are my family," Callum says. "And I will always put you first. Tonight, that means sending you away."

I shake my head. "No. I don't want to go. I'm going to text Kalani and she'll help me run away."

Callum chuckles. "If she was going to help you run away, she would have done it already. You won't run. When I return from battle, I expect you to be waiting for me."

"You are so dramatic."

He gives me a weak smile, which makes me wonder if there's even more he's hiding from me. Maybe he isn't overestimating the danger, but truly scared of what could happen. That puts a pit in my stomach which I desperately want him to comfort.

His hands move to my waist as if he can read my mind and despite myself, those hands comfort me.

"You won't run away," he says. "I can tell you're thinking about how to escape or how to wiggle out of this, but that can't happen, Zariyah. I need you to be safe. I *need* your safety."

He smells so good that I just want to agree with him so he doesn't get all grumpy and move away from me again. I don't want him to be serious, but I know he must be. *Damn it.*

"Okay," I say to him, nodding agreeably, although I haven't decided if I'll be holding to that yet. Callum's hands clutch my waist tightly and he presses his forehead to mine. His scent fills my nostrils and sends a gush of desire straight to my thighs. I wrap my arms around him because I don't want him to go.

"What's going to happen to Queenie?"

Callum bristles. "My sister Orla will be looking after Queenie."

"I've never met her."

"You don't need to meet her. She's incredibly annoying and Aiden wants her at a different safehouse from his children because of the smoking."

"She sounds like fun. I bet she has funny stories about you as a baby."

"There are no funny stories from that time period," Callum says. "I was a very serious baby."

"Whatever."

"Don't 'whatever' me," Callum says, kissing the top of my nose and sending flutters of warmth straight through me. "I just want you to be safe. I will return."

"When? In a week?"

Callum's body stiffens again. He kisses my forehead before replying.

"I will return when I can. Just trust me."

"And what if you don't come back?"

"For you, I will find a way to come back. I promise."

I HOLD onto him as tightly as I can, wanting to cling to him for dear life in a vague hope that I could make him change his mind, but Callum pries me off him and I feel my heart sink to my stomach.

This is really happening.

Chapter Twenty
Callum

It hurts to see the disappointment on her face. If I thought it could keep her safer, I would have her by my side, but the city has erupted with danger from every corner and bodies are piling up. I know she watches the news and I know she avoids the subject intentionally. I don't keep this away from her to hide from her.

I love this woman and I don't want to walk away from her tonight without showing her that. I reach for her chin and tilt it up to mine so I can kiss her on the lips. Her lips are so fucking soft. I don't know how long I can survive without these lips. She thinks this shit will be easy for me, but I beg to differ.

Grabbing her face with both hands, I pull Zariyah close to me and kiss her deeper. Aiden gave me an hour to prepare her, so hopefully we have time to pack her things when I'm done with her.

"I won't leave you without tasting you one last time," I say to her, keeping her cheeks firmly in my grasp. "I also don't want to leave without feeling your mouth around my dick, or your pussy around my cock."

"That sounds like a pretty long to-do list. It might take a couple days. Maybe even a week."

Unfortunately, there's no wriggling out of this one.

"It'll have to take less than an hour. Rian will be here to drive you to the safe house."

"Can I at least know where this safe house is? Upstate New York is bigger than you think."

"Mexico."

"Huh? I thought you said New York."

"Mexico, New York. It's a small town in the middle of nowhere with people who are too concerned with chewing dip and eating McDonalds to give any mind to us coming and going."

"This sounds grim."

"It's not grim. It's safe," I insist, drawing my fingers through her curls again. I pull her to me and kiss her again. I meant every word of what I said. I'm taking every inch of Zariyah Murray tonight, giving her something to remember me by. I don't know if we'll have to spend two weeks or six months away from each other. *If I do my job right, I'll see her again soon.*

I pull away from her and make her another promise. "I'll call you."

"I don't want phone calls," she whispers, reaching for the base of my hoodie. I eagerly take my hoodie off with my shirt, baring my chest, which feels sculpted and firm for her. I want her hands all over me so fucking badly.

I nearly cum in my pants when she touches me. Her hands feel so good on my chest. "I want you."

Those three words are almost everything.

Zariyah looks at me with those fierce brown eyes and then she adds three more words.

"I love you."

She breathes them slowly, in a nearly hushed tone. I grab her by the hips and carry her ass as far as I can make it, which ends up being the kitchen counter. I don't give a crap. Within a few minutes, I have her clothes off except for her panties. Watching her sexy caramel ass swallow those red panties makes this hurt even more.

I could die out there. This could be the last time I make love to her, but I can't let her know it. She's my woman and it's my job to protect her — not just her body, but to protect her heart and soul from pain. I am bound to her for life and those vows mean everything to me.

I slowly slip my fingers through the waistband of her underwear and pull them over her thick thighs. Zariyah has always had the sexiest legs out of any woman I've ever met. She naturally has a body that any woman would envy, a mixture of curves and definition. Once I have her panties off, Zariyah's scent lures me in.

Every woman has a natural scent down there and when you're with the right woman, everything about her pussy will be downright intoxicating. I drop to my knees between Zariyah's legs immediately. My instinct is to bury my face between her thick thighs and eat her out so well that her thighs squeeze together and keep my face firmly planted down there until she cums.

I spread her lower lips with my fingers first. As Zariyah gasps, I add my tongue, pressing it gently against her clit and then teasing her to a frenzied state. She gushes with juices and when I feel her thighs squeezing around my head, I tease Zariyah to the brink of orgasm with my tongue.

Her sweet juices taste fucking delicious, so I run my tongue enthusiastically over her lower lips until she cums and as she cums, I keep teasing her and licking her until her continuous orgasm turns her inner thighs red with desire. I kiss her thighs and lick her juices off them before diving between Zariyah's legs again.

My face is a fucking mess when I remove my head from between her legs. I worked up more of a sweat eating her pussy than I did hitting the bench press. No. Fucking. Regrets. Zariyah gazes down at me like I've done something wrong.

"What?" I grumble, waiting for her to slap me or some other outrageous shit.

"That was… more intense than anything we've ever done before."

Okay. Not upset. Stunned. I kiss the top of her thighs and she shudders. I feel victorious. I rise from my knees, eager to kiss her and touch her face, and the rest of her body, but Zariyah leans her head back, her thick curls cascading down her shoulders as she loses herself in just the lightest touch of my hand on her thighs and she says something that shocks me and excites me at the same time.

"I have never wanted to suck your dick so badly." She slowly climbs down from the countertop. Damn, she looks good and she's thick in all the right places. My dick aches with desire for her.

I have never been in a position before where a woman could make me cum just by saying all the right words. Zariyah has a perfect set of lips and feeling her full lips around my cock would be nothing but sheer perfection.

"Then kneel," I murmur, giving Zariyah a gentle peck on the lips, worried that more contact before I can steel myself will make me erupt immediately. "And take your time."

Zariyah gives me a concerned look, like she thinks I'll take this too far. But I just give her a reassuring kiss and wait patiently for her to sink to her knees before me. *Goddamn, she's hot.* From her position on her knees, Zariyah looks up at me with perfect, wide brown eyes. Her hands are eager to loosen the knot on my joggers.

Once she gets those free, Zariyah pulls the joggers down over my ass, taking her time to linger over my firm, muscular butt cheeks on the way down. My underwear feels uncomfortable from the sweat at the gym, but again, Zariyah doesn't seem to mind. She kisses the tops of my thighs slowly.

"Sweaty," she whispers. Yeah, and my thighs probably won't be as sweaty as my dick or balls. I'm too turned on by her kissing the top of my thighs to care. I groan as Zariyah gets closer to my dick. Her lips are so full and soft that any closeness to my cock makes me want to burst immediately. Controlling my orgasm grows more difficult when Zariyah's hands grasp the base of my cock.

She kisses the length of my shaft, her tongue jutting out against it with each kiss and she doesn't seem to mind how I taste. She makes a low noise of pure satisfaction in the back of her throat and then those sexy ass hands pump the shaft of my dick to complete arousal. Her grip provides just the right amount of tightness for my cock.

I groan with even more pleasure as Zariyah wraps her tight lips around the base of my cock. Her mouth is soft, the perfect depth and so damn tight around the head of my dick that I want to cum on the spot. She moves slowly, taking as much of my thick cock into her mouth as she can. Even if she can't hold much of me inside her soft, smallish mouth, she teases the underside of my dick with her tongue and holds me in the back of her throat, her suction getting me off perfectly.

"I need to cum inside you," I groan, when holding back gets too difficult, and I swiftly remove myself from Zariyah's mouth. Her face is tinged a reddish-cinnamon color from how deep she held my cock. Her lips are swollen red from stretching around my large hardness and everything about her makes me want to take her in our bed one last time before I leave.

Every time could be the last time when you're in this life. I turn Zariyah around so she faces away from me and kiss her shoulders slowly. She moans as my lips nibble her along her shoulder blades. From behind, I cup Zariyah's full breasts in my hand. Her tits are perfect. She has nice, large tits with these gorgeous, dark brown nipples. They have these thick, hard little buds sticking out of them that are fucking fabulous to suck on.

"You are so fucking sexy, woman," I growl, sucking on Zariyah's neck while I fondle her tits and press my dick into her back. *Mine. I want her to be mine for the rest of the night. I know we don't have that much time but damn, I could enjoy her body for a goddamn lifetime.*

Zariyah whimpers as I tease her nipples and then sink my teeth into her neck.

"I want you to be good when I'm gone," I murmur. "Promise me."

I expect her to resist me, but this time, Zariyah pushes her ass back against my cock, grinding against me so she keeps me rock hard. And she promises.

"I promise…"

"Good," I growl, spreading her lower lips and finding her entrance with my dick. "I love it when you're a good girl for once…"

I slowly enter Zariyah from behind, holding her hips with one hand to keep her steady as I slide my dick between her legs with a slow, smooth stroke. Damn, her pussy is tight. I grunt and push inside her to the hilt, filling her completely.

Zariyah's pussy tightens around my cock and it's almost impossible not to cum inside her immediately. I hold her close to me instead and fuck her slowly, using our combined sensitivity to slow down and feel just how perfectly her pussy fits around my dick. She makes low, pleasurable moans as I slide into her wetness. She's *so* fucking wet, making it almost easy to fit my large cock inside her.

Her pussy is an unholy combination of tight and juicy, driving my instinct to cum inside her wet hole to unrealistic proportions. Each thrust brings us new emotional closeness. I gently play with her breasts and kiss her neck as I take her from behind. This position has never been so close or romantic for me.

"I want to make a fucking baby with you," I growl, meaning every word of it. Zariyah thrusts her hips back and even if there's probably a part of her that will always want to resist me, she bites her lower lip as if to keep the resistance from spilling out of her.

Those final thrusts inside of her are fucking heavenly. She's so tight and pressing into her soft ass with each stroke only makes me want to cum inside her more. The euphoria I feel climaxing inside her is unlike anything I've ever felt before. She pushes her body against mine as she accepts every drop of my seed. I wait until I fill her up completely before removing my cock.

I land a little smack on Zariyah's ass. I'm gonna miss the hell out of that ass.

"Let's get you packed, baby girl."

Chapter Twenty-One
Zariyah

Callum says goodbye to me in the parking lot of the Costco in Everett, a few miles outside of Boston. He's acting like I'm on the verge of assassination. When I get into the car, I meet my fellow riders for the journey. The first is a woman around my age named Heavyn Murray who appears holding a baby. She's Rian's wife and she shows up accompanied by a middle-school aged girl with her brown hair cut into a short bob wearing a fierce scowl on her face.

"He is *such* an asshole," the middle-schooler says.

Okay, so she's a bad ass kid. Got it. I stay quiet as Callum guides me into one of the frontmost seats in the back of the black Escalade that will apparently be taking me away. Callum loads my bags into the back of another vehicle, but I don't see the person driving that one.

The man driving our Escalade is Rian Murray. I realize that he's the little girl's father and yes, this kid just called her father an asshole. I don't understand how they all fit together, but I understand they're a family and right now, they're fighting and we have a 5 hour and 31 minute drive from the Costco to Mexico, NY. Yup, that's where Callum sees fit to send me – to the middle of nowhere in some stupid tiny town in Oswego County, New York.

It doesn't take very long into the car ride for me to learn that the angry girl's name is Tegan because she calls her dad an asshole again before he admonishes her. That does it and they argue most of the drive up to Mexico, with poor Heavyn occasionally interjecting trying to calm them down. I can tell she wants them to be quiet because she's holding a baby and doesn't seem like she's too comfortable with Rian's speedy driving.

After hearing her life story through the back and forth arguing between Tegan and Rian, I decide that I like her. I'll be honest, it takes a better woman than me to be a stepmom.

"Hey," I whisper, turning around to talk to Heavyn after Tegan and Rian's fighting descends into stony silence. We still have two hours left. "Are you okay? I bet this drive is tough with a newborn and all."

"It is," Heavyn says, nodding.

"What's her name?"

"Ava," Heavyn smiles at me and nods, kissing the top of Ava's head affectionately. "Yeah. I feel terrible. Sorry I haven't been friendlier. I heard you were Callum's wife…"

I nod and we talk a little bit more until Heavyn falls asleep with her baby, who I find out is named Ava, cuddled against her chest. That leaves me with Tegan and Rian, who are still seething at each other. I don't know if I should try talking to Tegan. She seems really upset and I don't want to get involved and somehow make it worse. So my awkward ass just sits there. I'm ready to jump out of the car when we get to Mexico, even if our accommodations don't look anything like what you would see in Boston.

It's dusk where we get there and there are pebbles all over the ground in the pattern of what I think is supposed to be a driveway. It looks bleak and it feels like we're in a different country from downtown Boston. My immediate reaction is revulsion and then sadness.

Tegan says it all. "Is that a fucking trailer park?"

Heavyn sleeps until Tegan's comment. She yawns groggily and yawns. "I told you we would be roughing it, Tegan. And don't be rude. People live here or camp here or whatever, and they're perfectly decent people."

"I can't believe you haven't left him sometimes," Tegan says, half-smiling and half shaking her head. "We could go to a ranch in Idaho. You officially adopted me. It's legal now."

"I can *hear* you," Rian growls from the driver's seat.

"I don't care. You promised you would never do this again," Tegan says, yanking her car down open and jumping out of the car. Heavyn follows her and I follow her lead. Rian steps out of the car before slamming the door shut. Heavyn has baby Ava against her chest, but she's starting to gurgle, especially when she hears her father's voice getting all riled up.

"I'm done arguing. My job is to keep you safe, not to have you pestering me constantly," Rian snarls.

"I'm your kid," Tegan says. "I'm going to pester you until you die, old man."

"Tegan, can you chill?" Heavyn says sleepily. "Ava's waking up."

Tegan does not chill. We follow her dad all the way to the door of a double wide white trailer with blue shutters on the windows. I've never been inside one of these before, but it seems like it might be hard for all three of us to live there, especially considering Tegan seems to have a big personality.

When we approach the door to the trailer, Rian knocks on it in a special pattern. The door opens and I learn that apparently, we aren't staying here alone. This trailer already has a couple residents. Maybe even more than a couple. A woman with dark-skin and a pretty yellow dress. She's pregnant too, and much taller than the woman who appears behind her.

The woman behind her has a more copper skin tone and long reddish hair which she wears in a thick, long braid as she holds a baby boy against her chest.

Rian ushers us into the trailer and introduces us to each other. During the introductions, I learn that the woman in the yellow dress is Valentina, Aiden Murray's wife and the woman with the braided hair is Kamari. She's holding a newborn baby boy who she introduces as Colin. The babies are adorable. I feel a weird, warm squishy feeling that I've never felt before. Like I want a family too.

Kamari hugs Heavyn tightly once they're both inside the house, so

Zariyah

I guess they know each other too. If they all hang out together and know each other pretty well, they probably have so much in common. A real friend group and a real family. It makes me miss Sophia and Kalani.

They *all* seem to know each other and I feel silly and left out. I stand in the corner of the room, not sure of what to do or where to go until Rian guides me to my room away from everyone talking and greeting each other, and leaves me in the bedroom with a few short words. It doesn't even seem like they notice that I'm gone. *Sigh.* At least they're all black.

Maybe that's it. Maybe they don't like that I'm biracial. It seems stupid since they're all married to white men, so I push the insecurity out of my mind and focus on the little room Rian shows me. It's tiny, and instead of a king-sized bed, there's just a twin bed. It's clean and cute, but it's nothing fancy. It's nothing like what I left behind in Boston.

I miss Callum. I glance down at my phone for the first time since the drive here. I'm a little hungry, but I feel too awkward to go out there to eat. I don't have much in my suitcase, just a few clothes.

Callum: Be strong. I'll return for you soon.

His text doesn't make me feel any better. I wish that it would help, because I also want to see him soon. I feel so alone here, and everyone else out there knows each other. They seem too tired and wrapped up in their own lives to care about me. I guess I can stay here until morning.

I can hear Tegan arguing with her father outside my bedroom and I get the feeling I'll be able to hear everything happening through these walls. My stomach tightens in a knot. I won't be able to avoid people forever. I'll have to meet the mob wives in the morning. It takes me a minute to remember – I'm a mob wife too. I *belong* to Callum Murray.

I change into some sweatpants and a giant t-shirt I stole from Callum's closet. It smells like him, which doesn't comfort me as much as I thought it would.

I climb into the twin bed and wriggle around a bit until I find a comfortable sleeping spot. My phone lights up my face as I stare at the screen and try to figure out what the hell I'm supposed to do. It's not like staring at my screen ever works but… at least I can send texts.

Callum warned me not to try anything stupid and I *did* promise, but I still have to text Kalani.

Me: Hey.
Kalani: You made it?
Me: Yes.
Kalani: Cool. You heard from your brother?
Me: Uh. No. Everything good?

KALANI DOESN'T REPLY INSTANTLY like her other messages, so I go back to the chat with Callum and text him back. Kalani gets easily distracted and sometimes leaves people on read.

Me: What am I supposed to do here?
Callum: You're with your family. I know it must be scary, but you will be safe with them. I love you.

I DON'T KNOW what I want him to say, but I've never been able to appreciate Callum more than I do right now. I type back.

Me: I love you too.

Zariyah

. . .

WHY DO we have to be apart from each other when I just started to admit to myself how much I felt for him? I put my phone under my pillow and try to fall asleep. It's hard without Callum. It's especially hard when Rian eventually leaves and Tegan sobs so loudly I can hear her through the walls.

I can also hear Heavyn comforting Tegan and eventually a baby crying. Maybe three babies. The first baby is definitely Aifric, but then Ava joins him. Soon, Colin's crying is the loudest. Yup, three babies crying. We definitely have a full house and I don't know what to expect in the morning.

A FAINT KNOCK at my bedroom door awakens me in the morning. It takes a few seconds too long for me to realize where I am. I sit up and adjust to my surroundings. The knock gets a little louder.

"Coming."

I open the door to see Kamari and Valentina standing there with smiles on their faces. They look a little apologetic.

"Did we wake you up?" Kamari asks. "Heavyn made breakfast and we didn't want you to miss out. We just put the babies down and we were all wrapped up in our own mess last night, we didn't even say hi."

"That's okay," I say.

"It's not," Valentina says. "It's scary enough when they decide Boston is too dangerous and move us around. I know how you must feel."

I glance at her and from one look at Valentina's face, I can tell that she means what she said. She's been through something.

"We don't bite," Kamari says. "And we hate that we're here too. Our last safehouse had a bathroom for each of us."

"Come on," Valentina says authoritatively. "You can dress if you want, but we're all pretty hungry and we want to get to know you."

Even if I'm nervous, I head out there for breakfast and meet everyone properly. Tegan seems significantly calmer this morning, but I think that's because of Heavyn. I've never seen a stepmom so close to her stepdaughter, and it's heartwarming. Valentina serves me food and Kamari asks me questions, investigating my ties to Callum and then my ties to Boston because she's from Boston too.

"Your brother is famous," Heavyn interjects halfway through our conversation. "It took me a second to place you but... You're Lamonte Armstrong's sister, aren't you?"

"Who's that?" Valentina asks, genuinely confused. You don't meet too many people who don't know my brother. It might take people a while to realize we're related, but I'm surprised Valentina doesn't know him.

His name clicks with Kamari. "The football player?! I can see it! Oh my goodness. You are so down to earth."

He's the famous one, not me. I shrug and try to brush it off, but they gush over my brother's football career (except Valentina, who just nods along politely). As we eat and talk together, it doesn't take long before I start feeling like we're all old friends.

Tegan is the quietest one throughout breakfast. Once we're done eating and there's a lull in the conversation, Tegan lets out a dramatic sigh.

"How long are we going to be stuck in this trailer?"

"It's not too bad," Heavyn says.

"I have friends now," Tegan says with a little frustration. "Haven't I missed out on enough? I'm supposed to meet Ricardo to play soccer this weekend and now I can't go."

I don't know what Tegan might have missed, but I remember what it was like to be her age. Missing out on hanging with friends definitely sucked. Heavyn puts her arm around Tegan and pulls her close.

"I know it's tough, but you can text him, right?"

Tegan rolls her eyes, but rests her head on Heavyn's shoulder. "Texting is *not* the same."

Kamari brightens up. "Oooo, do you have a crush on him?"

Valentina wrinkles her nose. "She's twelve."

I see Valentina's point now, but when I was Tegan's age, I definitely had crushes. Sure, they were innocent and mostly involved wanting to hang out with a guy at the mall, but they felt super important to me.

"That's old enough to have a crush," Kamari says, dismissing Valentina's concerns about the appropriateness of a crush for Tegan.

Tegan turns red at the mention of a crush. The more I get a proper look at her, the more I see the resemblance to her father. Right now, she definitely has his scowl.

"I don't have a crush," Tegan mutters. Heavyn gives her a knowing side-eye, but she says nothing. That doesn't stop Kamari. She gets herself hyped up and excited with a gleaming expression on her face.

"Okay, well if you don't have a crush, you can tell us about him."

"Ew, I don't want to talk about him," Tegan says, turning even redder than before. "I don't even like him. He's just a friend and he's stupid."

"All boys are stupid," Kamari says. "We still love them. Your Uncle Darragh is very stupid and I love him."

She winks at Tegan, who giggles at Kamari's joke. She tucks some of her light brown hair behind her ears and sighs. "Ricardo is just the only guy who doesn't judge me for liking sports. I'm still a girl even if I play soccer."

"Well, duh," Heavyn says.

"It's just nice hanging out with a boy and not having to worry about stuff like my clothes. We just play soccer and talk about stuff."

"I think he likes you," Kamari says.

Tegan shakes her head. "No way. We're just friends."

"That's very good and appropriate," Valentina says. "There's no rush for you to find romance."

"I agree with Valentina. Sorry, Kamari. It's okay if you have a crush, though. It's just… no need to rush it," I chime in. At first, I'm nervous like I don't know if they will accept me and my opinions. I don't want to overstep my boundaries in talking to Tegan.

Heavyn nods though. "Well don't rush anything. Even friendship. He has to be a good guy to be your friend."

"He *is* a good guy," Tegan says. "I don't want to be in this stupid trailer park. My dad promised he would never do this to me again."

Chapter Twenty-One

She gazes down at her phone longingly. I can't help but relate. Cell phones weren't as big in my day as they are for kids now, but who can't relate to waiting by the phone for a guy to at least call back, if not text?

"Hey," Heavyn says. "Rian promised me too. But this is serious, Tegan. He promised we wouldn't be here long this time. Just a couple of weeks."

I can tell Tegan doesn't like that answer, but instead of fighting like she does with her dad, she slips off her chair, hugs Heavyn and excuses herself to the bedroom that they share with baby Ava. Once she's gone, Heavyn gives us all serious looks and gestures for us to come closer.

"I am *so* worried about her," Heavyn whispers. "Rian doesn't understand how hard this is for her and… I think she's planning to run."

"She can't do that," Valentina says. "We're in the middle of nowhere, at least an hour away from the nearest city."

"She's a Murray," Heavyn whispers. "I'm watching her closely but… I can't keep my eye on her 24/7. I need help."

"Shouldn't we just talk to her?" Kamari asks, glancing around nervously and keeping her voice low.

"I've tried," Heavyn says.

"She's a Murray," I add. "So I'm guessing she's a little stubborn."

Heavyn gives me a knowing look, which tells me I'm onto something. I can definitely relate to Tegan's frustrations and I won't lie, the thought of running away has tempted me once or twice. Callum's promises and the enjoyable company have made it easier for me to accept my circumstances, but I understand why Tegan might not want to.

"We can watch her," Valentina says. "We may have our hands full, but we're a family. We'll keep her safe and entertained so she can't even think about running away."

I nod in agreement. "You all have your hands full with babies and kids. I can help with looking after Tegan."

"That would be incredible," Heavyn says gratefully. "Thanks, Zariyah."

I HOPE I'm not putting too much on my plate. Tegan seems like she could have other Murray traits aside from stubbornness – like being a wily fox. I almost want to check on her in Heavyn's bedroom, but Valentina's baby lets out a loud wail, and the practicalities of daily life interrupt our conversation.

I like them. I hope they can accept me. I love Kalani, but it would be nice to have something more than that – a big family that looks after each other and makes me feel all warm and tingly inside. I enjoy those feelings more than I thought I would.

I TEXT CALLUM AGAIN.

I love you.

Chapter Twenty-Two
Callum

Aiden swigs from a dark brown glass bottle of Guinness with condensation dripping down the sides. He sweats as much as the bottle in the warehouse as he leans over the two plastic tables pushed together with a large physical map of Boston spread out over both tables.

Darragh stands next to me gazing at the figures on the map and Aiden's Sharpie drawings with his hands on his hips. Odhran and Rian stand together, my youngest brother eerily similar to what Rian looked like at his age, especially with the dyed black hair. Odhran has nails painted black tapping on the table from beneath an oversized black hoodie with white Japanese characters on the sleeve and a creepy anime design on the back.

Rian stands next to him with folded arms and a scowl on his face, occasionally fiddling with his wedding ring as he aims to match Aiden's focus. As the second in charge, they provide good balance to each other. Rian believes more in decisive, authoritative action against enemies, but Aiden's reluctance to commit violence makes him a good leader.

He's right not to want more bodies floating to the surface of the Boston harbor. He's right to put family first. That was where our father failed. He put tradition and hatred over family. But all our traditions, all our vows, they're meant to protect our bloodline. Racial purity is only one part of what makes our bloodline – and it becomes more unrealistic day by day.

We don't need our morals to fall along those lines the way we did before. We just need to know who belongs to us – who we need to protect. Look at Tegan. She might not be "racially pure" but she's our fucking family and we know it by looking at her. That's what matters. I can't make a damn thing out of Aiden's map, so I just keep looking at him, ready for him to give us orders, or at least explain more.

Apparently, Darragh makes sense of the map.

"We're surrounded on all sides and completely fucked. How do they have people on this many fucking streets? If we want to get from the Harbor to Cambridge, we gotta spend double the time taking side streets and avoiding blockades."

Aiden looks down at the map sternly.

"It's bad. Yes."

"I have football practice tomorrow," Odhran says. "Can this be done so I can get some sleep?"

Aiden's gaze flashes to him irritably. "Damn it, Odhran. Can you not see that we are having a family crisis? You're eighteen and dad would have wanted you initiated by now. There aren't as many opportunities. Football won't always be there for you. Family will."

Odhran nods. "Yes, Aiden."

If Aiden's response upsets him, he says nothing. Odhran, for all his moral deficiencies, doesn't struggle with obedience. He stops tapping his fingers on the table and stares at the map. I notice what Darragh sees, the blocked off streets, and he's right. We're trapped.

"We aren't trapped," Rian says calmly. "You can't put a nuclear bomb in a cage and call it a trap."

Aiden takes another long swig from his Guinness before setting it down on the table, near the map. He gives Rian a disapproving look.

"Unlike a nuclear bomb, we won't be blowing up everything in our path."

"Although," Rian says, definitely pushing his luck. "Two well placed kilograms of C4 here and here... we could fuck up a hell of a lot of Philadelphia fucks in a short amount of time."

Aiden stares at the map, probably to avoid turning his raging temper on Rian, who should know what Aiden's reaction will be to a suggestion like that. I spare Aiden having to say it.

"That could hurt innocent people, Rian. It's better if we are more targeted."

"I think it's better if we move quickly," Odhran says. "I don't even know why I'm at this meeting. I don't outrank Connor Doyle."

"You're here because it's time for you to get this tattoo," Aiden says, rolling up the white sleeve on his collared shirt to expose a claddagh tattoo on his inner bicep.

Odhran stares at him dumbfounded. I have one – mine on my lower back. Rian has one, and so does Darragh.

"I don't get it," Odhran says.

"You will after tonight," Rian says.

It's the tattoo you get after you kill alongside the boss, serving as his right hand as he engages in an ancient Celtic ritual we brought from the old world. I remember being a boy and seeing my grandfather's claddagh tattoo. I had no idea what it meant, but I always loved putting my hands on it and wondering what *ritual* he referred to. He was the greatest man on earth to me and even if he was dead for years by the time I earned my claddagh, I can't think about that night without thinking of him and how the tattoo connects us.

This isn't just a regular killing, but an important ritual with a basis in ancient Irish mythology. It's something that bonded a father and son in our family that we've been participating in for generations – a father teaching his son how to keep his people safe.

"Okay," Odhran says.

"You're with me tonight," Aiden says emphatically. He's taking on a role that would have been our father's. At least Aiden will be far more sympathetic to the situation at hand than our father would have been. Odhran will be in good hands.

"Bombs," Darragh mutters. "I mean... Bombs might not be a bad idea. Those motherfuckers bombed two of my new clubs. I don't want to be away from Kamari longer than I have to."

"You can't bomb innocent people just so you can be with your wife," Aiden snarls, barely containing his frustration. We all shut the fuck up, completely aware that a comment like that could have earned far worse from our father. Aiden has all his power, but he leads without leaning on fear. It's something we all respect. Something we would all be fucking foolish to take advantage of.

Our father might have raised monsters, but he didn't raise fools.

"We can warn the people," Darragh says.

"How?" Odhran says sarcastically. "A Facebook post?"

Darragh flashes him a middle finger, which Aiden pretends not to notice. That worries me. Aiden is the type to notice these things and point them out unless he has something more important on his mind. *Hm.*

"We won't be doing that," Aiden says. "What I plan is more complicated because it relies on each of us working independently. You can ask for one of our men to accompany you, but they must be initiated men – family."

"We'll do whatever you ask," Darragh says. "Even if I agree with Rian that explosives would be more efficient."

"I consider it a red flag that you're agreeing with Rian for once," Aiden says, his tongue fueled by more swigs of Guinness. "We know this particular clan has four brothers. They're each in control of blocking different parts of the city. We simply have to cut off the heads."

"Kill an entire family?" Darragh asks calmly.

"Yes," Aiden says. "They're unmarried, all under forty years old but... unfortunately, one of them has a daughter. She's staying with him. We will take the daughter. Orla will adopt her."

Rian snickers. "Are you serious? You're allowing Orla to care for a child? She's a chainsmoker."

"Orla contributes very little to this family while collecting a $7,600 paycheck from our businesses. I understand our father wanted women to have little involvement in our life, but I disagree. Orla is entirely unappealing to men, or not attracted to them, I don't care which. She's taking the child."

Odhran tilts his head to the side curiously. "How old is the child? Won't she run away?"

"It doesn't matter," Aiden says. "Her father and his people haven't just taken over parts of our city, killed and attacked several of our people, they're also infesting the city with dirty business. Fentanyl. Illicit pornography. Human trafficking. That's not the city we want to live in."

He's made up his mind, I can tell. Aiden has always known that the time would come that he might have to make an unpopular decision like this one. Leaving a child fatherless… Considering what our family has gone through, this decision is going to weigh on him.

His stiffening body and the way he opens his third bottle of Guinness for the night tells me that Aiden hasn't come to this decision lightly.

"Give us our orders," Rian says. "Everyone in this room ought to trust you with their life. And everyone in this room has a woman they want to go home to."

"Except Odhran," Darragh points out, winking at Odhran and elbowing him. Our sullen youngest brother doesn't smile, but he doesn't show any signs of rebellion either. He seems ready for this.

AIDEN GIVES us our orders and sends us off to work. He expects this to take us several days, but I want this to be over with quickly. The longer I risk leaving Zariyah alone, the more I risk her doing something that could get her injured, or worse.

It's not that I don't trust her change of heart. I'm an even better man than the one she fell in love with, and I've shed so many of my past demons that kept us apart. Just when I'm about to leave and begin my work, my phone buzzes. I assume the text message is from Zariyah at first, so I eagerly unlock my phone to read it, but the text isn't from her at all.

· · ·

Callum

THE TEXT MESSAGE is from her brother.

Lamonte: Do you think I'm ready to be a father?

WHAT THE HELL? My best friend chooses the worst times to pop up and ask me philosophical questions. I shove my phone into my pocket and get my ass to work. I need to see my wife's face again – *soon.*

Chapter Twenty-Three
Zariyah

The trailer is a madhouse. It's nice that Callum stays in touch, but it is *not* the same as having that big bear of a man lying next to me in bed. It's strange the things you miss about a guy when he's not with you. I miss his smell, the way he would put his arm around me and those nibbling kisses he would give me on my neck to wake me up.

Callum was always a pain in the ass, but maybe I liked that, maybe I just wanted him to be *my* pain in the ass. I miss him, and once this is over, I'll try not to take him for granted. We didn't get back together under the most 'normal' circumstances, but we're together, and somehow, this crazy shit is working.

Maybe it's time to tell Lamonte about our marriage. Every time I keep trying to talk to my brother, he sends me some dumbass GIF or a meme about sports. It gives me an excuse to keep my location and secret relationship under wraps, but I'm starting to wonder if Lamonte is hiding something from me.

Probably not. What the hell does Lamonte have to hide from *me*? I don't spend much time worrying about Lamonte and what he gets up to. What could he have to hide?

Since I'm the only one who doesn't have very young kids, I spend a lot of the days with Tegan. We've only been here three days, and I feel like we're good friends in such a short space of time. At first, I thought she was tempestuous for a kid and how she spoke to her daddy made me raise my eyebrows.

Getting to know her, I can tell that Tegan is highly intelligent and perceptive. She's as cranky as I am about being trapped in the trailer. One morning, we sit at the small table together while Tegan sketches something in a large leather-bound sketchbook. Heavyn sits on a reading chair nearby watching Ava nap on her tummy in the playpen.

I have lemon tea in a mug as I watch Tegan sketch and listen to the soft Claire de Lune lullaby playing from Ava's mobile.

Tegan's art is outstanding and watching her sketch distracts me from the one book I packed from Callum's apartment, a complete snore called *Clash of Civilizations* by Samuel P. Huntington. I don't even know why Callum has a book that manages to be both boring and have such strong racist undertones at the same time. The man needs some fiction in his life. Although I guess I've never seen him read, so I don't even know why he has this book.

Tegan is far more entertaining.

"You should try reading romance novels," Tegan says when I slam the book shut and roll my eyes. "Heavyn always reads romance novels and they always put her in a better mood."

"You don't have to put all my business out there," Heavyn says shifting uncomfortably and sliding her phone suspiciously between her thighs and the couch.

"I love putting your business out there," Tegan says mischievously. "Can I tell Zariyah how you and daddy fell in love? Then she can know all the hot family gossip."

"It is *not* hot gossip," Heavyn says embarrassed. "But fine. You can tell her."

Tegan tells me the story of how her dad and stepmom fell in love, glancing over at Heavyn for approval as she goes along. They have the closest bond of any stepmom and step-daughter that I've ever met. It's so sweet.

"They were keeping it a secret from me," Tegan says. "But I found out using detective work."

"That's not exactly what happened," Heavyn mumbles. "But we do *not* need to talk about the details, Tegan."

Tegan smirks and wiggles her eyebrows. "Embarrassed?"

"Oh hush," Heavyn protests.

Her newborn baby gurgles and Heavyn holds the baby to her chest, kissing Ava's forehead until she calms down. Ava is cute, with cinnamon colored skin, almost as dark as Heavyn, and with a shock of light brown hair. Biracial kids can have so many features. I came out with mostly plain, expected features for a biracial girl, but Heavyn's son is different. He has those brilliant sea-green Murray eyes too. *So cute.*

Valentina is with her kids trying to get them to sleep in the bedroom and Kamari sits on what passes for a back porch. We can't hang around anywhere outside facing the main road, but there's a nice thicket of trees filled with chirping birds and excitable chipmunks. Kamari sits there with Colin for as many hours as he can stand it.

"Ricardo and I have been texting," Tegan says, throwing her feet up on the couch, bringing Ricardo up "out of the blue" for the tenth time today. She totally has a crush, but I don't mind hearing about it, because it's almost nostalgic listening to kids talk about their experiences. I never gave much thought to wanting kids before, but the more time I spend around the big Murray family, the more appreciation I have for the life Callum wants.

I understand why he didn't see forced marriage as the worst thing in the world. To him, marriage means this – a house filled with women and babies… and *laughter.* It's not like I don't want a family, I just never thought I could really have one. When you're living to pay rent in New York City, and grieving all your lost lovers and lost friends, you stop thinking of a real future.

Maybe I could have that with Callum. Tegan keeps texting on her phone, a glimmer of a smile inching across her face. I'm watching reruns of *The Big Bang Theory* on TV. I'm not a fan of the show or anything, but it's the only thing on TV out here that is even remotely watchable. The only character I really like is Penny. Tegan isn't watching TV. She's too busy on the phone with Ricardo.

"He just gets me," Tegan says, a smile on her face as she draws the cell phone to her chest. She kicks her feet excitedly. "I wish I could see him."

"I wish I could see my boo too, trust me. But waiting will make him appreciate you more."

Hell, since I'm here, I might as well give her kid appropriate life lessons. Tegan nods excitedly.

"He won't have to wait much longer."

I glance over at Heavyn, nervous about Tegan's comment, but Heavyn is asleep with her baby clutched to her chest, also asleep. They look really cute together and I don't know if this is worth waking her up for. It's just a weird comment.

"I hope not," I say, trying not to act like her comment troubles me, which it does. "I haven't heard anything from Callum."

"I have my own plans," Tegan says. "I'm not going to do anything stupid, don't worry."

"When you say that, it makes me worry."

"Nothing to worry about," Tegan says. "We're all the way in Mexico. He's in Boston. There's nothing we can do to be together. I'm stuck here."

"Join the club, kid. Want me to change the channel?"

"Nope. Leonard is funny."

"Really? Leonard?" I respond, wrinkling my nose. I didn't even realize she was paying attention enough to recognize the characters on the show by name. And to have Leonard as a favorite is definitely weird. I guess he's sweet enough.

Heavyn yawns and wakes up from her brief nap. She mumbles something about going to put the baby down and Tegan gets up off the couch.

"I'll go take a nap in the room with the baby," Tegan says. "This episode is boring."

I didn't think the episode was that boring, but I can't blame her for wanting to nap. It definitely gets boring in the trailer. It can be hard to cope with not having control over our daily lives, honestly. Heavyn keeps herself occupied with Ava and Tegan all day, but I think she would be lost without Tegan. They're so close and Tegan is a fun kid.

"No problem," I tell Tegan as she follows Heavyn. "Don't forget we're having dinner at seven."

"I won't be asleep that long," Tegan says. "Don't worry."

HEAVYN RETURNS to the living room and yawns as she sits down again.

"Is Tegan okay?" she asks.

"She seems fine. She said something suspicious, but she's just napping back there, so I don't know. Maybe she was just being strange."

"What did she say?" Heavyn asks. I tell her and Heavyn seems worried. She glances back at the bedroom nervously. I don't want to make too much of it, but something about Tegan's tone as she said "I won't be asleep that long" still rubs me the wrong way.

I had my own sneaky moments as a kid and I couldn't blame her for plotting an escape if she were about to try something. Adults might be able to handle some boredom, but it must be hard on Tegan.

Valentina is probably the most patient out of all of us, but Kamari spends so much time just staring at trees because she hates feeling trapped in the house. Kamari prefers nighttime television to daytime television, so when she's done staring at trees all day, she comes in at night to watch television with us. She's fun to hang out with, even if she gets cranky from being indoors too long.

"Nothing that serious. She's probably just bored with everything. We can talk to her at dinner," I suggest. "We'll remind her that it's important not to try anything silly because we could all get in serious shit."

"What did she say?"

"Just that she wouldn't be asleep long."

Something funny happens on the *Big Bang Theory* and draws our attention away from overanalyzing Tegan's little comment. Heavyn doesn't seem too worried, which puts me at ease.

"Exactly," Heavyn says. "Is this a Penny episode?"

We curl up on the little couches and watch TV until Kamari comes inside with Colin. She kisses his forehead and whispers, "Is Valentina still in her room?"

I don't think Colin is asleep yet, but he's definitely headed that way as he rests his head on Kamari's slightly sun-damaged chest.

"Not anymore," Valentina says as she walks down the small hall-way. "Didn't you hear the weird noise? It sounds like Tegan's dancing in there"

"What noise?" Kamari responds. "I was just outside but her room is on the other side of the trailer from where I was."

Valentina's nose wrinkles and now she has all of our attention. Val glances over at Heavyn and continues, "Nothing. I thought I heard something strange while I was in my room but... I'm tired. Maybe it was nothing. I knocked on Tegan's door and she didn't answer. I was up all night with the kids and I really needed a nap. Maybe she has headphones on? Maybe I dreamed it all up."

Heavyn sits up, suddenly alert. I'm unsettled.

"She should be napping," Heavyn says. "She's all obsessed with texting Ricardo. I don't remember being *that* boy crazy when I was her age. But that wouldn't be noisy"

Valentina shrugs. "I was never boy crazy."

"I definitely was," Kamari said. "I had a crush on my brother's best friend."

"Relatable," I reply, nodding along with Kamari. I had a crush on my brother's best friend too. I didn't expect that he would kidnap me and force me into marriage years down the road. I didn't expect that I would fall for him.

Heavyn sits up and wrinkles her nose a little before saying, "Should we be worried about that noise you heard? Texting ain't that loud."

Valentina shrugs. "It's a trailer. It sinks. It expands. I hear all kinds of things. I can even hear Kamari on the phone with Darragh some nights."

That answer seems to satisfy Heavyn, who texts Tegan to make sure she's okay.

"I'll go check on her in a bit," Heavyn says. "She probably dropped one of those giant books she carries around."

"Probably," Kamari says. "Val, I'm so sorry for whatever you might have heard from me and Darragh. But the walls *are* paper thin. If it was something serious, you would have heard more than a bit of thumping."

"I do all that via text message," Heavyn muses. "Rian is great at multitasking, but very demanding."

"Are y'all talking about phone sex?" I whisper, making myself sound incredibly prudish. As the only childless woman, I want to respect the presence of their kids and not start screaming about sex. My dramatic tone makes them all giggle. Kamari nods. Heavyn shrugs and Valentina nods along with them.

Am I supposed to be doing that? Callum has never been much for words.

"Should I be sexting Callum?"

Kamari snorts and stifles a laugh. "Sorry, I'm not laughing at you. It's just a funny question. You can if you want to. Darragh is into it."

"So is Rian," Heavyn says.

Valentina shrugs. "Aiden has his moods."

"Just send him a naked picture," Kamari says with a shrug. "Show him all that ass and he will go crazy."

"I don't have an ass that would make a guy go crazy. You three are way better built."

Heavyn laughs. "Are you joking? I am beyond chubby. I keep gaining weight. Rian likes it, and it is what it is, but I wish I had a little less sometimes."

"A little less ass?" Kamari says with surprise. "Hell no. You work all that ass."

"You don't have to show off your body if you don't want to," Valentina says maturely. Kamari playfully rolls her eyes.

"Why shouldn't she? She's damn fine and Callum… I mean… that man is the size of a tree. I can't blame her for considering it. Ask him for a dick pic next."

"Ew," Valentina says. "What is the point of a dick pic? What can you do with a picture of a man's penis?"

"Marvel at its beauty," Kamari says. "Heavyn knows what I'm talking about."

"What? How did I get dragged into this?" Heavyn asks, getting suddenly very nervous and shifting in her seat.

"I see you walking funny sometimes," Kamari says. "Rian must have a big one."

"No, no!" Valentina says. "We're done here. I think you all need Jesus."

Even if she's chastising us, she has a smile on her face. We all burst into laughter and then we keep talking for a few more minutes before a loud knock interrupts our conversation. We freeze. None of us are expecting any visitors. We barely spend any time outside, we haven't needed more supplies yet, so we haven't arranged any deliveries with Aiden. Nobody here has so much as ordered pizza.

So who the hell could be knocking on the door?

Valentina jumps out of her seat and offers to answer the door. We all quickly stand up as well. None of us were ever going to let her go alone.

"I told these idiots they should have left us some guns," Kamari hisses. "All we have for a weapon is a damn filet knife. I guess we could make it work…"

"Shh," Heavyn says, attempting to peer out the trailer window as we approach the door in step behind Valentina.

. . .

Chapter Twenty-Three

"STAY BEHIND ME," Valentina commands before bravely opening the door. The person standing at the door poses no immediate threat. A portly white woman in her sixties with waist length gray hair and a tie-dye t-shirt on over thick khaki cargo pants stands on our doorstep out of breath and red in the face.

"Is everything okay?" Valentina asks her.

"Sorry to bother y'all," she says, gasping for breath between each word. She's rather hefty, and really red, so I'm guessing she ran all the way up here. "My name's Julie. I know y'all keep to yourselves, but I just saw the little girl in the window with the pretty blue eyes get into a vehicle up on Route-104 and I don't know if y'all knew that but... I figured I should come let y'all know. If you want more information, I got the license plate and the car... Oh hell, can I come in and sit down?"

We aren't supposed to let anyone in, but we don't really have a choice. Valentina nods and ushers Julie into the house. My throat tightens.

THE GIRL with the blue eyes. *Tegan.*

I LET her go back there into that room and she either ran away or got kidnapped. This is my fault. And *anything* could happen to her. She already feels like family and I already feel like I fucked up.

Chapter Twenty-Four
Callum

Aiden offers us the choice to use backup, but I prefer working alone. I track the motherfucker Aiden assigns me. He uses an alias, which slows me down, but once I peg the guy, it's easy to follow him. He spends his night with violent, vile motherfuckers. It's hard to stay undetected, but I know our city too well. I can stay hidden when I need to. Hell, if I can stay hidden in New York City, I can stay hidden here.

After the motherfucker gets completely wasted, I follow him, lure him into an alley, knock him out and drag him into the truck cab before driving him to the warehouse that used to house Darragh's old strip club. I have my instructions. I kill him, take his ear and cut him up before disposing of him.

It's hard, heavy work and it's not worth describing. I get dirty. Very fucking dirty. But I get the job done and when I finish, I text my brother. I want the orders to go to Mexico and be with my wife again. Zariyah...

I can't imagine leaving that woman alone for long and not expecting immense amounts of trouble. I half expected to get a phone call from Aiden that she's run away and if she does that again, both of us will be in a boatload of trouble.

Chapter Twenty-Four

I'll take my truck to our cousin's shop on the South Side tomorrow to get it cleaned more deeply, but I get most of the smell and the blood out with some bleach. I miss Zariyah. Queenie must miss her too, poor girl. And I miss my dog. I can't wait to be done with this so I can get them both back.

AIDEN: 4 hours, Orla's place.
Callum: Yes, boss.

YOU DON'T QUESTION the boss, even if your muscles hurt. Lifting weights causes soreness and aching, no doubt, but there's something especially strenuous about handling the human body. Even stiff with rigor mortis, bodies never quite do what you want them to do and they always feel heavier than they are, even to a guy who can deadlift 800 lbs off the ground.

At least four hours allows plenty of time for me to rest before driving over to Orla's place. Killing wears a man out. I sleep shirtless on the couch and set my alarm so I have plenty of time to drive over there. This early morning meeting will happen a couple hours before Orla goes to work and implies that Aiden followed through with both the ritual killing to initiate Odhran and taking the child from our enemies.

Hm.

I fall asleep easily. Waking up is the problem. My alarm sounds like it's yanking my eyeballs out from the back of my head. I just want the noise to stop so I can sleep a bit longer. It would be so goddamn easy just to sleep… longer… I close my eyes and nearly fall asleep again when fear over Aiden's reaction to me being late grips my chest and forces me awake.

After dragging myself off the couch, I throw on a hoodie and sweatpants. I wish I had time for Dunkin'. Hopefully Aiden has the good sense not to show up without any coffee or donuts. Rian will probably protest donuts since he hates everything that brings joy in life, but I crave a sound helping of sugar and enough caffeine to wake up a rhino.

The truck smells too much like bleach, so I drive to Orla's with the windows down and listen to *Real Country* by Upchurch. The music soothes me, reminds me of a place I can never be – out there in the wild away from the noise and mess in Boston. I don't have any interest in leaving behind my family duties. I'm content to just listen to the music. I might not be country, but there's something relatable about the fierce pride in the music. They might not be Irish like us, but they feel like our people.

I can hear arguments carrying on inside once I stop the truck engine. Orla could get into an argument with a nun if you let her, and she could probably provoke the nun to smack her first. I brace myself for whatever insults my sister will inevitably throw my way once we're face to face.

Rian stands in Orla's front door with the door open a crack, as if he plans on running away himself the second he gets the chance. He offers me a sympathetic look as I approach.

"Darragh's late," Rian says. "He says he's on the phone with Kamari and there's some emergency going on."

Before I can probe further, I hear Aiden bellowing at Orla.

"Christ, Orla. You are not naming the child *Cinnamon*. She will have a traditional Irish name and she will be baptized."

Hoping to break up the tension and to follow the smell of coffee that hits me when I enter Orla's place, I greet both of them in a booming voice.

"Any of that coffee for me?"

They continue fighting as Queenie lets out a sound that's a mixture between a howl and a bark, accidentally makes herself fart and then comes waddling over to me with her white-tipped tail wagging furiously. I crouch down and scratch behind her ears, letting her have some love as my siblings continue their senseless argument.

"Our mother chose traditional Irish names. Now we're stuck with idiots like *Callum* and *Odhran*. What sorts of names are those?"

"I like my name. I went by Cal in elementary school for a while. That wasn't bad either."

"Our names are just fine," Aiden says. *"Irish* names are just fine."

He emphasizes the word Irish like it's the worst thing in the world to consider a name from another culture. He still has a strong sense of Irish pride, even with the changes to his character over the years. Orla clearly has a problem with Irish names. She raises her eyebrows and then dramatically rolls her eyes.

"You got a normal fucking name like Aiden. I got Orla! I have a right to want *my* daughter to have a normal life."

"You have known her for *five minutes,*" Aiden hisses. Rian yawns pointedly, but they ignore him. He surprises me by walking over to me instead and nudging me aside so he can get to the donuts. What the fuck? Since when does Rian eat donuts?

"Don't you dare take that glazed one."

I nearly smack his hand away. What the fuck is he thinking? Glazed donuts are my favorite. Orla and Aiden continue arguing about names in the background. Rian takes the glazed donut and I defer with a grunt to the less delicious strawberry frosted donut. At least he's not giving me shit for enjoying a sweet treat this time.

"Since when do you eat donuts?"

"Tegan keeps forcing me to try desserts. I swear she wants me to get a gut."

That doesn't stop him from eating the donut. I enjoy mine and wash it back with some black coffee. I can't imagine living anywhere without a Dunkin'

"What do you think, Callum?" Orla asks as if I've been paying attention. "Do you think I should name my daughter Caoimhe?"

"Kwee-va?" I repeat. "How do you even spell that?"

"See!" Orla says. "You are fucking ridiculous. What about something *normal* and Irish like Bridget. She doesn't deserve to get teased."

Aiden smirks. Orla doesn't notice, but I see how she just stumbled into Aiden's trap. He suggests a ridiculous Irish name that would most likely lead to a child in Boston ending up on the receiving end of severe bullying. Orla responds by suggesting a name Aiden has a chance to approve of.

"I think we had a lesbian great aunt in Galway named Bridget," Rian says confidently, even if I'm sure he's making it up. "That'll please our mother."

"This would be a lot easier to decide if I could have cigarettes. Can't I smoke while the kid is sleeping?"

"You can *vape* while the kid is sleeping and not in the same room," Aiden says. "And you will *not* disobey or I'll give you a job where you actually have to get out of bed before nine in the morning."

"Being a mother is the hardest job in the world, Aiden," Orla says smugly, rolling up the sleeves on her button down and folding her arms sassily.

"You barely met the damn kid," Aiden grunts. "Don't give me a lecture about parenting. Just promise me you'll help her adjust to... everything."

"She's two years old," Orla says. "She just needs toys, hugs and a mom who gives a crap about her. As long as I can still have coffee and those vapes, I'll be fine."

A loud yawn interrupts our conversation and makes me aware of Odhran's presence. He was asleep so soundly on Orla's couch under several thick down blankets, that I didn't notice him. Odhran moves like a cat sometimes – too fucking quietly.

"Coffee.." he grumbles, shedding the blankets and exposing fresh black ink on his wrist. *The claddagh.* That means the ritual happened. I don't know why Aiden chose Odhran's wrist to tattoo him, but the ink looks good. Red and unhealed – but good. I pat Odhran on the back and bring him coffee. After what he just witnessed, he'll need it.

"Is Darragh back yet?"

"Good point," Aiden grumbles. "Orla, why don't you check on Bridget? I'll go outside and find out where the hell our brother ended up."

Aiden wanders outside to look for Darragh and probably chew his ear off. I have another donut. Odhran nibbles at a donut and takes a reluctant sip of coffee.

"How is Six?" I ask Odhran. My brother has been dating an Irish girl since he was twelve-years-old. Now that he's done with high school and moving to college in the fall, I don't know how he's going to handle Six. He should marry her. They've been together for six years. Our mother would have probably given him permission to marry her when he was seventeen.

"She's fine."

"Six? Who the fuck is Six?" Rian asks, snooping around for more of the donuts. He's spent most of Odhran's life behind bars, so it makes sense. Odhran turns red. He doesn't like talking about her, but I don't mind answering and making him blush more. My emotionless brother showing any emotion at all brings me joy, so I don't mind pushing him about his girl. I'll answer for him.

"Aisling Cunningham. She's from the North side Cunningham family."

Rian nods knowingly. The Cunningham family has been close with ours for years. They helped our father during the struggle for Irish pride in Boston during the eighties when Italians threatened to take over our city.

We've stood together through the influx of Puerto Ricans and black folks, and a marriage between Odhran and the Cunningham girl guarantees our family's continued allegiance in the future.

"Is she related to Charlie Cunningham?"

"Youngest sister," Odhran answers. "Can we stop talking about her?"

"What kind of stupid fuck doesn't want to talk about their woman?" Rian says. "I would do *anything* to be with Heavyn right now. I need to get her pregnant again…"

Before I can make a joke about Rian's comment, Aiden opens the door to Orla's place accompanied by Darragh. They're both completely red in the face and my stomach sinks when Aiden turns his perpetual and senseless frustration towards me.

"Fuck's sake, Callum. Why can't any of you keep your shit together?"

He doesn't need to say anything else for me to know that somewhere, somehow, Zariyah has done something – probably tried to escape. That means she must have lied to me. She promised she would take this seriously and she wouldn't run away. *Fuck.*

Darragh is the one who gets straight to the point. "Rian, your daughter ran off again and Callum's wife disappeared chasing after her instead of waiting for us to turn up. We can get there faster if we can access a private jet."

Rian turns to Darragh and slowly turns deep red as he pushes his tongue into the corners of his mouth like he's trying not to turn this into a Murray family brawl. Sensing chaos, Orla emerges with her daughter Bridget in her arms. I don't know how long she expects to keep the baby quiet.

"Do you expect me to pull a private jet out of my ass?" Rian snarls at Darragh. "Tegan should have known better not to run away. But sadly, I knew my daughter would most likely defy me. I put a tracking device in her cell phone."

I'm relieved to hear about Tegan, but I didn't think so far ahead. I foolishly trusted Zariyah.

AND SHE'S BROKEN that trust.

Chapter Twenty-Five
Zariyah

It's my fault. Tegan showed clear warning signs that she was planning something and I basically let her pull the wool over my eyes. They told me not to blame myself, but how could I not blame myself? Callum trusted me not to run away, but he also trusted me with his family. If anything happens to that little girl - I will never forgive myself.

This little girl became my family in a few short days. I'd rather lose Callum than lose her. *He would understand, right?*

Valentina disagrees that I should go after her, but I can't just sit there and listen to Julie recount the same story over again. I know what vehicle she was in, I know what direction she went – I need to go after her. I barely hide that I'm running off. I make some excuse about checking the main road to see if Tegan is on her way back and then I just... *go.*

They don't start calling me until I'm over two hours down the main road. I keep stopping at RV parks along the way and talking to people, just in case anyone saw something earlier. I'm thankful that the summer sun means I can get a lot of ground covered before night-fall. Callum will probably want to divorce me after this. He made it clear how he feels about promises and what happens when they're broken.

I feel like I have to do this. I didn't fight like this for Sophie and I don't want to lose anyone else like that. I don't want anyone else to know the type of loss that I've known. If Callum doesn't understand, then I'll have to let him go…

There's nothing I have to hide about my search, but when I try to answer the phone call, the call drops and then I lose all of my phone signal. This place is peppered with dead zones and cell phone signal is only occasional and in places like gas stations or more populated areas. The phone reads "SOS Only". *Fuck.* I have to trust that Aiden won't send them after me due to the danger involved and I can just keep going and use the extra time to get closer to Tegan.

Since my phone isn't even connected, I turn it off, but that means I can't keep track of the time. All I know is by the time I get close to an answer, my stomach growls furiously. I'm hungry and I can feel that my gentle sprinkling of melanin hasn't been enough to keep the sun at bay. My arms and chest look red. I can't imagine what my face looks like.

But I finally talk to someone who has answers. Someone who saw something. A young man sitting in a camping chair at the front desk of an RV park waves me over with a big smile on her face.

"Jeff told me a strange woman would probably be coming up my way," he calls out to me in one of the strangest accents I've ever heard. Folks out in rural New York sound oddly country. I walk up to the man who apparently expected me, and he hands me a bottle of water.

"I've seen something," he says. "My name is Mark Fish, by the way."

"I'm Zariyah."

I take the bottle of water greedily and step as far off the main road and out of the sun as I can. Mark has the good sense to set up his camping chair under a large maple tree.

"You're looking for a little girl in a black Jeep Grand Cherokee with a license plate KCW6673?"

I nod. I've said it so many times that apparently it's become a part of some country ass group chat.

"You've been causing a stir at all the campgrounds up here. We don't get many strangers and we don't get many missing people. You gone to the cops?"

"I can't," I gasp.

Mark nods. "I understand. We have biker gangs all 'round here and certain folks don't take kindly to cops. Well, I saw the Jeep heading North earlier and when I heard there was some woman coming up this way, I text messaged a few of my friends. This the Jeep?"

He sticks out his cell phone and there's a grainy picture of a black Jeep. The photo might be grainy, but the license plate definitely matches.

"Where is this?"

"Five miles up that way at the *Lakefront RV Campground.* They don't know anyone is on to them. Do you think they're dangerous?"

"No. I think my… niece… just wanted to meet up with a boy and ran off."

"Can I help you get up there?" he offers.

"No… I couldn't ask that…"

"Sure you can!" he says. "It's a hot day today and I know the area. Come on."

I don't see that I have that much of a choice, honestly.

"If you drop me off near the entrance, I'll have the element of surprise. Do you think I'll get a better phone signal up there?"

"Oh definitely. Where we're at now is a dead zone," Mark says. "Once you get to Lakefront, it should be much better. Are you sure you don't need me to load up the old shotgun?"

He laughs, so I assume he's joking and I laugh along with him. I hope I don't need a damn shotgun.

"How long ago did you get that picture?"

"Not too long ago. Come on, little lady. I'll take you up there."

They could still be there then if Mark didn't get the picture too long ago. I have time, so I let Mark take me there.

Mark insists that I get into his truck and he takes me all the way to the entrance of the *Lakefront RV Campground*. I jump into the truck without thinking, trusting that this salt of the earth white guy around my dad's age isn't going to do me any harm. It's a risk, but it's worth it if I can get Tegan back before anything bad happens.

Just because she somehow arranged running away with Ricardo doesn't mean she's safe. If Callum finds out about this and thinks it's about me not trusting him, I hope he realizes that's not why I'm doing this. I believe in the danger, but I also believe it's my job to protect our family too, not just his.

Mark drops me off at the campground entrance and I insist that he drive away. I'll figure out a way back without him and I don't want to compromise our location more than we already have. I feel like I'm finally reaching Callum's level of paranoia. I wait for Mark to drive away before I walk up the gravel road through the campgrounds. I don't know where the Jeep is parked and Mark's friend isn't at the front gate anymore.

Mark explained that he was probably strolling through the campgrounds making conversation because he's a pretty chatty guy. I nod along because it seems to me like everyone up here is pretty chatty. I can't imagine anyone caring this much about a missing kid in New York City or Boston.

As I walk through the small campers and RV's, I scan for the Jeep. Before I come across the Jeep, I hear a loud, blood-curdling scream that I immediately recognize as Tegan's. The scream comes from the shoreline, about seven rows of RVs down from where I'm standing.

I run towards the sound without thinking. She's in trouble and this campground is oddly empty. Too empty. Was I too careless? Panicked thoughts rush through my head as I sprint towards the lake shore.

As I draw closer to the rocky Lake Ontario shoreline, I see Tegan standing with a boy who I assume is Ricardo... but she's screaming because the boy isn't alone. There are three large men standing over him, holding a gun to the boy's head. Tegan doesn't notice me approaching, but it's not because I'm quiet. I attract the attention of the armed men, but Tegan is fixated on Ricardo.

Chapter Twenty-Five

"If you hurt him, my dad will KILL YOU!" Tegan shrieks. "LET HIM GO!"

"Tegan!" I yell at her, being foolish and instinctive. I want her to have a chance to run away and I hope that calling her name can give her a chance to run and provide a distraction. It's not like I don't care about the boy with her, but Tegan is my family. She was my responsibility and I could never forgive myself if someone hurt her.

One of the men immediately turns a shotgun on me and I freeze in place, throwing my hands up. I know he might shoot me anyway, but I don't have a choice. Tegan doesn't run away or leap into the water. She rushes to Ricardo and wraps herself around him, holding him in her arms and covering him from any potential gunfire. Ricardo hugs Tegan back as he starts crying.

"You should have run," he says. "Tegan…"

"WHO THE FUCK ARE YOU?" the man holding the gun says to me. "You ain't one of these fucking hillbillies."

"I'm not. And you can put your gun down. I don't know what you're doing here, but you have no business with that little girl and if you hurt her, I will be the least of your fucking problems."

"I'm not leaving without Ricardo."

The man holding the gun glares at me. I can tell from the look in his eyes that he could end my life in a fucking instant without a second thought. Who the fuck are these people, and why do they have Ricardo? I search for clues. They aren't Irish.

That's the first thing that stands out to me. I never thought I would really care much about Callum's culture, but I can't help absorbing a thing or two. The tattoos are in Spanish, which makes me wonder…

"Are you Ricardo's family?" I ask the men. They don't all look very Puerto Rican. That's what's weird about it. Ricardo looks how you would expect. He's not like Tegan. He has darker skin, slick black hair…

"Who the fuck are you, woman? Before I put a bullet in your fucking head, I want to know who the fuck I'm talking to."

A taller man standing with a gun pointed at Ricardo and Tegan silences the man threatening me.

"J.P., we don't have time to question the bitch. We need to get the ceremony going."

"What ceremony?"

The man holding the gun at my head scowls like I'm being too damn useless. I don't care. I'm not here to answer questions and even if I'm scared, I had to face the truth a long time ago. We don't get to choose when it's our time. God calls us when he's ready. I learned that from losing a best friend at a young age. If Sophia is out there at all, if any part of her spirit is alive, I know she'll look after me. Even if it's my time to go, I know she'll be there on the other side.

"I asked you a question. Are you too cowardly to answer my questions before you kill me? Don't you have all the power here?"

My heart races. I know I'm acting crazy, but I just have to hope that this time, being crazy will work.

"We're taking the Irish girl and marrying her to one of our own. Her family is a bunch of shitheads and they fucked with our people. Then to make matters worse, their territorial disputes have spread to our streets. Our boss is sick of this shit and we're sending the Murray assholes a message. This shit has nothing to do with niggers."

Did this man just call me the n-word? He's pale, with dark brown hair and the other men have similar features. Maybe they're mixed race too – half Puerto Rican and half white. I can't really tell and analyzing their racial heritage has to be the least of my concerns. I just want to know why this is happening and how I can get Tegan out of it.

"It may have nothing to do with me, but you can't marry off a little girl. Even if she likes Ricardo. They're too young to get married. This is insane! Do you really think her family would let you get away with this?"

The man holding the gun grins. "By the time we ruin her, it won't matter. This isn't about logic, woman. It's about revenge."

"Raping a little girl? If that's what you think makes your people look strong, you are fucked in the head."

"It doesn't matter if I'm fucked in the head, woman. I'm the one holding the gun."

I glance at Tegan. She's still holding Ricardo, but she's looking at me. Waiting for me expectantly. She knows just how bad this is, but that fierce little girl, through all her fear, still won't abandon her friend. Even if she knows his family is doing this to her. They used him to get to her.

This might be her first heartbreak and it kills me that she has to go through it like this. I have to get her out of here.

Once I'm sure I have Tegan's eye contact, I take a deep, slow breath and prepare myself for the inevitable. I'm going to die. I'm going to do something crazy and I'm going to die.

BUT IF I'M LUCKY, my death will save Tegan Murray's life. *I'm sorry, Callum. But when you married me, you made me your family. And this is what family does.*

Chapter Twenty-Six
Callum

Rian and I hear the gunshot at the same time and leap out of the rented truck. Our families, our mess to clean up. Aiden, Darragh and Odhran are still in Boston. We're in the right place, but we're too late. Rian runs towards the shore because a loud scream follows the gunshot.

Tegan. I've heard Tegan howling at the top of her lungs enough to recognize her screams. I pull my gun out. *Zariyah. Why isn't Zariyah screaming?* I follow Rian, but he's smaller, lighter, and significantly faster than me, so he gets to the beach first. Just as I situate myself on the rocky beach, Rian fires three quick shots.

I hear more screaming but then it all fades away when I see her lying there with blood spilling from her arm. Not just her arm. It looks like it's everywhere. I can't describe the hurt that courses through me. I lose my shit.

"ZARIYAH!"

Every complicated emotion that I've ever felt for Zariyah comes forward. I don't even think. I run to her and drop to the ground to analyze the wound quickly. The first gunshot must've hit her.

"Callum..." she croaks out several seconds after I call her name. She doesn't look good. I need to get her out of here.

"You stubborn fucking woman."

"I'm sorry…"

"Don't be sorry," I murmur. "Just stay alive."

Rian fires several more gunshots. Once he stops, I hear him say, "Open your eyes."

I'm glad he at least didn't kill people in front of his fucking daughter. I hope I'm never in the situations that Rian finds himself in. Once the gunfire stops, I hear Tegan shriek, "Daddy!"

My reunion doesn't feel quite so fucking sweet. Zariyah doesn't have a lot of time. I hear Rian jogging over.

"Is she alive?" he asks calmly. I don't feel so fucking calm.

"Yes. But she's losing a lot of blood and is going into shock."

"I dealt with shit like this in prison," Rian says. "I'll get her safely into the car and we'll take her to the nearest hospital."

"In fucking Syracuse?"

"There's a clinic near here," Rian says. "Calm down, Callum. I know you love her. I won't let you lose her. Come on. Let me have a look."

I don't want to let go of Zariyah's hand. Letting go of her feels like giving up. Rian doesn't make me stop holding her, but he crouches next to Zariyah and moves her arm. She groans in pain and blood gushes from the wound. Blood has never made me feel so sick before.

I've failed her. I'm furious with myself for failing her.

RIAN MOVES her arm and more blood gushes out. My stomach twists into a large knot. I could really lose her. Zariyah looks so weak and so pale. I've come to expect her to be loud, larger than life and constantly on fire. But she's not on fire right now. I can see the life draining out of her.

"She's going to be fine," Rian says, even if she doesn't look like she's going to be fine. I want to throttle the fuck out of my brother.

"Then why does she look dead?"

"I need fabric and pliers. I can get the bullet out and then we need to get our connections in Syracuse so we can get her to the hospital."

Callum

I have pliers, but I don't want to waste any time.

"Are you sure this will work?"

"It'll work if you hurry the fuck up," Rian says impatiently. I head back to the truck and return with pliers. Rian has his shirt off and Tegan stands back with Ricardo, facing away from her dad while holding Ricardo's hand.

"I don't need her seeing more shit than she has already," Rian growls, noticing my glance at Tegan. "I swear, I don't care if Heavyn disagrees, I'm going to consider bringing a wooden spoon into the equation to teach Tegan how to behave properly. Remember when great aunt Aoife beat us senseless that summer in Glengarriff? We fucking learned our lesson quickly."

If Heavyn is anything like Zariyah, I doubt she'll take too kindly to Rian's notions of parenting, but he makes a point about the current generation. Even Zariyah, only a few years younger than me, responds very well to having her butt spanked.

Rian grumbles to himself as he works. Even if I tell myself I don't want to watch, I couldn't bear something happening to Zariyah and not having her hand in mine. Her lips turn blue and she sweats as Rian removes the bullet and then presses fabric to the wound.

"The bullet didn't hit anything vital. But she still needs stitches and she's losing too much blood. Come on. I'll keep her arm out of trouble and we'll put her in the truck."

I help Rian move Zariyah into the backseat of the truck. Ricardo and Tegan ride in the truck bed and we drop them off at the family trailer before Rian hits the highway down to the nearest hospital, thirty-something miles away in Syracuse.

I sit in the backseat with Zariyah's head on my lap. I need to feel her heart beating. She's still sweaty and unconscious, but Zariyah's breathing and the bleeding seems like it's slowing down. When Rian gets us to the emergency room, a nurse with a celtic knot tattooed on her exposed forearm immediately meets us at the entrance.

One of ours. She leads us down a hospital hallway pushing Zariyah on a gurney. The hospital wing initially appears abandoned, but seems to just have quiet, private rooms. This place is dead compared to the hospital in Boston. She turns to us once she has Zariyah in a waiting room.

"She'll need surgery. Doctor Flannery will be with you shortly."

"Thank you," Rian says. I'm in too much shock to say much. I want to scream at them to hurry up. But nothing can make this process go any faster. Rian says I worry too much and we argue about his coldness until the doctor appears. Zariyah goes into surgery and it feels like time slows down to an unbearable pace until the Irish nurse returns with a somber expression.

"THE DOCTOR WANTS to have a conversation with you, Mister Murray," the nurse says, gesturing towards me rather than Rian. She's my wife, so I suppose it makes sense I would be the one they call. Still, Rian outranks me in the mob, so I glance at him for permission. He nods.

I follow the nurse and she leads me into Zariyah's hospital room. Doctor Flannery is older than I expected, in his late seventies, with thick glasses and a gold claddagh ring on his ring finger above a gold wedding band. I don't know his connection to the mob specifically, but he's one of our people.

And apparently he's still willing to treat Zariyah despite her race. He doesn't bear any signs of disgust or concern for her mixed heritage, which brings me some relief. Older Irish folks aren't above giving a politically incorrect lecture and right now, I just want her to survive. Zariyah is awake, but she isn't looking at me. She casts her gaze down.

Doctor Flannery sticks to the business at hand and starts speaking before I can address Zariyah and ask her how she's doing myself.

"Your brother is a surprisingly good field medic. He removed the bullet and kept the wound under enough pressure that I could give her some stitches and pain medication. She can leave the hospital tonight if she makes it through the next four hours."

"So she's fine?"

Zariyah might not be able to look at me, but I can't take my eyes off her. She might look pale and out of sorts, but she's so beautiful. Her hair is so thick and dark, and I just want to press my nose to those pretty curls and appreciate Zariyah for what she is – my beautiful, chaotic, disobedient, gorgeous ass woman.

"She will be. She needs to rest and she won't be able to use her arm for a while. She'll need someone to change her dressing but based on the work of your field medic, I suspect you're more than capable of handling it."

"Thanks, doc."

"You're lucky. If your brother hadn't removed the bullet you would have lost her and the baby. This shouldn't affect her pregnancy, but if you notice anything strange, call your local doctor."

That gets Zariyah's attention right away.

"I'm sorry, what?"

"Didn't I tell you, dear?"

"I'm pregnant?" Zariyah says with a shrill voice, giving me a guilty expression as if her getting pregnant would somehow be all her fault. I don't know what to think about the doctor's news, so I say nothing intelligent.

"We'll call the doctor if anything goes wrong. Thanks."

"I can't be pregnant," Zariyah blurts out.

Doctor Flannery gives us a half-interested smirk. "I'll return if you need me. It seems this is a private conversation. Congratulations."

He leaves the private hospital room. Zariyah is still stuck in bed, thank goodness, with an IV in her arm giving her fluids. She can't leave until she's done with those, so I have until then before she tries running away or beating me over the head.

She doesn't seem happy.

"I'M PREGNANT," Zariyah whispers, like she doesn't believe it. She shakes her head. "No way. I can't be pregnant. Not now."

"What's wrong with now?" I feel gruff, but also intensely protective of her. I hate the distance I feel between us. There shouldn't be distance between us. Zariyah is my woman and after what she's been through, all I want to do is keep her in my apartment and look after her until the baby comes. The thought of anything happening to her rips my heart out.

She's the one woman I've ever loved. I'm not capable of loving another woman. It's a sick, twisted realization that no matter how much Zariyah fucks with my head – I'm not letting her go. That woman could set me on fire and I would let her do it. She has me more than wrapped around her finger.

She owns my heart.

"I disobeyed your commands. This is it for us. You kick me to the streets and I end up a single mother. If CPS finds out I'm a single mom getting shot at, it'll be a matter of time before they snatch my baby up and this is all over."

"Care to lighten up, Zariyah?"

"No!" she says. "I know I didn't listen. I messed up. I *keep* messing up. Even when I try to be the type of woman you want me to be, I'm just… a mess. You shouldn't have trusted me to listen."

"This is good news, Zariyah," I say to her firmly. *My wife.* Does she really think one little episode of her impulsive behavior is enough to scare me off? She's having a baby. A baby is bigger than my rules. A baby is bigger than our family traditions.

A baby is good news. *Very* good news. Still, I understand her sense of panic. She's younger, she's been injured, and I've hurt her so badly in the past. I've abandoned her when she needed me. But, I won't let her go. *She was mine the day she turned eighteen and Zariyah will always be mine.*

Zariyah gives me an even more confused look. "I broke your rules, Callum. I know what this means. We're over. I ran away, I got shot. I messed everything up after you trusted me."

"What the hell are you talking about?"

Zariyah gives me a fierce look like she wants to slap me. "You made yourself clear, Callum. You expect obedience. But I'm never going to be a perfect obedient mob wife. Tegan was in danger and everyone just wanted to wait but that's not me. I trust you, but my trust in you just makes me want to fight harder for myself. Because I know you'll be there."

"I don't need you to be perfect. Or obedient. Not all the time. You were trying to save Tegan's life. I'm not going to send you away or give up on you because you thought you were doing the right thing."

"I ran away. Your brothers' wives didn't run away. They trusted their husbands. I know I messed up. You don't have to feel bad for me because I got shot."

"You're not my brothers' wives, Zariyah. You are a lot more fucking trouble than that and it's exactly why I love you."

Her gaze flutters to mine and those giant brown eyes melt me completely. Does she really think after all the bullshit she's put me through I'm going to let her go?

"You still love me?"

"You still loved me," I tell her. "Even after you found out the worst things about me, you still loved me."

"No I didn't," Zariyah says, still argumentative despite her gunshot I'm pleased to find. "I left you and I never looked back."

"But you still loved me. If you didn't love me, there's no way in hell I would've won you over. There's no way in hell you would've risked your life for my family. Your heart is so goddamn big, Zariyah."

"You call it having a big heart. Some people call it impulsive and reckless."

"Your big heart makes you impulsive and reckless. You make me better because of it."

She rolls her eyes and flops back. For a moment, I worry that I've done something wrong.

"We're having a baby…" I say to her, moving closer and kissing her on the forehead. "That is much more important than my rules."

Her large eyes gaze up at me and captivate my soul entirely. She makes me entirely fucking weak. Vulnerability that would have felt horrifying to me before comes naturally to me now. I run my fingers through her curls. They're so soft and long. If we have a daughter, I know she will be just as beautiful as Zariyah.

It's hard to think that a younger version of me could have ruined this with my father's old beliefs – beliefs that don't have a place in the world we live in.

"I just want to get out of here," she sighs. "Are you going to help me escape?"

"You're the mother of my child. I'm not going to let you scamper off and get into more trouble."

Zariyah wrinkles her nose. "You're really happy about this?"

"Aren't you?"

"After all that time in the trailer, I definitely wanted a baby of my own but… are we really ready?"

"We got married the first day we saw each other after years. Falling for you happened in an instant and we've made it work this far. We'll make it work."

I kiss her forehead again. Zariyah sighs and a relaxed smile spreads across her face. "I'm glad that you're happy."

"If I had my way, I'd keep you pregnant," I murmur.

"If you help me escape, I'll let you," she teases, her mischievous gaze locking with mine. I touch my beautiful wife's cheek. *I can't wait for us to have a baby together, but I won't let her put herself in danger.*

"Not a chance," I whisper, giving Zariyah another loving kiss on the forehead. She sighs and gives up on her escape plan. *Good.*

"Will you sit with me then?"

"Yes, ma'am. I don't think I'm ever going to leave your side…"

"Well, you'll have to," Zariyah says.

"I'd like to argue with that," I grumble, glancing around for any potential escape hatches Zariyah could find her way into.

"I need you to do something for me," she says seriously. "So stop looking for escape hatches."

I raise my eyebrows. What does she want me to do for her? Miss independent over there wouldn't even wait for me to come rescue her.

"It's been too long since my brother and Kalani have replied to my texts. I asked the nurse to check my phone. I need you to drive me down there the second I get discharged."

"You're still pale as fuck and you're worried about tracking down your brother? He's a celebrity, Zariyah. He can handle himself."

"He's an idiot," she says with a groan. "You have to help me, Callum."

"You just lie there and get better," I grumble. "Once the doctor says you're better, your wish is my command."

"I should get shot more often," Zariyah says sassily. "This is the fastest I've ever won you over."

"Hm," I grunt. I'm pretty sure that woman is wrong. She has me wrapped around her fucking finger and that's exactly how I like it.

Chapter Twenty-Seven
Zariyah

Callum slides into bed next to me and holds my hand while I let them pump me with fluids. I want to escape, but I admit that I feel a lot better once I'm done with the IV bag. Callum sticks to his promise to drive me back to Boston once the doctor dismisses me.

His brother Rian wants us to stay at the family trailer park for one more day before we drive back to Boston. I'm nervous about facing the family and even more nervous about what could be happening to my brother and Kalani. Rian dismisses my concerns and claims that they're too far removed from his family business to get killed.

I don't share his confidence. When Lamonte was playing professional football, he would drop off the face of the Earth, but we were in regular contact up until the point I went up to Mexico. Now that I know Tegan is safe and that I'm mostly fine, I just want to find him.

Despite my fears, returning to the family trailer isn't as bad as I thought it would be. We get there early in the morning, just after everyone in the trailer wakes up. I barely slept all night, so I look forward to crawling into bed and sleeping away the rest of the day.

First, everyone wants to see how I'm doing. Word spread about the gunshot wound and I'm not sure what response everyone else will have. Even if I felt like I was doing the right thing, I still betrayed them and scared the crap out of them.

Everyone greets me with warmth and positivity, soothing my fears about my screw up. Kamari congratulates me in a whisper for running off after Tegan. Heavyn doesn't outright thank me for running away, but she gives me a big hug and shares some of the jam tarts she made for dessert with me. Tegan is glued to her side and Rian glued to her side. If they're going to have a blowout fight over Tegan running off, it hasn't happened yet.

Valentina just seems glad that I'm safe, but she's too busy with the babies and preparing breakfast for us to have as a family to stop for too much conversation. She's the only person in the room who wants to return to Boston as much as I do. I think she misses Aiden.

Callum makes idle conversation as Valentina serves pancakes, chopped strawberries, whipped cream and maple syrup in the kitchen, giving us all our plates and directing us to assigned seats around the table – which can't hold all of us – and then to spots on the couch nearby.

I get a seat at the table near Callum, who seems weirdly nervous for a man about to dig into a stack of pancakes.

"Did you leave any pancakes for anyone else?" I ask Callum, giving his stack of pancakes a skeptical look. "There's about a pint of maple syrup on there."

"It's called a cheat meal, Zariyah."

"Okay… Well as long as that meal is the only thing you're cheating on."

Callum gives me a nervous smile instead of laughing at my dumb joke. Why is there something suddenly wrong with him? I'm done with that big bear's cranky ways. I hold my fork up and try to find a good part of Callum's meaty hand to stab with it, hoping to shock him into an attitude adjustment.

Before I can poke his ass, he blurts out, "Zariyah is pregnant. We're having a baby. It's finally happening. I finally knocked up my wife."

Okay. He had a good thing going there, but he screws up with the last sentence which gives far too much information. I stab Callum's hand with my fork, but he's clutching the table so tightly and grinning so excitedly that he doesn't even feel it.

"Congratulations," Valentina says, clapping her hands excitedly. Kamari lets out the loudest scream-whisper she can afford with sleeping babies in the trailer and hugs me. Heavyn does the same thing.

Rian gives me a pat on the back and warns Callum, "Be careful. Your arms are big enough to crush a newborn easily."

"He'll be fine," Heavyn says, glaring at her husband. "Don't freak them out. This is good news."

My excitement builds once I share it with my new friends. They're not even really friends. They're *family*. They treated me like family from the day we met and now I feel like we're about to share something else. Something bigger. Our celebration continues until we finish eating.

I finish eating long before Callum who looks like a literal beast as he chows down on pancakes. Syrup drips into his strawberry blond beard and even if he looks partly like a gross caveman, there is something insanely sexy about watching a man lose his shit while he eats. *I love his big appetite in every context.*

Once he's done eating, Callum doesn't waste another moment on polite conversation.

"I'm taking her pregnant ass to bed," he says. "I know it's early, but she needs rest. I'm assigning us an entire day of sleeping in the trailer."

I give Callum a funny look. I don't know how he expects his exceedingly tall self to fit in my bedroom. It's still just a trailer and the more bodies you add, the harder it is for us to all fit and move around.

There were already too many of us before Callum and Rian needed accommodations (and food).

"You had me up all night," he says when I suggest the bed might be too small for both of us. "You'll sleep on my chest if there isn't enough room. But I'm getting some peace of mind."

"I won't have any peace of mind until I talk to Lamonte."

"Are you really so eager to talk to your brother?" Callum grumbles. "We're probably going to have to tell him about us considering the news..."

I haven't given myself permission to think about "the news". Callum and I have been acting reckless in bed together since day one, but I pushed thoughts of pregnancy away until I couldn't anymore. Until now.

"That's the last thing on my mind. Someone tried to kill me, so for all we know someone might have tried to kill him too. He could be dead."

"But mercifully, you're alive," Callum murmurs, coming up behind me and touching my good shoulder. He kisses it gently, careful to avoid my arm, which is still very tender despite the pain medication. His lips feel so damn good on my shoulder.

His kiss only distracts me for a second, although I'm pretty sure Callum wants to serve as a permanent distraction.

"Maybe he doesn't want to be found," Callum suggests, kissing my shoulder again as we stumble forward into my small room. He uses his foot to close the door behind us. I'm still facing away from him, enjoying the parts of Callum I can appreciate without even looking at him. His scent. How warm he feels. His size. The softness of his lips. They're never too wet or too gruff.

"Or he could be hurt. People get hurt all the time."

"They do," Callum murmurs, kissing my shoulder. "You're hurt. So it's my job to distract you from that hurt until tomorrow. You can worry about your brother and everyone else then. Today is about you..."

"I'm sleepy," I whisper.

"I bet you are. Come to bed," Callum murmurs. "I want to feel you sleeping on my chest. Every minute in Boston without you was pure torture."

"Really? You didn't appreciate the peace and quiet or the lack of arguing?"

"I missed all those things about you. Now come to bed..."

. . .

Chapter Twenty-Seven

I WAKE up feeling achy despite Callum's best efforts to avoid messing with my arm. He administers more pain medication and then solemnly informs me that he needs to dress my wounds. When I complain about the dressing, he becomes very stern again and informs me that I have no choice but to obediently sit there and allow him to administer medical care.

Callum dresses my wounds in the trailer bathroom shortly before Heavyn and Kamari finish cooking up a storm for dinner. Rian watches all the kids including Tegan while Valentina takes a much needed nap. I never saw Rian as much of a fatherly guy, so walking out there and seeing him holding Valentina's baby makes him look warmer than I expected.

Tegan sits near him still using her cell phone, but Ricardo is nowhere to be seen. I want to ask about him, but I don't want to cause a scene or anything so I tiptoe over to where Heavyn serves up plates of food and ask her if she knows anything. Family came for him, she says, while I was at the hospital. Rian and Tegan apparently got through all their arguing then.

Heavyn doesn't go into details, she just seems pleased that they're getting along now. I try to help her serve dinner but she insists that because I'm injured, I need to get 'princess treatment'. I hate feeling like I'm weak, but absolutely no one is on my side. None of them let me help and they treat me like I'm a baby bird. I have to admit after a while that it's not bad to get treated nicely.

I give up on fighting. Callum promises that we're leaving in the morning, so I make the best of the night. I don't announce to anyone that I'm pregnant. I want to come to terms with the news on my own before I run around telling people. If it were up to me, I would leave Lamonte out of it for as long as possible. But I'm worried about him. I don't get why Callum keeps acting so calm. *Men…*

AFTER DINNER, Callum takes me back to our room for more sleep. I'm *way* too tired to argue with him. I just want to be next to him tonight. He saved my life and more than that... he loves me enough to understand why I ran away. That's a pleasant surprise.

I feel like I ended up with the right guy, but he doesn't feel like the man I ran away from all those years ago. He's right. He's different. I see a way that I can let Callum in without losing my mind. We fit better together than I thought. Even with all the fighting.

My arm aches as I lie next to Callum. If it weren't for the pain, I would totally jump on him. He's a saint, though, and he doesn't even bring up having sex with me. He's too worried about me to rush into things, but I wouldn't mind if Callum found a creative way for us to join our bodies together.

I missed him. Hell, my body still misses him. And now that we're having a baby together, everything feels so real. The hardest part will be having to confess everything to Lamonte. That will definitely suck. But right now, I can't even worry about how angry my brother will be when I don't even know where he is – or if he's alive.

I don't share Callum's certainty that everything will be okay, or that finding Lamonte will be easy. In the morning, Callum stays true to his promise. When we wake up, my arm hurts a lot less, even if it's still in a bit of pain. Callum ensures I have my prescription medication before we leave. He makes breakfast and does an *insane* number of pushups before we leave the trailer. It's harder saying goodbye than I thought, even if I know the folks I'm leaving behind will always leave my family.

I just need to know that everything is okay with my brother, especially if the Irish mob stuff bleeds into our personal lives. Callum wants me to trust him, and I do, but I also trust that he would say anything he had to if he thought it would protect me.

I fall asleep on the drive to Boston, but I don't stay asleep the entire time.

Once we're close to the city, I'm too nervous about Lamonte and Kalani to stay asleep. I have my forehead pressed against the window like I can will Callum to drive faster. I don't think it would be legal for him to drive any faster than this, but I wish he could just to make sure my brother is safe.

Chapter Twenty-Seven

Callum suggests I call my parents to ask, but I don't exactly want to drop the news that I'm pregnant to them first. Lamonte's my older brother, and at one point, we were best friends, and we've hidden this from him for too long anyway. What if something happened to him and now we'll never have the opportunity to confess the truth? ?

After losing Sophia, I let go of the illusion that people are going to be with you forever. There was a part of me that felt dark after her. I didn't even want to connect with anyone. I couldn't stand to be in the same city as Kalani. Something drew me back to her and then Callum's family pushed me even further – they forced me to come out of my long period of isolation.

I can't hide away in Brooklyn and pretend that losing my best friend as a teenager didn't nearly break me. I have to face the people I care about – face that I might lose them. With Callum, I don't have to do that alone. Letting him back into my heart was the hardest part of coming back to Boston. He was my biggest risk and my biggest reward.

I don't want to run away from love anymore. Not from Callum. Not from my family. It's not like I don't still feel the pain of losing Sophia, it's just that I look at it differently now. Love can hurt, but it can also heal.

I finally give in to Callum's suggestion to call my parents, even if I really don't want to. They probably don't know anything about Lamonte and I don't want to accidentally let any information slip that I'm not ready to share. But Callum essentially makes me call.

"Hey, mom…" I say into the phone. Callum glances over every few seconds, but he doesn't say anything throughout the phone call, letting me do the legwork on my own. I avoid the subject of my pregnancy while giving my mom an update that I'm "seeing someone" after she presses incessantly and refuses to give me any useful information.

"Is it Callum?" she asks excitedly. "I was hoping you would reconnect in Boston and when Lamonte said he ran into him…I had my suspicions."

I confess that the person I'm seeing is Callum and she sounds excited. Despite her previous contact with Lamonte, my mom hasn't heard from him in a week. I make her promise that she won't tell Lamonte about Callum. I had to let one secret go, but I don't want it running rampant.

My mom clicks her teeth. "It's none of your brother's damn business who you decide to date. Callum Murray is a fine brick of white chocolate."

"I'm going to throw up now."

"I said what I said," my mom says.

I make a hasty excuse to hang up when she starts getting a little too detailed about *her* fine brick of white chocolate. I'm not ready to hear her talk about my elderly dad like that. I don't have any problem with the elderly getting their freak on, but nobody wants to hear about their parents.

Plus, she doesn't know where Lamonte is and I want to find him before she starts to worry. Just like Callum, she doesn't seem worried. Before I hang up, her one suggestion is that Lamonte might be with a woman.

Who could that be? I try to think about any celebrities or models he has been associated with publicly. My brother has been renowned in the media for always having an extremely thin and extremely blond white woman hanging off of him. I've never liked his girlfriends, but he's never been good at hiding them considering he's a famous athlete and a complete dope about handling the press despite his years of experience in the spotlight.

I asked my mom if she's seen him photographed with anyone recently and she said that she hasn't.

Once I hang up, Callum turns to me with a grin on his face like my brother's disappearance is funny or something. I scowl immediately.

"How was Mrs. Armstrong?" Callum asks.

"Why are you not freaking the hell out?"

Callum shrugs. "Because I've got you. As long as I've got you, I know everything will be fine. Plus... we're having a baby."

My stomach lurches. Right. I haven't completely gotten used to the baby idea yet. Part of it scares the crap out of me. I mean, am I responsible enough to have a baby? I literally just walked into gunfire. Great. Callum chooses the perfect time to make me more nervous instead of less nervous.

When he realizes he screwed up, he doesn't say anything. He just puts his hand on my thigh for the rest of the drive to Boston, silently protecting me. I might want to kick him in the butt sometimes, but I love Callum Murray. He was my first love for a reason. Strong. Tall. Incredibly handsome. Mischievous. Disciplined. Loyal.

I think he'll be a good dad. I hope we can be good together…

CALLUM PARKS his truck a couple streets down from Kalani's apartment. When he's about to jump out of the truck, I look at him like he's crazy.

"What, Zariyah? Aren't you in a hurry?"

"I don't notice you packing a pistol."

Callum gives me a stunned look. Has he not read the situation? I got shot and I don't plan on getting shot again. He knows his way around a gun.

"We're going to your best friend's house."

"If she was in there or if Lamonte was in there, don't you think they would answer the phone?"

Callum gives me a funny look.

"What?"

"Nothing. Let's go check on them," Callum says. "I'm not bringing a gun."

He's pretty firm about not carrying a gun and even if I try arguing with him, nothing works and he won't even let me bait him into a fight over it. He just threatens to throw me over his shoulder, which would definitely break the news to Lamonte in the worst way possible. So I just screw my face up and walk alongside Callum to Kalani's apartment.

As we get closer, I stop being quite so mad at him and slip my hand in his. The nerves about what we could potentially be walking into are starting to build. I'll never forget what it felt like hearing the news about Sophia. I can still feel the pit when I slow down too much and let the grief creep in. It's always there, but it gets easier to manage. Sort of.

"See?" Callum says. "Kalani's car. Lamonte's car."

Sure enough, both of their cars are parked in the lot outside Kalani's place. How can Callum not see how this makes my suspicions worse. I squeeze his hand and solemnly remind him.

"They could be dead in her apartment, Callum. When we walk in there unarmed and get blown to pieces, I hope you regret choosing peace."

"You're *pregnant*," Callum growls. "I'm not letting my pregnant wife stumble into *another* gunfight. Everything will be fine, Zariyah. I promise."

I want to believe him.

I DON'T KNOW how he sounds so sure of himself, but it's messing with my head. I don't feel certain about anything at all. We ascend the stairs and Callum rings the doorbell. My breath hitches. I swear I hear scrambling around, but then there's nothing. Silence.

"Did you hear that?" I ask Callum.

Callum knocks on the door again and rings the doorbell. I swear I hear giggling. Okay, that must be Kalani. Although I wouldn't really consider Kalani the type to giggle. Still, no one comes to the door. Callum sighs impatiently.

"I'll just pick the lock," he says.

I knew he was a gangster, but I didn't know it was that serious. Callum makes me keep watch just so no nosy neighbors or passersby call the cops, but it's Boston – no one here gives a shit about what anyone else does unless they're wearing a Yankees cap (a cardinal sin).

It takes him a while, but Callum picks the lock. Once he puts his hand on the door handle, I take the lead and shove it open. Mistake. Huge mistake.

The source of the giggling becomes immediately apparent, but it's worse than that. Kalani's apartment looks like a pleasure den. Like no one has cleaned up here in ages. And my best friend is naked, bent over her kitchen counter, with my equally naked brother positioned behind her.

I scream. I scream so damn loud that they jump apart from each other like how bugs scatter when you shine a light on them. Kalani shrieks in response as my brother howls out a series of expletives. If Callum has any response at all, I'm screaming too much to notice.

"OH MY GOD! THAT'S MY BROTHER! KALANI!"

My brother has always had a type. With pale, caramel skin and annoyingly light eyes that attract everyone's attention, he's had his pick of women and he's always settled for blonds. I've even heard him speak disparagingly of black women which yes, I've torn him apart for since our own damn mother is a black woman.

"What the hell is happening!?"

My best friend surely knows my brother's reputation in the press as a player, and not just any player, the type of guy who chases white women like Usain Bolt chased world record sprints. They can't even find their clothes. Callum mercifully covers my eyes, but that doesn't stop me yelling. With my eyes covered, I can at least pay attention to something else aside from the horrific scene in front of me.

I saw my brother's dick and my best friend's apparently pierced nipples and… oh my God. I want to die. Not my naked brother! EW!

I scream loudly, "EW! OH MY GOD THIS IS DISGUSTING!"

Callum on the other hand is chuckling like this is funny. It's easier to turn my outrage on him.

"Do you really think this is funny?!" I yell at him. "Did you *know* about this?!"

The image won't leave my mind and I wish I could pour bleach on my eyes. Why don't I carry my emergency eye bleach knowing the type of friends I have?!

Callum snickers. "They're clothed," he says after a few minutes.

He drops his hand away from me, but I still don't know if I want to look at them. There are some things that can't be unseen.

"Listen, Zariyah. Your brother is fine as hell. I'm sorry you had to see all that but... I don't regret it."

I'm more stunned than upset. I mean... I don't want to be a hypocrite because of what I came here to do, I just didn't expect this.

Callum clears his throat. I should have known that was a red flag, but in my stunned state, I can't think. It's like I'm frozen in an odd stupor. My brother and Kalani? Since when? Has this always been going on? I don't feel betrayed, but I definitely feel like I missed something. We all grew up together and they barely said two words to each other. My brother certainly never gave a crap about my uncool bookworm friends.

"Zariyah," Lamonte says, in his commanding older brother voice. "I swear to God, this just happened. I never looked at your friend that way and it was only when I came back to Boston that... well... fuck it, I'm tired of hiding from you. I'm in love."

"You're in love?!" Kalani squeaks. I finally look at her. I probably won't be able to look at my brother for ages because of witnessing his gross genitals. With Kalani, it's a bit easier, but I still can't get the image of her bouncing titties out of my head and since I won't be able to drink for the next ten months, and while I breastfeed my baby, I'll probably be haunted for quite some time. I have to get used to looking her in the eye despite that, don't I?

"Yes, baby," Lamonte says. "This isn't how I wanted to tell you but... I fucking love you, girl. I've been with some of the baddest bitches, but none of them are as bad as you."

"Lamonte seriously?" I chime in. "Is that the best you can do?"

"No," Lamonte says. "But that's only because my jeweler ain't done with the ring yet. Kalani, baby. You're gon' be mine forever."

He goes up behind her and wraps his arm around her. I stumble into Callum, pressing my hand instinctively to his chest. Kalani grins at me and bites her lower lip. It's the slightest touch, the smallest revelation, but my brother notices instantly.

"Wait a minute," he says so quickly that it sounds more like *wayment*. And then he repeats it five more times before finishing up. "Why the hell are y'all over here?"

Chapter Twenty-Seven

"Because you wouldn't answer your stupid texts," I snap at them. "I thought you idiots were dead, not screwing like rabbits, more alive than ever."

Just thinking about what I saw again makes me want to throw up. Then again, maybe this is my first experience of morning sickness. I snap my hand away from Callum.

Callum clears his throat again – that first red flag.

"Zariyah and I are married," he says to Lamonte. "And she's pregnant with my baby. So there. I suppose we have everything out on the table."

THAT'S what you would assume, right? We both have secrets, they both come out, and everything settles. But no, that's not how my brother reacts.

"You fucked my baby sister?" he asks Callum, the joyful and relieved expression falling from his face. Kalani and I exchange glances. The vibe shift is obvious and if these two gigantic motherfuckers start fighting over bullshit, there's no way we can pull them off each other.

Oh hell no. This isn't how it's about to go down.

"We're married, Lamonte."

"What the fuck?" Lamonte crosses the room, but he doesn't go to Callum first. He stares down at me with outrage. "You fucked my best friend?"

Why the hell is he coming to me and not the *man* who acted on his urges with me? I won't say I was innocent or anything, but it's typical Lamonte to blame me instead of the grown ass man who put the damn baby in me.

"Are you fucking kidding me?" I yell at my brother. "At least I had the decency to do it in private and not in the damn kitchen and get caught."

"It's different!" Lamonte says. "I can handle myself. Do you even know who the fuck Callum Murray is?"

"I'm not a child, Lamonte," I yell back at him. "And why are you mad at me? He's older than me. Technically, this is Callum's fault."

Great. That was stupid to say. Kalani looks at me like I lost my mind. Lamonte turns his attention to Callum and I can see my *husband* looking all ignorant with his hands balled up into fists like he's really going to fight my brother. I don't mind a little arguing, but we can't let this come to blows.

"Listen," Kalani yells. "Y'all better not throw hands or I will call the police."

"If you call the police, this place will be swarming with paparazzi," Lamonte says truthfully. "You can't do that. You're my girl, Kalani, and I won't have the general public speculating about my damn private life and getting all up in my business anymore."

"Then you'd better back off that white boy right now."

"My best friend married my sister in secret. Zariyah's right. This is his fault. She was just a kid. And you know that your people would never accept her. So why the *fuck*, Callum Murray, did you get involved with my damn sister?"

"Certain things are beyond my control, Lamonte. Shit got outta hand."

"Beyond your control? What the fuck are you talking about?"

"I'm pregnant!" Kalani screams, completely distracting both Callum and Lamonte from the fight at hand.

What? I can't tell if Kalani is just doing this to stop them from fighting or if she's really serious about being pregnant. I mean, it was a damn good idea to stop them from fighting. Lamonte turns around to look at her.

"I'm not lying," Kalani says to me, seeing my expression of disbelief. "And I don't want y'all fighting in my house. Next thing you know, the stress takes me and the baby out."

"The baby? I mean, how far along are you? Can stress affect the baby already?" Lamonte asks, his expression changing to one I haven't seen in a *long* time. Growing up in the world of football and then going pro, Lamonte wasn't exactly rewarded for showing his emotions. It didn't help that he was light skinned and pretty skinny before he started playing football, so he couldn't show any emotions without being picked on.

But I'm his sister, and I can see when my brother loves somebody and the way he looks at my best friend shocks me. He's paraded a ton of his fancy girlfriends in front of our family and he's never once looked at any of them the way he looks at her. It's like Callum and I don't exist. He takes her hand and they kiss.

It would be cute. But I'm still not ready to see all that after the scene that unfolded previously. Especially when the kissing starts to involve a lot of tongue. I clear my throat dramatically hoping they'll remember that Callum and I are in the room, but it doesn't seem to work. At all.

"AHEM," I say dramatically. The kissing noises get louder. My stomach turns. I don't have a choice. Callum puts his hand on my shoulder protectively and while I appreciate his presence, I can't take watching them kiss anymore without flashbacks to seeing my brother and best friend naked together.

Lamonte pulls away from Kalani slowly. And then he walks up to Callum, calm as ever, and punches him in the face.

"Are you crazy?!" I scream at him. He seemed like he was handling everything well. This is out of control. Blood sprays out of Callum's nose as Lamonte throws another punch. It's like Callum isn't even fighting him. *Boy, beat his ass!* I try to jump in the way, but Lamonte easily removes me without causing me any harm. I scream, Kalani screams, and Callum just stumbles back holding his face.

"What the hell is wrong with you, Lamonte?!" Kalani says. "I'm having your damn baby and the first thing you do is assault a fucking mobster? I'm not trying to have a baby daddy in jail."

"I'm not trying to be your baby daddy," Lamonte says. "What we have is real, Kalani. I'm trying to tie the knot. But I won't leave any of my business unfinished."

He tries lunging for Callum again, but I jump between them without thinking. Lamonte barely misses my head when he swings at

Callum, but Kalani grabs his shirt and attempts to drag him back. I stumble backwards as I duck to avoid my brother throwing hands and land smack against Callum's chest.

Kalani drags on my brother's clothing and pulls him away from Callum. She puts her hands on Lamonte's shoulders and I watch as my best friend effortlessly calms my brother down. Why the hell do they look kinda cute together? I mean, it's still gross as hell that she's into my brother, but I like how he looks at her.

My best friend deserves a guy who looks at her like he's obsessed with her.

"Chill out, Lamonte," Kalani says.

"I had to do something," he says. "That's my little sister."

Kalani rolls her eyes and drags my brother even further away from Callum. "You're being a damn hypocrite. Why don't we all accept that we found love in an unexpected place and nobody has to fight anybody."

"That sounds fair," I say. "But I wish y'all replied to your damn texts. I thought you were dead."

"We're fine," Kalani says, smoothing her hair out and trying to regain her composure throughout the entire situation. She keeps casting suspicious glances at Lamonte in case he starts acting up again. But I can tell he's accepting the situation. He wants to make Kalani happy. That's different from Lamonte too. He likes getting his own way. "No need for you to panic."

"I told you," Callum says, putting his arm around my shoulder. "But I'm glad we came down here so your brother could unnecessarily punch me in the face."

"Listen, man… the bleeding already stopped. We good?"

They make eye contact, shrug, and nod. Is this what men consider to be communication? Callum spreads his arms wide and Lamonte gives him a big bear hug. When the step apart from each other, Lamonte sizes up Callum and then sizes me up.

"Are you really pregnant?"

"Yes."

Kalani squeals. "So we're pregnant at the same damn time!?"

"Uh huh. I don't know how we pulled that off…"

My best friend hugs me and she won't stop screaming and jumping until I join her in her excitement. We squeeze each other tightly and then I feel Callum coming up behind me. He gives me a big hug and I let him hold me. Then Lamonte joins us and we all stand there together, one big family.

"I can't wait to get back to the bookstore," I whisper. "We are going to have so much fun girl bossing and becoming moms together."

"Uh huh," Kalani whispers back. "I think Sophia would be proud of us."

"I know she would."

"She encouraged my crush on Lamonte, you know," Kalani says. "I never would have looked twice at him if it weren't for her."

"If one of us has a girl, we'll have to name her Sophia," I say firmly. "It just makes sense."

"What if we both have a girl?"

"We'll figure it out then…" I say. "But we have to do something to honor her."

Kalani and I agree and slowly, we all pull away from our hug. Callum insists I need rest now that we've confirmed my brother and Kalani's survival. I can't argue with him. Whenever my pain medication wears off, my arm feels terrible. Callum takes me back to *our* place. His house feels more like home now that I've been gone.

I miss how Queenie smells and when she waddles up to me with her wagging white-tipped tail and ears dragging on the ground, I crouch down and give her the biggest hug and scratch behind her ears. *I missed her.*

Once I say hello to Queenie, Callum leads me to the bedroom and tucks me in, forcing me to have a cup of tea, a sandwich for lunch and more pain medication. I'm too tired to argue from all the traveling and worrying about my brother to argue with Callum. I obey his commands and let the grouchy giant play nurse.

. . .

CALLUM FUSSES over me for about two weeks before he allows me a measure of real independence. I work at the bookstore with Kalani and help her little sister get ready for her fall semester at university. Onika starts at one of the popular liberal arts colleges a little over half an hour outside of Boston. She's a quiet type who prefers video games and take out to partying, so I think she'll be just fine there.

When I tell Callum about my day and about helping Onika get ready for college, he tells me that Odhran is about to enter his junior year there.

"Should they meet?" Callum asks. I don't know much about Callum's younger brother except that he dresses in all black, dyes his hair black, plays the organ, and he just had to quit the school football team because of a gunshot wound.

"They should *not* meet under absolutely any circumstances," I warn Callum. "Just pretend you don't know this information."

"Odhran has a girlfriend," Callum says. "He has been engaged since he was about twelve years old and he's more traditional than Aiden. With a stern warning, he could look after her and protect her. He might be a piece of shit, but he's at least obedient."

I appreciate where Callum is coming from. He wants to look after my best friend's little sister, but even he knows that his younger brother is creepy and terrifying. He's said so himself. I attack the only part of the argument that I know will end the conversation quickly.

"Traditional? Like the tradition of racism?" I ask Callum. He drops the subject and finally agrees not to mention his brother to Onika at all. The less she knows about the mafia, the better.

Once my two week period of intense observation ends, Callum doesn't fuss as much and I settle into a gentle routine. Callum takes me to the gym with him in the morning after I spew my guts out from morning sickness. I just go slowly on the elliptical where I can watch him get all sweaty and sexy in the mirrors out of the corner of my eye. He is *so* sexy. Once we're done with the gym, Callum makes me breakfast every morning, satisfying all my pregnancy cravings. Once I eat, I meet Kalani at the bookstore and we work on our promotions, events and general sales responsibilities. We will probably need a few months to get on our feet, but it feels nice to work on something that's ours again.

We keep Sophia in the bookstore's back office on a shelf in a nice urn with fresh flowers next to it. I had to fight Kalani who worried about the bookstore becoming haunted, but I don't think I could do this without my best friend's spirit. *I'll always love you, Soph.*

After closing up the bookstore in the evenings, I meet Callum at home and we cook dinner together, which normally ends in us having sex before dinner, after dinner or *while* we cook. Everything is peaceful, normal and just feels… *regular.*

I don't even feel like I have a mob husband, just normal Callum. Just the sexy Irish man I dreamed about when I was eighteen years old.

Everything feels so normal that I forget how quickly it can all change in the matter of one night. One Friday night Callum knocks me out with some truly mind-blowing oral sex, furthering my complete surprise that something different from our normal routine happens.

I don't even realize that I fell asleep until I hear a loud noise. Not just any noise. The sound of Callum slamming his hand on something that startles my ass right out of my sleep. My bonnet damn near flies off as I shoot straight up, dragging my blanket over my bare breasts.

"This is *not* a fucking game, Odhran!" Callum growls. He sounds angry. I climb out of bed immediately. If Callum wants me out of his business, he'll lock me in the bedroom. I wrap my blanket around my body and approach the bedroom door, slowly opening it and trying to get a bit closer to the argument. I didn't know Callum was having his brother over.

I FREEZE in the hallway when I hear Callum say, "You have to leave her alone, Odhran. What you're doing isn't right."

"I don't want to do this anymore," Odhran says, his voice sending a chill down my spine. He's so damn terrifying that I second guess tiptoeing down the hallway to hear more.

Zariyah

Callum's younger brother has always scared the crap out of me. I change my mind about interrupting their conversation and slip back into bed... I don't want anymore violence or any mob drama. I trust my husband to handle that stuff and I'll handle this stuff – the bookstore, our baby, our home.

I don't want the drama anymore. I just want Callum...

Chapter Twenty-Eight
Callum

I can't stop thinking about my conversation with Odhran. Aiden won't listen when I suggest he's neglected Odhran's upbringing since our father died. While I can warn Odhran about the consequences of his immoral actions, I lack the authority to discipline him. And I have bigger problems, like my pregnant wife.

She gave no signs that she overheard my conversation with Odhran. Knowing Zariyah, if she had, we would have had to stay up all night talking about it.

She wouldn't understand how I could forgive Odhran for being the monster that he is. So it's probably for the best that I keep some secrets from her, just for the sake of keeping her safe and happy.

I don't want to give this up. Her. Our bed. Her smooth stomach moving with each slow breath. I could watch Zariyah sleep forever. I kiss her cheek, hoping to wake her up. Hoping to hold her. Three weeks ago, I sent Odhran away with a stern warning, and I just have to hope he doesn't do what his instincts tell him to. I hope he doesn't hurt a woman.

The thought that he could makes me sick. And when I feel like this, there's only one person who can bring me back to life. Her lashes flutter open as I kiss her cheek again and then her neck.

"Are you going to wake me up for sex every morning?" Zariyah murmurs, raking her fingers through my hair and pulling my face closer as I keep lavishing her neck with kisses. She's so fucking beautiful.

"Yes."

"I'm pregnant. Eventually, I won't be able to move."

"Then I'll wake you up by eating your pussy…"

Zariyah groans sleepily and makes a half-hearted attempt to roll over.

"Oh no you don't," I murmur, pulling her back over to me and rolling Zariyah onto her back.

"Callum," she complains as I spread her legs and position my body on hers. "I smell like sleep."

"You smell like my woman," I whisper, kissing her neck. Once I kiss her neck and move my hips against hers, Zariyah forgets her protests and kisses back. She forgets that she loves morning sex as much as I do. If I *do* neglect her for one morning, she's the one who pounces on me. Her thighs wrap tightly around my torso and I start kissing her lips instead.

I have her exactly where I want her right now, except for the layer of clothing between us. She runs her toes along the backs of my thighs, feeling the contours of my muscles as her palms clutch my back.

"You are so evil," she murmurs, her fingers moving from my back to my hair. I haven't cut it in ages and it's a mess. I look more Irish with long hair.

"No. Just horny."

"I'm supposed to sleep more so the baby can grow."

"You've been asleep ten hours."

"Have I?"

I slide my hands underneath Zariyah's light pink lingerie until I get to her breasts. She stifles a moan as I tease her nipples with my fingers. Watching her sleep gets me rock hard and kissing her while her hands roam all over my body makes the situation worse. I need to feel her.

"This is some sexy ass lingerie," I whisper, moving the light pink strap over Zariyah's shoulder and planting a kiss on her collarbone. "I can't wait to take it off."

Zariyah stifles another whimper as I kiss her neck in the sweet spot that drives her crazy.

"Don't hold back, baby. I want to hear you moan."

I slide my fingers into her panties and find her just as wet as I expect. *Fuck, she's slick.* My fingers rub Zariyah's pussy until she can't hold back her moans. Her body is perfect. I can't wait to watch her change with my baby. I can't wait to keep her pregnant. Once I get her nice and wet, I slip a finger inside her, slowly spreading her folds apart and entering her deep.

Her gooey center is tight around my finger and my dick almost explodes. I urgently need her. Kissing her and touching her becomes an art of working us both up to a fever pitch. We strip each other's clothing off quickly enough that I don't lose my patience, but slowly enough that I can appreciate both the softness and the warmth of Zariyah's bottle.

She's still so little compared to me. And so sensitive. And mine forever...

"I love you, baby girl," I murmur, running my tongue along the length of her neck until she moans from my finger working inside her with a steady rhythm. She loses herself in moaning and clings to my neck as I finger her tightness. When she cums, she moans my name and I go fucking wild. I add another finger inside of her and tease her until she gets close to another climax.

When Zariyah approaches release all over both my fingers, I remove both of them from between her legs and rub her juices over her thighs as she shudders with frustration.

"You are such a tease," she whispers.

"Hm," I grunt. "Says the woman who married me and acted like she hated me for months when all I wanted was to make love to her."

"Oh quiet," she whispers, raking her fingers through my hair. "I just want to feel you, daddy."

Daddy? That's new.

"Daddy?" I murmur, my dick strained with desire for her.

Zariyah smiles, her brown eyes gleaming mischievously. "You're right. You're even bigger than a daddy. You're more like... big poppa."

"That sounds..."

"Shhhh," Zariyah says. "If you have a corny nickname for me, it's only fair that I get to have a corny nickname for you."

"And you're going with 'big poppa'?"

"You're 6'8" and weigh as much as a horse."

I don't weigh as much as a horse, but I also don't bother arguing with her. I like the way she's touching me. Right now, I'd let her call me anything she wanted as long as she let me put my dick inside her.

"Fine," I whisper. "Just let me make love to you."

"Since when have you asked for permission," she whispers with a mischievous look on her face. "I'm yours to take, Callum. So do it... make love to me like I'm yours."

The hairs raise on the back of my neck and all over my forearms. Fuck, how does she know the right things to say to me and exactly the right times to say it? I press the head of my large cock against the tight entrance that always resists my large member's invasion.

Zariyah gasps with the hint of pain as the tip of my cock pushes against her entrance. I hold her gently and push into her slowly. She's so tight. So warm.

"I love you..."

Our bodies move together as I slip into her deeper. She cries out from the pain, but Zariyah doesn't stop me from moving until I bury my dick inside her to the hilt. Once I'm inside her, she has flushed skin and an expression of both pain and pleasure on her gorgeous face. I fucking love her features. Her cheeks. Her eyes. The roundness of everything.

"Fuck me," she pleads. "Fuck, you feel so good."

I ease my fingers between her legs again and rub her clit as I make love to her slowly. Despite taking my time with her, we both can't hold back for long. We cling to each other and enjoy our bodies moving together for as long as possible. Zariyah climaxes first with my finger rubbing her clit and my cock stretching her and stimulating every inch of her wetness.

Zariyah's pussy tightens around me as she cums and I can't hold back. I bury my cock in her deeply and allow myself to fill her with my seed. I grunt with pleasure and pump into her with a few more fierce strokes. She is so goddamn tight. Fuck. I'm lucky I lasted this long.

As she comes down from her orgasm, I take Zariyah's hands and pin them over her head. She squeals in surprise as I hold her down and keep my dick inside her.

"Callum," she gasps. "What are you doing?"

"Preparing you for round two," I growl. "I'm going to pin you to the bed and make you cum again… so you stay right there…"

"I don't have a choice."

"Good," I murmur. "Perfect…"

I MAKE love to her until we both can't anymore. Zariyah insists on cooking me breakfast and she brings me eggs and white rice mixed up with soy sauce. I eat for my muscles, not for the flavor. She has something far tastier, but I don't judge her as she sits in bed with her two-day old glazed donut which she dips into black coffee.

"What did your brother want a few weeks ago?" she asks.

Shit.

"Did you hear our conversation?" I ask tepidly. I try to act calm about it, but I assumed I was already in the clear with Zariyah. I should have known she would sneak up on me with something. She's not the type to let something go. It's a part of why I love her but… I've tried to keep this away from her on purpose.

"No," she says. "Something told me I didn't want to hear it."

"You didn't," I say, trusting that she's telling me the truth. "Odhran is very troubled. I don't want you around him and frankly, I don't think he should be around anyone."

"Ouch," she mutters. "Harsh judgment from a murderer. No offense."

"None taken," I respond with a shrug. "My brother was born

different. He doesn't think like other people. Without guidance, without structure, he will kill, he will rape, he will cause more harm than all of us combined. Since my father died, he has no guidance. I worry about him."

"Did you ask him to come here?"

I nod, although I don't want to admit that I put Zariyah at even the slightest risk. I just think someone ought to do something before Odhran's actions come back to bite us in the ass. He needs proper guidance.

"Why?" she asks.

"I want to help him. He's engaged to an Irish girl but… I think he hurts her. I don't know. Whatever it is, I want it to stop."

"Can you bring it to Aiden?"

"It seems too small to bring to Aiden," I admit.

Zariyah wraps her arms around me. She makes it all feel better.

"Everything will be okay," she whispers. "You're a good big brother and you're twice his size. I'm sure you can scare the crap out of him and get him to behave."

"I doubt that," I whisper back. "But I'd rather stay in bed with you all morning than deal with my family today."

I JUST HAVE to hope that Odhran sticks to his word. I have to hope he stops himself before it's too late. *If he doesn't kill that girl, he'll kill another one.*

AND THEN WHAT will happen to our family? We could lose our respected position in our community if he hurts one of our own. Even if he hurts an outsider… I can't help but worry. Even Zariyah's fingers running through my hair can't take *all* the worries away.

There are still dark hearts in Boston.

. . .

AND THE DARKEST Murray by far is my younger brother. *Odhran Murray.* We all think he was born that way, especially Rian, who seems convinced that he has more than a few screws loose. Odhran never needed training to embrace the darkness. His fury, his violence, his deranged delight in causing pain were innate.

He's the perfect mobster. The perfect killing machine.

A SOULLESS MONSTER.

THE END

Onika & Odhran's story, *Mafia Stalker,* Book #5, will be released on September 5th 2023.

Click here to order the book.
bit.ly/bostonirishmafia5

Click here to receive text message updates when the next Jamila Jasper book releases:
bit.ly/textjamila

About Jamila Jasper

The hotter and darker the romance, the better.

That's the Jamila Jasper promise.

If you enjoy sizzling multicultural romance stories that dare to *go there* you'll enjoy any Jamila Jasper title you pick up.

Open-minded readers who appreciate **shamelessly sexy romance novels** featuring black women of all shapes and sizes paired with smokin' hot white men are welcome.

Sign up for her e-mail list here to receive one of these **FREE hot stories**, exclusive offers and an update of Jamila's publication schedule: bit.ly/jamilajasperromance

Get text message updates on new books: https://slkt.io/gxzM

Dark Mafia Romance Preview #1

Sample these chapters from my Amalfi Coast Brotherhood Italian mafia romance series while you wait for the next mafia romance series.

If you enjoy dark & twisted mafia romance stories, you can binge the entire completed series on your eReader.

Enjoy the free chapters.

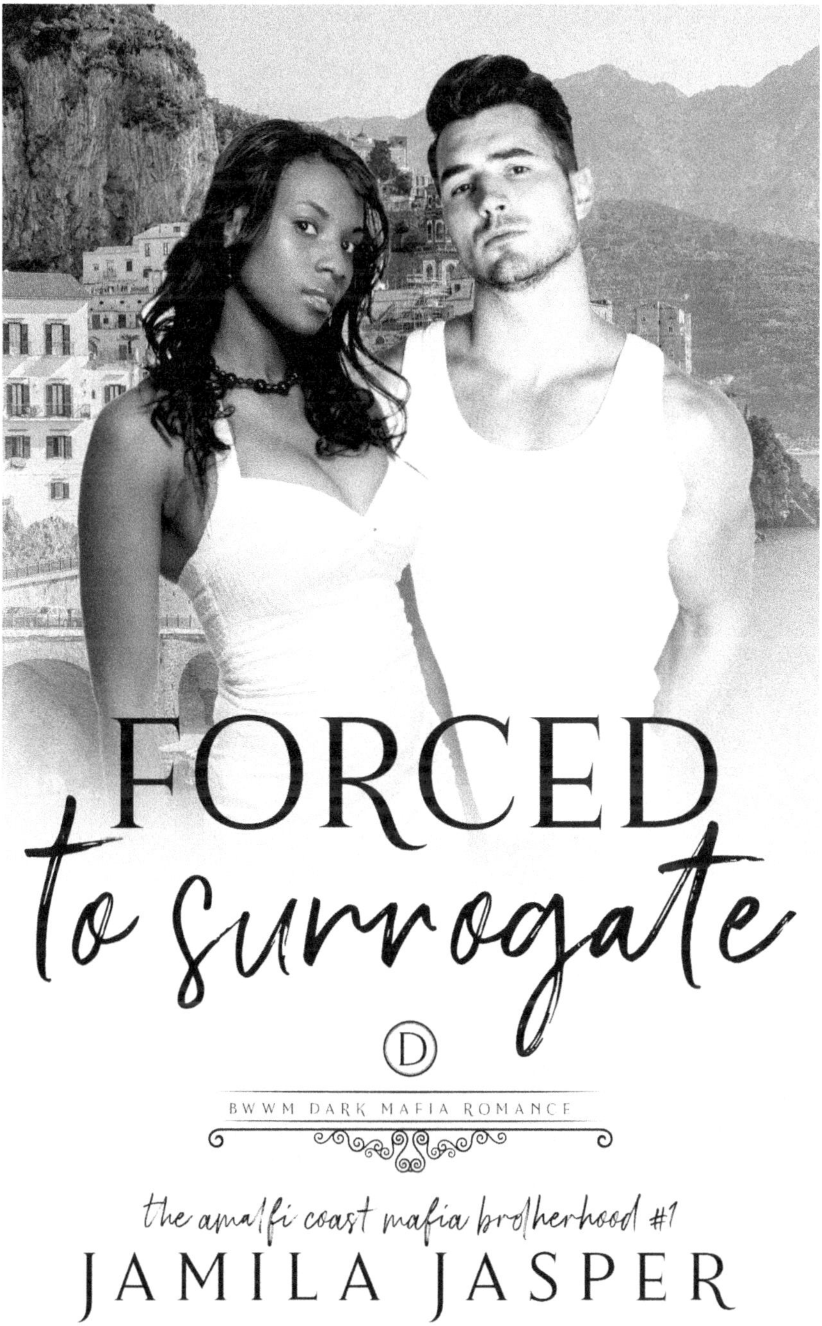
FORCED
to surrogate
D
BWWM DARK MAFIA ROMANCE
the amalfi coast mafia brotherhood #1
JAMILA JASPER

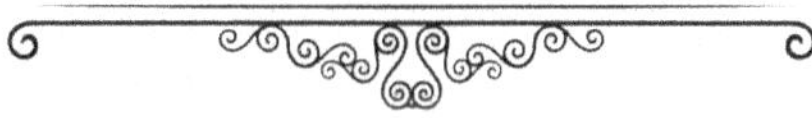

Description

The last thing Jodi remembered was a shot of tequila.
Next thing she knows,
Italian sociopath Van Doukas has her chained in his basement...
And he's claiming she agreed to become the mother of his child.

There's a detailed contract and everything... with her signature.
Jodi will do whatever it takes to get away from him...
But she doesn't count on the 6'7" Italian Stallion being skilled with his
tongue and excellent in bed.

Series Titles

Forced To Surrogate
Forced To Marry
Forced To Submit

Content Awareness

Chapter 1
Produce A Pure Italian Heir
Van Doukas

There aren't enough cigarettes in the world for meetings with my father. The boss. Tonight, I meet with him to discuss something 'very important'. He calls everything 'very important', but tonight, I know exactly what he wants from me.

He wants me to kill again, this time for my foolish sister, who can't seem to keep herself out of trouble. Everyone in the family heard about what happened to Ana by now. That idiot Jew was foolish enough to put his hands on her with witnesses and expect nothing to happen? That's not how the Doukas family works, which he'll soon learn.

You mess with the Doukas family, we retaliate. If the Jew had any wits about him, he would disappear from the Amalfi Coast and head for the mountains or Sicily, or somewhere we don't have ears. He could go to Albania like Matteo. Maybe then we wouldn't find him. But fuck, I don't want to carry out another hit. Why can't that lazy fuck Enzo do it? Or better yet, Eddie. I carried out my first hit when I was two years younger than him. We spoil the new generation and wonder why our family falls apart.

None of this would be my responsibility if Matteo would get over himself and come down off his fucking mountain.

Van Doukas

I stop my motorcycle and approach my father's front door. The all white old European style mansion sits on an excessive and opulent lot on the coast, right above the cliffs with a long path to the beach, a 'fuck you' to the tax collectors and the government who want to stop us from doing business.

Most of my siblings still live here, but I prefer keeping myself far away from papa and his... associates.

I can hear the party from the entrance. Seriously? On a fucking Tuesday afternoon? I assumed he called this meeting because he was working for once. He's intertwined in a different business based on the noise filtering outside. Please, Lord, let me not walk in on my father having sex with a model... *again*.

I open the front door to our old family home without knocking and immediately regret it when a completely naked foreign woman runs giggling toward the door, too high and drunk to feel self-conscious, exposing her completely nude body to a stranger. At least I didn't find her twisted in bed with papa, although this isn't much better.

"Oh! Good afternoon, sir!" she teases me in crude Italian, spinning around to show off her assets. *Whore. Foreigner. Her tricks possess little interest to me.* My brothers Lorenzo and Matteo would sway more easily.

"Where's my father?"

She giggles and spins around again. Fucking hell, I wish the ground would swallow me up. My father's prostitutes do not interest me.

"Your papa?" she says, standing to face me with her legs slightly apart, daring me to ogle more of her body. I have no interest in whores and I want her to answer my fucking question.

Before I can answer, another one of my father's toys saunters into the foyer, naked. This one is young—she looks eighteen just about— far too young for my father. I grimace and keep my gaze firmly fixed away from the nude females. Just because the men in my family are bastards doesn't mean I have to follow suit.

If we don't conduct ourselves with respect, how can we expect the respect of the Amalfi Coast?

"Yes. My father. Sal," I grunt, failing to hide the irritation in my voice.

The woman ignores my irritated tone with her response.

"Oh, he's in the back with Boyka. I can take you there after we take you to bed upstairs."

How much is he paying these women? We're still struggling to get Jalousie off the ground and he spends all his money on Slavic hookers.

"Not interested. I have a meeting with him."

"Are you sure?"

I don't dignify them with a response. I walk past the girls, keeping my eyes away from their bodies. Where the hell is my father? I pass the long hallway with the family portraits and follow the loud music and the louder giggling from near the pool. The familiar sound of pool jets betrays papa's location.

He's in the fucking hot tub again, I know it. He spends all fucking day in the hot tub, dishing out orders and expecting work to happen without him lifting a fucking finger. It's a fucking miracle anything gets done around here.

My father chuckles loudly, and I brace myself before approaching him. He's the boss and you don't question the boss, even if he's your father and even if he cares more about partying and women than our family — than our future.

When I enter the back patio, the pungent smell of tobacco and marijuana surrounds me. Judging by the bottles of vodka on the ground, the piles of cigarette butts and the other piles of detritus, they've been at this fucking party since last night.

Fuck. I put the cigarette tucked behind my ear into my mouth and approach my father's outdoor speakers, unplugging them and stop-ping the little dance party happening around his hot tub. Three women, each wearing next to nothing with their tits out belly dance for him while he chuckles loudly, his fat stomach causing waves in the hot tub. When the music stops, they stop too and look up at me indignantly.

They don't have to ask who I am. The ones who don't know Van

Doukas can tell that I'm related to Sal. I have my father's eyes, but thankfully, I don't have his overweight body or his bald head. The girls make booing sounds at me, but I brush them off.

"I'm here for our meeting," I say sternly to papa.

He chuckles and nods. "Yes. The meeting. I almost forgot."

Almost? He doesn't look like he's fucking prepared for a meeting.

Papa dismisses the girls, except for one — Boyka. She slides into the hot tub next to him, twirling his thick plumes of chest hair around her fingers and sliding his freshly cut cigar between his lips. Nauseating. Papa coughs after a puff and taps the cigar over the edge of the hot tub.

"You're early."

"I'm twenty minutes late."

"Oh?"

"Papa, you said it was important. Shouldn't we conduct this business alone?"

None of the girls are dumb enough to rat on Salvatore Doukas, but unlike my father, I don't see the sense in taking risks.

Boyka's hand moves down my father's chest and I don't want to imagine what sorry shriveled part of him she touches next. I just want my orders so I can get the fuck out of this bachelor pad.

"I'm getting old, Van," he says. "I'm getting old."

He didn't call me down here to bitch about his old age. I furiously puff on my cigarette, waiting for him to get to the fucking point. Papa grunts as Boyka touches something… sensitive. Cristo…

Watching my father grunt through a hand job might be the only thing worse than watching him stick it to a woman.

"Do you mind postponing your fucking hand job until later?"

Boyka's hand rises guiltily from the water and I choke down bile. She really was touching the old fuck. I shouldn't swear at him or set him off. Papa might seem old, but he can have me killed. Any of my brothers would do it if he gave the command. Tread carefully, Van.

"Maybe I should leave," Boyka says, giving me a flirty glance as she plays with her tiny pink nipples.

"Yes," I snap. "Please get the fuck out of here."

Papa scowls. "Be respectful, Van. Boyka is a very dear—"

"I said please."

Papa smirks. "Boyka, return in thirty minutes. If we're not done…"

"We'll be done," I interrupt, glowering at my father. I don't have all afternoon for his games when I have the club to attend to.

Boyka reluctantly leaves.

"Are the women in this house allergic to fucking clothes?"

"None of them are allergic to fucking anything."

I'm not doing this with the old man today.

"Why did you call me here?"

I start another cigarette. I keep swearing I won't touch another, then I spend five minutes around papa and change my mind.

He leans back in the hot tub, displacing several pints of water over the edge.

"I'm tired, Van," he groans, leaning back and rubbing his forehead.

"From working?"

My father doesn't pick up on the sarcasm. He hardly leaves his fucking hot tub anymore, and he hasn't done anything even remotely resembling working at either of the nightclubs, restaurants, apartment complexes or construction sites around town.

If it wasn't for me and Enzo, he wouldn't have the fucking time to boink Boyka or whatever the fuck he does with all these young Slavic women.

I still have to tread carefully around him. He's still my father, my boss, and I must obey him.

"Yes," he says, coughing. "From working. I need someone to take my place and lead the family soon. I want to retire, Van. You and I both know I need a break."

He spends every fucking day on vacation while his sons and nephews run his businesses. Vacation? We're the ones who need a fucking vacation.

"Perhaps you should contact Matteo about that."

My older brother spent his entire life preparing to be the boss. It's not my fault he fucked off, leaving his worthless children with us, I might add. I'm already halfway through my fucking cigarette and he hasn't closed in on the point.

Papa scoffs. "Matteo hasn't left Albania in four years. He left his children, his business, his fucking money, and he's not coming back. Give up on him."

"You're the one who trained him for the role. Send Enzo after him. Better yet, send his fucking son."

I don't want to go into the mountains to bring my jackass older brother back and I don't want to have this conversation with my father.

"Why don't you go to Albania?"

"Every time I'm in the same room as Matteo, he tries to kill me," I remind papa. I love Matteo, but he isn't exactly easy to get along with.

I'm surprised a woman tolerated him long enough to allow him to give her Eddie.

"Fair. But I need a replacement, Van. I don't want to be the boss anymore. I can't take the stress much longer."

Stress? What stress? Does my father seriously think sitting in his fucking hot tub banging whores counts as a job?

"Have you considered the role?" He asks before I can spew something disrespectful in my father's direction.

"Why would I want to be the boss of this fucking family? It's filled with degenerates, fuck-ups, people who need more violence to be kept in line. I kill enough as it is. You don't want me to be the boss and nobody in this fucking family wants me as the boss."

"People respect you, Van."

"People fear me. There's a difference."

Papa nods. "Exactly. Personally, I think you would make a good boss."

"I disagree."

But I don't completely. Yes, the job would be horrific and I'd have even more blood on my hands than I do now by the end. I could bring honor back to our family, clean the streets of our scum, stop the Jews from fucking with our shit... but I can't. Not with Matteo gone. Even in the fucking Albanian countryside, he would find out what I did and Matteo would kill me.

"No," Papa replies calmly. "You don't. But I agree with your assessment that you're not quite ready."

"I never said that. I said I didn't want the job."

Nobody smart wants my father's job. He spent twenty years walking around with a target on his back before he built up enough trust, enough loyalty, enough captains in the streets of Italy to ensure his safety. I don't want to lose my freedom.

"You didn't have to say anything. I know my son."

"Hm."

Arguing with my father is entirely senseless.

"You need an heir, Van."

"What?"

"I will give you the leadership of this family without the ritual, without the sacrifice and without the financial investment required. All I want is an heir."

"Why don't I go up to fucking Albania, then? Because I can't produce a child out of thin air."

Papa chuckles. "Don't you have women? If you want a woman… I filled this house with them. I have very young ones too. Eighteen. Nineteen. They make good mothers."

"I am not interested in fucking teenagers."

"Then find a whore like that old Greek Pagonis fuck. I don't care how you get the heir. You can prove how serious you are by giving me a child. I'll be generous. I'll give you a year."

"I don't want this role," I snap. "So the likelihood I'll produce an heir is slim."

Papa laughs, which only infuriates me further. There's nothing funny about bringing a child into the world.

"You can't lie to me, Van. You were always the most ambitious child. Maybe it's because you were smack in the middle and we didn't pay any attention to you. Who fucking knows?"

My father spent little time raising any of us, except for Enzo, and look how that fucking turned out.

"Thank you for the psychoanalysis."

Every time I visit my father, my desire for alcohol increases exponentially, along with my cravings for nicotine. He brings the worst out of everyone, especially me.

"No problem," he says, again ignoring my sarcasm.

"What happens if I don't produce an heir? Eh? You still need someone to take your place."

"I make this offer to Lorenzo if you don't produce what I want."

"What?" I would have at least expected him to mention one of our cousins, one of the very obedient captains from the northern coast, or even fucking Eddie, Matteo's 18-year-old son, would be better than my irresponsible fuck of a brother. That old fuck really knows me well because he just said the only thing that could get me to reconsider his stupid fucking offer.

"You heard me."

"Lorenzo would ruin this family. For fun."

"I know. And it would become your responsibility to save it. You would have to act as the boss to save Lorenzo from himself. You might as well earn the position."

Fuck this old man...

"I don't want a family life, papa. I don't want the fucking wife or the fucking family. I want this life. It's what I'm good at. Business. Killing. More killing. That's who you taught me to be."

I'm not a man who can picture himself kicking around a football with my children or taking them to the beach. I'm not built for seducing women for more than a night and dealing with the danger of introducing them to my life or worse, hiding it the way papa did with our mother.

He can pretend it's not his fault what happened to her, but we all know the truth. No woman deserves our life. I can't afford to react. He loves when he can draw a reaction out of me.

Papa continues, as if my reaction is irrelevant. "Part of this life means having a family. I can't expect my other children to carry on my bloodline."

"Matteo has a son. You have a fucking bloodline. Why don't you make him the fucking boss?"

"Eddie? Eddie will not survive long the way he lives."

"That's a way to talk about your grandson, eh?"

"Have another cigarette, Van."

I'm already on my fucking third. But I'm not in a position to turn down his offer, considering the shit he wants me to deal with right now. An heir? I thought he wanted me to kill someone. Producing an heir in a year… It's just fucking impossible. I stick the cigarette in my mouth and light it.

"You can't let the family fall apart. We aren't the only people who would suffer. What would happen to our people, good Italian people, when the only people around they can get money from are the fucking Jews, who hate our guts?" He says.

I can't let his guilt trip work on me.

"I want an heir."

"Hm."

"Consider what you would sacrifice by turning down my offer, Van. It's not just about the family. It's power. You act like you're a fucking saint, but you are my son. You enjoy power. You're just too much of a stuck up cunt to let yourself enjoy it."

"Thanks papa."

"You're welcome. Now, onto the matter of the Jew."

Fuck. I hoped my father would only piss me off one way today, but if we're discussing the matter of the Jew, I won't leave here tonight without an assignment. Someone else could easily do this job, but he wants me to kill. Because I'm good at it.

"I suppose none of my other brothers have the free time to do this?"

"I don't care. I need you to do it. The cunt offended this family."

"Perhaps we waste too much time retaliating for every offense. Ana told you to drop it."

I'm taking a risk just questioning his order, but he's pissed me off so much that I stopped caring.

"Decision making isn't women's work. It's our work. The man

signed his own death warrant. I want it done soon. Call me when you finish the job."

"Hm."

"If you don't like the way I run this family, Van, you know what to do. I want to retire. Make an old man happy."

Drugs and whores are the only things that make my father happy.

"An heir," I scoff. "You want me to have a fucking bastard child to continue your bloodline? A bastard won't have any loyalty to his family. Children have a mother and a father, a mother they spend all their time with. If I fuck some poor woman, you won't have an heir. You'll have a problem on your hands."

"Then get creative. If you need to get the baby and kill the mother, do what you must."

What's happening to this family? When did we lose our way and talking about murdering women for our own ends? Papa... This life changed him. It was slow, but it changed him completely. Too bad there's no getting out.

"Thank you for the advice."

"You're welcome. Now get Boyka back in here and get the fuck out. I need relief."

"Good evening, papa."

I drop my cigarette on the ground without bothering to step on it. Maybe my father's right — it's time for him to retire. But how the fuck will I get an heir? I need help.

There's one person I can call on for assistance in these matters. I don't like involving the Greeks in Italian business, but... they're our cousins. She answers after a few rings and it sounds like she's at a nightclub. She has an inordinate amount of time for parties...

"Ciao?"

I can barely hear her over the sound of the music.

"Miss Pagonis. It's Van."

She giggles. "Duh. What's happening? You finally have work for me?"

"How soon can you come back to Italy?"

Chapter 2
Single AF On The Amalfi Coast
Jodi Rose

I'm the last single woman in my family.

Three months in Italy, and I haven't had so much as a kiss, but my younger cousin Raven gets married to her college boyfriend and he looks like a dream. I drop a congratulatory comment on her photo, but my heart sinks.

You ugly, Jodi. Get used to it and stop chasing all these men out of your league. Settle with Kyle. He's the best you can do. Maybe mama was right. I'm not the marrying kind, anyway. I spent all my dating years focused on school and look at where that got me…

"Edo!"

The bartender gives me a sympathetic look. Ugh. Edo is so hot. Too bad all the hot guys are gay, especially in Italy, apparently.

"What happened?"

"Look at this."

I show him my phone and Edo cracks a smile. "Beautiful! Is she your sister?"

"No, my cousin. She's getting married and here I am… single… again."

And I'm running away from my problems with a one-way ticket to

Italy. When my family finds out I'm not coming back, they're going to lose their minds. Everyone already thinks I'm crazy for leaving Kyle...

"Fuck your ex, Jodi. Seriously, fuck him," Edo says with all the passion of a best friend, even if we barely know each other.

I have major regrets about getting drunk my first night here and spilling all the drama about my ex-boyfriend to a bartender, but at least it made us fast friends. Although I'm not sure if Edo just likes the fact that Americans tip, unlike our Italian friends. He always has a way of scamming some extra euros out of me. At least he's a damn good listener.

I groan and dramatically lean against the bar as I make a proclamation that I wholeheartedly believe.

"I'm never going to get with another guy again. This is it. I'm dying alone."

I've read the statistics. Or at least I've read what women on Lipstick Alley say about the statistics. I'm a thick, well-educated black woman who is tired of the dusties and has real ass standards — according to the internet, I'm dying alone.

Edo grins and shakes his head. Since he learned I was American, he's done everything in my power to take me under his wing since I got here. I just hate getting too far out of my comfort zone, so I've ditched all his invitations to visit the local clubs in favor of spending my nights drinking cocktails alone and checking social media. I'm in Italy. I should have daily adventures and bread. I can't forget the delicious ass bread.

"You will not die alone," Edo says. "At least not without trying... my latest cocktail creation."

Edo does a dramatic dance before revealing some clear beverage that looks like some horrible mix of vodka, vermouth and orange juice.

Good. I want to get completely fucked up.

"That looks... clear."

"You'll love it, I promise."

"Will drinking really make the pain go away?" I muse, twirling the glass around so the little orange peel swirls inside it. Kyle. Why do you always miss the ones who fuck you up the most?

Hopefully, this drink will get my ain't shit ex off my mind, but let's be real. What I really need is a summer romance. Ha. Like that's going to happen in a country where half the people think I'm a prostitute because of my skin color.

"Yes. It will. Absolutely." Edo replies with a wink.

"Cheers." I swirl the drink around despite Edo's repeated claims I ruin his creations by doing that. I pour it down my throat and taste a pleasant citrus flavor before a powerful vodka burn. It takes everything in my power to get the rest of the drink down my throat. Whew! That was a damn burn.

"What the hell did you put in that?"

Edo winks, but offers no response. Tricky ass Italian.

"My shift ends in ten," he says. "I'll take you out tonight to Jalousie. No getting out of it this time to watch *Empire* in your apartment."

How the fuck does this skinny ass white boy know me so well already? I shake my head, prepared to reject his offer to take me to the club, but Edo won't let it go. He wriggles his brows suggestively.

He loves regaling me with stories about all the shenanigans that go down at the Amalfi Coast nightclubs. I'm not really a nightclub girl. Small bars like this one fit me better, but didn't I come to Italy to have fun? Meet someone? I should put in some effort.

The only men who give me any attention are the creeps on the beach who say so much nasty shit to me in Italian that I'm glad I don't understand.

Maybe I'll meet better men at the club, especially a club with a fancy ass French name like this one. Jalousie. Wait… Edo's mentioned Jalousie to me before in the past.

"Ain't that the club with the mafia shootout you told me about?"

I don't believe half the shit that comes out of Edo's mouth, but he loves regaling me with stories about the real Italian mafia, which he claims is apparently far worse than any mafia in Long Island or Staten Island. How could anyone who lives in one of the most beautiful parts of the world hurt and kill other people? I think he likes telling tall tales to impress tourists.

I get people on Staten Island killing each other, but the Amalfi Coast? Hell fucking no. The sea is perfectly blue, the air smells fresh constantly, and it's plain peaceful out here. Italians have a rich culture, amazing food, better wine and the guys here are hot.

Not every guy, but when you walk down the streets here, you definitely encounter more than a few hotties. They all dress like supermodels, too. I've never seen so many regular ass people sporting Gucci and Fendi.

"Yes," Edo says. "But you're here for 9 more months, right? Have a fling. Don't tell him your real name… and disappear. You can find a hot and incredibly rich man to spoil you during your trip."

"Wait… is this a gay club or my type of club?"

Edo chuckles. "The guys are hot. I didn't say they were gay. You haven't earned your way into going to a gay club with me yet."

"Wow, Edo. I thought we had something going here."

Edo shrugs. "My private life is my private life. That's how it is in Italy. Your private life, on the other hand, is my playground. I'll introduce you to people. I know people who frequent Jalousie."

"Hot guys?"

"Eh…"

"Hot straight guys?" I correct myself before he answers. I don't want Edo tricking me into going out for nothing.

"Not exactly… I have a girl friend in town who goes all the time — Cassia Pagonis."

He says the name like I'm supposed to know who the fuck that is.

"Who the fuck is that?"

Edo chuckles. "A very fun girl with very hot brothers."

I perk up a little until Edo tells me they're all married. Great.

"Great. They're married…"

Before Edo can reassure me (again) more customers wander into the bar and Edo scurries to the other end of the bar to take orders.

I gaze into my phone again, looking at pictures from Raven's wedding. My cousin looks gorgeous, but I can't help a twisted pang of envy. I know it's wrong but... will that ever happen for me?

My homegirls from college keep sending me articles about the sorry state of marriage for black women. Alyssa says that we need to divest completely from marriage and just have fun.

My idea of fun isn't keeping a collection of all "my dicks" in a private folder on my phone. I want the real fucking thing! Even if the world loves reminding me that 'the real thing' only happens for white women or black women with the lightest dusting of melanin... I want to believe in love.

I scroll past Raven's pictures and my feed is all babies, new puppies, new jobs, new houses, new apartments, new husbands... new everything. Before Italy, I was just doing the same old shit. I wanted to shake things up. I don't know why my life hasn't transformed entirely. I'm in the prettiest place on earth — the Amalfi Coast.

Edo's shift ends, and he calls my name from the other end of the bar, beckoning me over to the cash register.

"Any tip for me today?"

"I saw you slip that five euro note out of my wallet. I think we're good."

Edo shrugs. "Sorry, this job doesn't pay well."

"I get it. I'll pay for our drinks tonight. Happy?"

"Incredibly."

I shouldn't be offering to pay for anyone's drinks, honestly, but I tell myself that I'll worry about all the damn money I'm spending once I get back to America. I have nine months of freedom and then I can worry about these damn bills and loans and everything else.

Edo drags me off my stool, and we step outside into the cobblestone street. I'll never get over how beautifully blue everything is here. The streets smell like the ocean, pastries, wine and cigarettes, of course. People sell jewelry and fruits on the streets and the Italian accents are... gorgeous. My Italian's still crap, despite Edo's best efforts to teach me a few phrases.

At least I don't have to hear all the street harassment thrown my way, which is plentiful. Edo replies defensively to a grey-haired man who calls something lewd in my direction and grabs me tighter. "Fuck these guys," he says. "You aren't that fat."

I swear, I'll never get used to how fucking blunt they are. But I appreciate Edo doing his best to defend me. We can hear the music from Jalousie echoing down the street before we get close.

"Isn't it early for the club?"

"Why are you so fucking American?" Edo asks, linking arms with me. "Relax."

"EDOARDO!" A shrill voice with a strange accent calls from across the street. I know Italian accents by now, at least how people from the Coast sound when speaking English, and this girl sounds different.

"That's Cass," Edo says to me, a smile breaking out across his handsome face. "Chin up. She'll love you."

Edo waves to the girl across the street and she struts over to us, sticking her hand out to stop the cars making their way down the cobblestone streets. They don't even honk as she passes.

The first thing I notice about her is how striking she is. She's tall, with curly dark brown hair pinned up out of her face and flowing down her back. She's wearing crazy high heels, like all the European girls do, a short leather skirt and a tight black leather crop top.

With her dark red lipstick, she looks like a film noir femme fatale… and she stares like one.

"Edo… is this your American friend?"

She turns to me and smiles. Shit, her accent might be strong, but her English is perfect. Cass's hair falls over her shoulders, her curls carrying a soft eucalyptus scent.

"Jodi Rose," I say, happy to have some female company around here, not like there's anything wrong with Edo. "Nice to meet you."

She takes my hand, three silver Cartier bracelets sliding down her wrist. Wow. Her bracelets aren't the only expensive item of clothing she has.

"Cass Pagonis. I'm sure Edo has told you all sorts of horrible stories about me."

"I did not!"

Edo definitely did. But Cass doesn't seem like a crazy party girl. She rolls her eyes and brushes him off.

"I'm here on the Coast working for my cousin's family," Cass says. "I'm from Thessaloniki. My idiot brothers want me back next week, unfortunately. But I could use a night out before I go."

Edo claps his hands. "Yay! Party time. Too bad Jalousie only caters to the most chauvinistic mafia pigs you can imagine."

"I thought you said they were hotties?!"

"They are," Edo says. "But they might be assholes."

Now he tells me. Edo would have said anything to get me out of my damn apartment. I hope I don't regret it.

"Watch it," Cass cautions, an impish smile on her face. "Those chauvinistic mafia pigs are my cousins and brothers."

Edo shrugs. "Fine. Fine. But I need dick too. Gay rights."

Cass swats his shoulder.

"Edo, why don't you let me take her for the night? There's no one at Jalousie for you, and you can go meet up with Klaus or… that other one."

Edo suddenly straightens his back and reminds both of us that just because he's gay doesn't mean he's given up on old world chivalry.

"I can't send Jodi off with a stranger," he says.

I appreciate the sentiment, but I don't know if Edo would do much damage against… any man who weighed more than his slight 108 lb frame.

"I'm fine," I tell him. "Seriously."

"I'm armed anyway," Cass says. I think she's joking, but neither of them laughs. Is she serious? She doesn't look armed, and she looks more like a model than someone who knows how to use a weapon.

I could use a female friend in my life over here. I've got plenty of female friends back home, but they all want to talk about Kyle and my "healing journey". They don't want to hear that I'm still lost after all these months.

Edo shrugs. "If you insist."

"I insist," I tell him. "You've done enough taking care of me. Plus, I'll get to know my new friend… Cass."

"Exactly," Cass says. "Jodi… I think we can become wonderful friends. We can swap stories about Edo."

"There are no stories about Edo," he chimes in. "Because Edo is an incredible friend and a better bartender."

"Shoo," Cass says. "I can handle things from here."

Edo doesn't quite walk off, but he checks his phone and begins texting furiously to plan his next move.

"It's the last time they have DJ Fat Camel playing here. We'll dance, drink and later, I'll take you home, yes?"

"That sounds good to me."

"Well, you have my number if Cass abandons you on the top of a Ferris wheel," Edo says as he swipes four times quickly across his screen and then shoves his phone into his pocket.

Cass rolls her eyes. "I have done nothing of the sort. Get out of here, you big drama queen."

"Ciao!"

Cass and I say "Ciao!"

Edo walks down the cobblestone streets and lights a cigarette before disappearing around the corner. Cass breathes a sigh of relief and turns to me.

"I just think you're perfect," she says.

Weird comment to make, but I mumble a gracious thank you, assuming something got lost in translation.

"Do you have friends with you?" Cass asks, taking out a hand mirror and fixing her bright red lipstick.

"No. I'm here solo tripping. Had a quarter life crisis and… here I am."

"Do you like Italy?" she asks genuinely. Her eyes are so intense.

"It's beautiful."

"Not as pretty as Greece," Cass says. "But I agree. Shall we go in?"

"We should head to the back of the line," I say, my stomach knotting as I see the line stretched around the block. I hope we can even get into the club.

Cass grins, unperturbed by the growing line outside Jalousie.

"My cousin owns the place. Come on, we go in through the back."

Before I can protest, she takes my hand and we walk around a back alley that smells like trash, vomit and again — cigarettes. Cass drags me over to a door and surveys me once before touching the handle.

"Very proper outfit. Excellent. Let's go. Ready to dance?"

I nod, even if I'm nervous. Sure, I'm trying to have an adventure tonight, but I just met this chick. How do I know she isn't crazy? Well, she has Edo's backing, so at least she'll be a good time. Edo definitely knows how to have fun if his clubbing stories are even 55% true.

Cass punches in a six-digit code and the back door to the club opens. I can smell the club before I hear the music and Cass drags me in through the back before I can second guess myself. What am I really doing? I don't know this chick at all and I agreed to go clubbing with her? Is Edo's word really enough?

Once we're in the back door, a man appears. He's tall, with dark brown slicked back hair, tattoos all over his arms and grey eyes. He has broad shoulders, but is otherwise lean and very muscular. He's handsome, but it's too bad he smokes. I can smell the cigarettes from a distance.

"Cass? What the fuck are you doing here?" he asks, seeming genuinely upset.

"Shut the fuck up, Enzo," Cass snaps, her expression changing suddenly into a disapproving scowl. "I have business here."

The man smirks. He's around Cass' height, but he looks... greasy.

"Is that her?"

"Mind your fucking business."

Cass pushes him hard so we can get past him. The grey-eyed man's eyes land on me and he runs his hand over his jawline before snickering.

"He's going to kill you."

"Shut up," Cass snarls. Enzo laughs and raises his hands in defeat.

"Enjoy your night," he says to me in a sing-song voice. For the first time, I feel real hesitation. But Cass grabs my hand and drags me inside of the club.

Cass drags me all the way to the tables and chairs surrounding the dance floor, chatting excitedly and peppering me with questions about

America. I struggle to understand her accent at first, but then I get into the rhythm of her voice and it's easier for us to communicate.

I have to listen in so hard that I barely scan the room we enter. At least the nightclub has a nice interior, and it doesn't seem like any ghetto shit might pop off. Another Edo exaggeration, it seems. I relax as Cass sets me up at a small, two-person table.

"I'll get you a drink. Wait here. If anyone comes to talk to you, tell them you are with Cass Pagonis. That will shut them up."

Before I can protest, or offer to come with her, Cass disappears. Shit. I guess I have to wait here. I already have five texts from Edo about the hotties he met at the club a few doors over. Damn, he moves quick. I've been here for weeks already and I still haven't met a heterosexual male who hasn't been an incredibly old and excessively horny man offering for me to be his 'African prostitute' — offers I have obviously declined.

Cass returns quickly, before I have any time to worry with two shots, each one with some blue flavoring at the bottom.

"Okay, Jodi. This is to a long and beautiful friendship between us, starting with one crazy night, yeah?"

I nod. "Hell yeah. I've never done anything like this before."

I blurt out the last part nervously, but Cass has a way of soothing me. She just smiles and nods. "Don't be scared! I'm a good Greek girl. Now come on... we'll take the shots together."

She counts us down.

"1... 2... 3..."

I take the shot — and it's the last thing I remember about that night.

Click here to keep reading:
https://bit.ly/amalficoast1

Extremely Important Links

ALL BOOKS BY JAMILA JASPER
https://linktr.ee/JamilaJasper
SIGN UP FOR EMAIL UPDATES
Bit.ly/jamilajasperromance
SOCIAL MEDIA LINKS
https://www.jamilajasperromance.com/
GET MERCH
https://www.redbubble.com/people/jamilajasper/shop
GET FREEBIE (VIA TEXT)
https://slkt.io/qMk8
READ SERIAL (NEW CHAPTERS WEEKLY)
www.patreon.com/jamilajasper

JAMILA JASPER

Diverse Romance For Black Women

More Jamila Jasper Romance

Thank You Kindly

Thank you to all my readers, new and old for your support with this new year.

I look forward to making 2022 an INCREDIBLE year for interracial romance novels. I want to thank you all for joining along on the journey.

Thank you to my most supportive readers:

Cortney, Yolanda S., MonaGirl, Dianna, Mary, Nysha, Fayola, Ty, Shyra, Andi-Mariee, Keisha, Jennett, Fredericka, Candece, Lydia, Sabrina, JM, Jackie, Mo, Ashaunte, Tolu, Lori, Dionne, ZLB, Nicol, Elbert, Jesi, Brenda, Desiree, LaShan, Only1ToniD, Debbie, Tiffanie, Shawnte, Lisema, Christine, Trinity, Monica, Juliette, Letetia, Margaret, Dash, Maxine, Sheron, Javonda, Pearl, Kiana, Shyan, Jacklyn, Amy, Julia, Colleen, Natasha, Yvonne, Brittany, June, Ashleigh, Nene, Nene, Deborah, Nikki, DeShaunda, Latoya, Shelite, Arlene, Judith, Mary, Shanida, Rachel, Damzel, Ahnjala, Kenya, Momo, BJ, Akeshia, Melissa, Tiffany, Sherbear, Nini, Curtresa, Regina, Ashley, Mia, Sydney, Sharon, Charlotte, Assiatu, Regina, Romanda, Catherine, Gaynor, BF, Tasha, Henri, Sara, skkent, Rosalyn, Danielle, Deborah, Kirsten, Ana, Taylor, Charlene Louanna, Michelle, Tamika, Lauren, RoHyde, Natasha, Shekynah, Cassie, Dreama, Nick, Gennifer, Rayna, Jaleda, Kimvodkna, Jatonn, Anoushka, Audrey, Valeria, Courtney, Donna, Jenetha, Ayana, Kristy, FreyaJo, Grace, Kisha, Stephanie E., Amber, Denice, Marty,

LaKisha, Latoya, Natasha, Monifa, Alisa, Daveena, Desiree, Gerry,
Kimberly, Stephanie M., Tarah, Yolanda, Kristy, Gary, Janet, Kathy,
Phyllis, Susan

<u>Join the Patreon Community.</u>
<u>www.patreon.com/jamilajasper</u>

Patreon

Instantly access all six seasons of *Unfuckable* (Ben & Libby's story) with 375 chapters.

For a small monthly fee, you get exclusive access to my all this & my recently completed serial Despicable (275 chapters) ⬇

www.patreon.com/jamilajasper

Patreon

Patreon has more than the ongoing serial and previous serial releases...

INSTANT ACCESS

- NEW merchandise tiers with <u>t-shirts, totes, mugs,</u> stickers and MORE!
- <u>FREE paperback</u> with all new tiers
- <u>**FREE short story audiobooks**</u> and audiobook samples when they're ready
- #FirstDraftLeaks of Prologues and first chapters **weeks** before I hit publish
- Behind the scenes notes
- Polls and story contribution
- Comments & LIVELY community discussion with likeminded interracial romance readers.

LEARN MORE ABOUT SUPPORTING A DIVERSE ROMANCE AUTHOR

<u>www.patreon.com/jamilajasper</u>